THE BRIDESMAID

By Beverly Lewis

HOME TO HICKORY HOLLOW

The Fiddler

The Bridesmaid

THE ROSE TRILOGY

The Thorn • *The Judgment* • *The Mercy*

ABRAM'S DAUGHTERS

The Covenant • *The Betrayal* • *The Sacrifice*

The Prodigal • *The Revelation*

THE HERITAGE OF LANCASTER COUNTY

The Shunning • *The Confession* • *The Reckoning*

ANNIE'S PEOPLE

The Preacher's Daughter • *The Englisher* • *The Brethren*

THE COURTSHIP OF NELLIE FISHER

The Parting • *The Forbidden* • *The Longing*

SEASONS OF GRACE

The Secret • *The Missing* • *The Telling*

The Postcard • *The Crossroad*

The Redemption of Sarah Cain

October Song • *Sanctuary* (with David Lewis) • *The Sunroom*

Amish Prayers

The Beverly Lewis Amish Heritage Cookbook

www.beverlylewis.com

THE BRIDESMAID

BEVERLY LEWIS

BETHANYHOUSE
a division of Baker Publishing Group
Minneapolis, Minnesota

Published by Bethany House Publishers
11400 Hampshire Avenue South
Bloomington, Minnesota 55438
www.bethanyhouse.com

Bethany House Publishers is a division of
Baker Publishing Group, Grand Rapids, Michigan

Printed in the United States of America

Library of Congress Cataloging-in-Publication Data

Lewis, Beverly
The bridesmaid / Beverly Lewis.
p. cm. — (Home to Hickory Hollow)
ISBN 978-0-7642-1052-5 (alk. paper) — ISBN 978-0-7642-0978-9 (pbk.) — ISBN 978-0-7642-1053-2 (large-print pbk.)
1. Amish women—Pennsylvania—Lancaster County—Fiction. 2. Women authors—Fiction. 3. Amish farmers—Indiana—Fiction. 4. Man-woman relationships—Fiction. I. Title.
PS3562.E9383B75 2012
813'.54—dc23 2012013185

Scripture quotations are from the King James Version of the Bible.

Cover design by Dan Thornberg, Design Source Creative Services
Art direction by Paul Higdon

With love
to my beautiful cousins—
Cindy, Diana and Sharon,
Shelley and Brenda,
and Kendra.

Prologue

Three times a bridesmaid, never a bride."

That's just what my younger sister said about me—in front of our engaged cousins, no less—most of them planning to marry come Amish wedding season. A mere five months away.

Seventeen-year-old Cora Jane's words echoed in my head . . . and rippled through my heart. *Jah*, she was as superstitious as many of us in Hickory Hollow, but to be so glib about announcing it?

There I was, sitting on the sand at Virginia Beach, surrounded by oodles of *Englischers*—families with little children, young couples, and singles like me. All had come for the sunset. Some were celebrating more than others, relaxing on their portable beach chairs with cans of soft drinks.

Meanwhile, my younger Witmer cousins, Malinda, Ruthann, and Lena—first cousins to each other—and my fair-haired sister Cora Jane were up yonder on the boardwalk, laughing and eating cotton candy. Sighing, I recalled Cousin Malinda earlier today, looking mighty excited when she asked me to be in her wedding. We had been packing sandwiches with Cora Jane and the others for a picnic lunch when Malinda leaned over to ask me, her face pink from more than the June sun. If I was to agree, it would be the third time I'd be a *Newesitzer*—side sitter, or attendant in a wedding.

"It just ain't schmaert, Joanna," Cora Jane warned, her big blue eyes flashing. *"You're already twenty-four, ya know!"*

And still a Maidel. I shrugged away the wretched thought. Drawing a long breath, I tried to relax on the beach, alone with my writing notebook . . . away from Cousin Malinda and other relatives who'd come to attend tomorrow's funeral for my great-uncle Amos Kurtz. We'd traveled in large vans to honor the eighty-eight-year-old deacon, who was revered in Hickory Hollow and the Shipshewana, Indiana, church district where he later lived. As a result, many Amish had come to pay last respects and to offer comfort to his elderly widow. Years ago Amos and Martha had retired here in Virginia, joining a growing community of other aging Amish near the ocean they loved.

My thoughts returned to Cousin Malinda's upcoming wedding—and her kindly request. Although I'd once yearned for a beau and marriage, I'd given up on love. And I wished I'd never confided in Cora Jane about any of that. I rejected her pity—and anyone else's, for that matter. Goodness knows, I've dished out enough of that on myself!

Opening my notebook to the end of the last scene in my current story, I pushed my bare feet into the warm sand, still wearing my green dress and matching cape apron. My white organdy *Kapp* was safely in the hotel room—no sense in getting it unnecessarily soiled. Even so, as I sat fretting and looking ever so Plain amongst all the folk in skimpy bathing suits and shorts, I knew I must be a peculiar spectacle. The years of wearing Amish attire at market and elsewhere outside the confines of the community had led me to accept the fact there would always be curious stares.

But soaking up the ocean spray and salty scent was worth any amount of attention. Oh, the wonderful-*gut* feeling of the sea breeze against my hair, still up in a tight bun. How I longed to let it down . . . let the wind blow through it. Still, I didn't want to add to the misconceptions far too many Englischers already had about us, some even from novels they'd read.

My pen poised, I played my favorite what-if game as I began to write. The squeal of a sea gull caught my attention as the sun fell, faster now it seemed, behind me, over my shoulders, its gleaming rays fanning out to the clouds high above. I leaned back and stared at the evolving light show above me, letting my mind wander as I watched beachcombers and shell collectors. Certainly I hadn't meant to be rude, ignoring Malinda's request.

Yet, dare I accept?

Out of the corner of my eye, I noticed a tall Amish fellow walking barefoot in the foamy surf, snapping pictures every few seconds. A curious sight, to be sure! His black pant legs were rolled up, and he was minus his straw hat. His light brown hair fell below his ears, longer than that of the young men in the Hickory Hollow church district back home. I could scarcely pry my gaze from him.

"What's he doin' here?" I whispered, observing his amble through the gentle breakers, his handsome face aglow with a rosy cast.

Then, surprisingly, he glanced over at me.

"Hullo there." He smiled in the fading golden light.

I almost looked around to make sure his greeting was meant for me. "Hullo," I managed to reply, quickly closing my notebook.

As the sky dimmed, he moved away from the water and walked right toward me. "Mind if I join ya?"

"*Nee*, not at all."

He sat down beside me, pointing to a black ship on the horizon.

"Jah, awful perty." I felt too shy to say more.

We sat, not speaking, amidst the smell of popcorn and sea air while beams of red, pink, and gold sprayed the sky from the west.

"No wonder people thought the earth was flat, back before Columbus," he said quietly.

I nodded. "Sure looks that way from here."

"Ever see anything like this?"

"My first visit to the ocean," I admitted. "So, no."

He turned slowly, unexpectedly. "I'm Eben Troyer, from Indiana." His smile was disarming.

"Joanna Kurtz . . . from Hickory Hollow."

"Ah, Pennsylvania, where some of my cousins grew up. But I've never been there—unique name for a town, jah?"

We talked further, and I soon learned that soft-spoken Eben had come here for his deacon's funeral. I could hardly wait to say that it was the same service my family and I had come to attend.

"Well, how's that for a coincidence?" he said, his features growing faint in the twilight.

He showed me his camera, saying he took mostly pictures of landscapes and animals, same as our bishop, John Beiler, allowed. "Rarely pictures of people," he remarked . . . although the way Eben brought it up, he almost sounded like he wanted to take *my* picture.

His attention flabbergasted me, but it was ever so pleasing. No one had ever sought me out like this. For sure and for certain, my family and every last one of my girl cousins had written me off as destined to be an *alt Maidel*.

"How long are ya here for?" he asked, his smile warming my heart anew.

"Three days, counting today."

Then Eben surprised me again, asking if I'd like to walk with him to the fishing pier down yonder. I agreed, and he politely offered his hand as I got up from my sandy perch. Oh, glory be, we must've walked for miles into the night. So far and so long we got ourselves plumb lost trying to find our way back.

Following the funeral the next day, Eben and I hurried again to the beach. There, we waded into the ocean up to our knees—in our clothes, of all silly things. And later, after the sun and wind dried us out some, we rented a bicycle built for two and rode up and down the boardwalk, the warm air on our faces. We ate chili dogs and ice cream under the fishing pier, and his eyes rested on me when he said, "I've never known a better day, Joanna."

My heart pounded in my ears.

That evening and the next, we met at sunset, laughing together and talking about whatever popped into our heads until, wonder of wonders, Eben reached for my hand! My heart beat so wildly, I wondered if he sensed it. All I could think of was our interlaced fingers.

But all too soon, we had to part ways, our private time together at an end. He asked for my address, and I happily gave it. In such a short time, we'd become so dear to each other. I tried not to cry.

Our meeting on the beach—as romantic and special as it was—birthed a renewed hope in me. After all, it was nearly a blight on any Amish girl to still be single at my age. *Ach*, but Eben Troyer had surely changed all of that. Surely he had. . . .

Then and there, I decided it was safe to go out on a limb. I agreed to be Cousin Malinda's bridesmaid, hoping with all of my heart to prove wrong my sister's pointed warning.

Chapter 1

If Joanna hadn't witnessed it, she wouldn't have believed Cousin Malinda would break down and cry on the morning of her wedding. Certainly all the preparations were stressful, and November's weather was also quite unpredictable—today was undeniably disappointing, with rain making down in sheets. *But is that reason to shed tears on your wedding day?* Joanna wondered.

Neither of the other two brides Joanna had stood up with had wept before going downstairs to make their marriage vows. But then, neither of those weddings had taken place on days with a cloudburst and deafening thunder.

Standing before the bishop with Malinda and her tall, brown-eyed Andrew, Joanna hoped her cousin wasn't moving ahead with something she might later regret. Once the sacred promises were made, there was no looking back. Marriage was to be honored for life.

Surely Cousin Malinda's tears were related instead to something other than second thoughts or cold feet. Oh, Joanna hoped so. Something to do with a blend of many emotions, maybe?

Through the windows, she saw the last vestiges of leaves falling in the downpour, the sky a slate gray. It nearly looked like nightfall, even though it was closer to noon.

Returning her attention to the bride and groom, Joanna was relieved to see Malinda look up adoringly at Andrew just as Bishop Beiler pronounced them husband and wife. "In the name of the Father, the Son, and the Holy Ghost."

After the tears, only love remains, Joanna thought, aware of the reverent spirit in the temporary house of worship. So many church members were present today, as well as extended family from other districts and even Englischer friends.

O Lord, bless Cousin Malinda and her husband, Andrew, with your loving care, Joanna prayed silently.

All during the wedding feast and the fellowshipping that afternoon, the rain continued, pouring over the eaves and streaming down the windowpanes. Then, lo and behold, it turned to sleet . . . and later to snow, with thick flakes filling the sky.

"Such a lot of weather for a single day," Joanna overheard Malinda's mother saying to Andrew's, a heavyset woman in her late fifties.

"Makes things interesting, jah?" Andrew's mother replied, making note of the edible wedding novelties for the bride and groom at the *Eck*, the special corner of the wedding table. Besides sticks of chewing gum and wrapped candies, there were little animals made from Rice Krispies and candy. And miniature buggies made from marshmallows, hitched with toothpicks to animal cracker horses.

Joanna nodded absentmindedly from the corner where she and several other single girls, including her golden-haired cousins, Ruthann and Lena, stood talking and nibbling on sweets.

Cora Jane was there, too, looking exceptionally pretty in her bright green dress and white apron. "To be honest, weather ain't the only thing amiss today," she said, looking askance at Joanna.

For goodness' sake, thought Joanna, letting the remark slide over her, even though it felt like an ocean wave threatening to topple her. True, this *was* the third time she'd served as a bridesmaid, but now that Eben Troyer was in her life, she wanted to set foolish superstition aside and just enjoy the day.

Joanna thought back to the beautiful beach where she'd met handsome Eben. How she yearned to hear his voice, the way he'd said her name as they walked together. It was easy to fall into that daydream; she missed him terribly. She would not soon forget the delightful day at the mailbox last summer when she'd laid eyes on Eben's first letter, her name and address written in his strong hand. It was the beginning of their long-distance friendship, now blossoming into something so much more. She secretly treasured that special letter, having read and reread it before tucking it safely away in a wooden letter box in her hope chest. It was there that Joanna kept her most treasured possessions, including her writing notebooks.

Around midafternoon, copies of the German hymnal, the *Ausbund*, were passed around, and a special wedding Singing began for the newlyweds' enjoyment, with the courting-age youth sitting in pairs at the feast table. *Such a happy time*, Joanna encouraged herself, out of place though she felt at such gatherings anymore.

She put on a smile when she spied good-looking Jake Lantz, also known as Freckles Jake, sitting across the front room. The nickname arose from the freckles dotting his nose and cheekbones. His tall, robust frame proved he was hardworking, the kind of young man any Amish girl would welcome as a beau. His sandy hair and hazel eyes were identical to those of his younger brother, Jesse, who sat nearby, singing with other fellows in their late teens. Though Jake was twenty-three, both brothers were still quite single—according to the rumors, Jake had scared off a couple of girls on the first date, wanting to hold hands too soon.

Remembering that Eben had taken her hand in his the last evening they'd been together, Joanna couldn't help but smile as she sang with the others. Eben's gesture had been so natural, an outgrowth of their shared affection.

Between songs, Joanna chuckled over the candies made to look like little airplanes that decorated the table in front of her. *When did make-believe planes become the norm at Amish weddings?*

Suddenly, she was again aware of Jake's gaze and felt a wave of pity for him, feeling as sorry for him as she had for herself last year around this time, at her first wedding as a bridesmaid. No doubt Jake just wanted to marry and get on with life. *Maybe if he'd had a sister, he'd know better how to treat a girl. . . .*

Later, Joanna poured her heart into the gospel song "I Love to Tell the Story," one of her favorites. But she wasn't able to put Jake out of her mind for long. Several times over the course of the afternoon he caught her eye, and as Joanna learned later, he even went so far as to ask Malinda to pair him up with Joanna for the evening barn Singing.

"He's awful sweet on ya, cousin," Malinda herself revealed to Joanna in whispered tones prior to the evening meal.

But Joanna gave no indication she'd heard . . . nor did she say she was no longer available. Best to hold to tradition and keep Eben a secret—at least till the proper time.

After the wedding supper, Joanna and the other courting-age young folk headed to the barn for the regular Singing. The evening was still, without a hint of a breeze. If it were summer, she might be sitting out by the pond beyond their barn, bare feet in the water . . . her writing notebook on her lap. Out there, with the occasional breeze, she could keep her stories from prying eyes, especially Cora Jane's. It was one thing for Joanna to keep a daily journal, but quite another to write made-up stories, since fiction was frowned upon by the ministerial brethren.

All of that aside, Joanna had for some years delighted in spinning her imaginary yarns. There were just so many interesting ideas flitting through her head!

She glanced at her younger sister, who stood in her usual cluster of friends and cousins. Here lately, Joanna had suspected Cora Jane was getting close to a marriage proposal. Truth was, with her golden hair and big blue eyes, Cora Jane knew how to get a young man's attention, something she'd even shared back when they were confidantes. Since Joanna had met Eben, however, their sisterly chats had become a thing of the past. And maybe it was for the best, with such a secret to keep.

Joanna remembered clearly what her sister had whispered during one nighttime conversation: that it was important to let a fellow know you were interested, holding his gaze and hanging on to his every word, interjecting a comment here and there while letting him do most of the talking, especially on the first date. And all of that had come so naturally to Joanna with Eben . . . something that had never happened before.

The minute the songs were finished, Jake looked Joanna's way again, and so as not to encourage him a speck, she visited with Cousin Malinda's younger sisters. She wanted nothing more than to slip out of the barn for home, unseen. Feeling a little guilty about her deliberate aloofness, she returned his smile when she again found him looking her way. Her toes curled in her shoes.

Will he take it wrong?

Then, as if by some miracle, Cora Jane, and Malinda's younger sister, Mary Rose, walked over to the other side of the barn to talk with Jake. Feeling much relieved, Joanna wondered if Cora Jane had, perhaps, observed the silent exchange of smiles and sensed Joanna's uneasiness. Had her sister stepped in on purpose?

Looking about her, Joanna saw that she could at last exit discreetly. So she pushed open the barn door and left to walk home through the chilly night. She didn't mind the snowflakes that sprinkled her nose and lips; Joanna simply pulled her coat tighter around her, glad for her scarf and gloves.

In that moment, she had an unexpected thought, one that warmed her heart. What if she and Eben were to marry next wedding season? Which two girls would *she* choose for her bridesmaids? Joanna laughed to herself—she was putting the carriage before the horse again. She was known to have a vivid imagination, something even *Mamma* had pointed out since Joanna was but a little girl. So now Joanna questioned herself: Was it merely wishful thinking to hope her beau might propose, perhaps even via letter? Or was this just the stuff of the romantic fiction she dearly loved to read . . . and write?

Wonderful as it was to anticipate and receive Eben's letters, they were a frequent reminder that her beau lived way out in Shipshewana, where he and his extended family had farmed for generations. She was curious about his parents and siblings—his entire family, really—but hadn't had the gumption to ask, not wanting to appear forward. She sometimes feared she might mess up and write something awkward, spoiling things between them. So she was careful to see that her own letters dealt mostly with daily life and happenings in Hickory Hollow.

Joanna had taken care to capture every detail of her own beloved little hollow there in Lancaster County. She'd also written Eben about the dear folk, like Samuel and Rebecca Lapp, and Paul and Lillianne Hostetler . . . and Ella Mae Zook, the old Wise Woman so many in the area turned to with their problems. Joanna hoped she hadn't gone overboard with her portrayals or the descriptions of the landscape. It was just that she loved everything about Hickory Hollow and was holding her breath that Eben might come *there* to court her, to settle and eventually marry. So far, though, he hadn't said anything of the kind.

Picking up her pace now, she thought of Cora Jane and her steady beau, Gideon Zook. She'd seen him drop her off late at night after a long buggy ride. The memory of Cora Jane's mirth rang out in Joanna's mind—that appealing, melodious laughter.

"Do I laugh enough?" Joanna whispered into the darkness, unsure how to share her lighthearted side in letters to Eben. But there had never been a need to work to impress him. Why, joy of joys, recently Eben had started signing off, *with love*.

A mighty gut sign!

And tomorrow evening at seven o'clock, Eben had said he'd call her, having asked for the phone number of the community phone shanty situated in one of *Dat*'s fields.

So much for Cora Jane's admonition, Joanna thought with a smile.

Then a sudden concern presented itself, and she couldn't help wondering what Eben wanted to discuss by phone. *And why now?*

Chapter 2

Joanna slipped into bed well after ten o'clock that night, but she awakened before dawn with such curiosity and expectation for the day that she got right up and lit the lantern. She hurried across the room, her bare feet chilled by the draft creeping through the floorboards. Then, taking her notebook from the three-ring binder stored in her hope chest, she curled back up in bed and wrote for a good hour, till it was time to shower.

Her thoughts today were on one thing: the phone call from Eben tonight. Oh, to hear his voice again!

After dressing, she brushed her hair more than a hundred times, caught up in the notion that she wanted to look her very best, even though Eben couldn't possibly see her. Joanna was to use the outdoor phone meant primarily for emergencies and calling for a driver—necessary things that didn't include talking to a beau. Yet lots of folk did small things behind the bishop's back, saying by their actions, *What the strict bishop doesn't know won't matter*.

Even so, what *would* happen if Joanna were ever caught using the phone for personal use? Was it truly a transgression?

Parting her hair down the middle, she tightly twisted the sides before pulling her blond hair into a thick bun. Then she placed her white Kapp on her head and hurried back upstairs to make her bed and put away her writing notebook. She'd taken an unnecessary risk, leaving it out in plain sight on the bed, of all things. For sure and for certain, the phone call tonight had her all but *ferhoodled*.

She still had no idea why Eben wanted to call. Was it just because he missed her? His letters certainly indicated his lasting affection. She hoped hers sent the same loving message back to him.

After breakfast, she put a roast in the oven, then set about sweeping Mamma's big kitchen floor with the stiff-bristled broom. She got in the corners real good, as Mamma had taught her back when she was a little girl, scarcely as tall as the broom itself, finishing out in the catch-all utility room, which was as cluttered as she'd ever seen it. *How does such a mess happen in a single day?*

Once the floors were spotless, Cora Jane brought in a pile of mending and sat down at the kitchen table without uttering a word to Joanna or to their pleasingly plump mother. Right away, she set to work patching, not giving anyone so much as a glance. Joanna figured it was best to keep out of her sister's way, especially considering how Cora Jane had acted at Cousin Malinda's wedding.

Around ten-thirty, Joanna wiped her brow and went to wash up before peeling potatoes for a generous pot of beef stew. Taking into account Cora Jane's attitude, she'd rather cook on her own. Mamma had undoubtedly noticed the tension between them, but Joanna hoped things might calm down somewhat, now that Malinda and Andy's wedding was past. *Now that I've served as a bridesmaid yet again.*

Joanna began cutting up the potatoes, musing. If she could do anything in the kitchen, she'd choose something other than cleaning. Cooking was altogether different, because she didn't equate making meals or baking bread with housework. To her thinking, one was humdrum and uncreative, the other enjoyable. She smiled, thinking how she'd feel cooking for Eben each day.

Just at that moment, Cora Jane looked over at her. "You happy 'bout something, sister?"

Mamma turned to look, as well, blue eyes shining. "Are ya makin' enough stew so we'll have leftovers tomorrow?"

"Oh, there'll be a-plenty," replied Joanna, thankful for Mamma's intervention. "This is a double batch."

"G*ut*, 'cause I really *hate* peelin' potatoes—it's the worst thing ever," Cora Jane complained.

"Now, dear," Mamma said sweetly. "No need to say 'hate.'"

Cora Jane clammed up, eyes blinking fast. At her age, she knew better than to say things to set Mamma off, yet sometimes Cora Jane just seemed bent on being disagreeable.

But Joanna knew it would do no good to fret over her sister. She returned her attention to cutting up the roast beef, then browned the cubes in butter. When that was done, she added two large onions, canned carrots from last year's family garden, and the seasonings. She'd made the meal so many times, there was no need for a recipe. All the while, she wondered what Eben's favorite meals were. Joanna could scarcely wait to learn all there was to know about him!

Her father's intense gray eyes were fixed on the steaming bowl of stew Joanna set before him, though he characteristically said nary a word. He leaned his tall frame against the chair at the head of the table, and the four of them offered the silent table blessing. They enjoyed the hearty meal, complete with cottage cheese, fresh-baked bread, and Mamma's wonderful apple butter. For dessert, Joanna served the rest of a pumpkin pie Mamma had baked yesterday afternoon following the wedding.

Cora Jane ate without making a peep. Dat didn't say much, either—generally he said little unless he had good reason. Mamma, for her part, tried to make small talk, mostly about the cold weather and the coming snow. Joanna cherished her own private thoughts as she spooned up the delicious stew, relieved in a way that Cora Jane wasn't as talkative as usual.

Looking around the largely empty table, Joanna tried to picture Eben sitting there. Could *he* manage to get Dat talking during dinner? Very few folk could. Not even Michael Hostetler down Hickory Lane, their neighbors' genial son, who until recently had worked part-time for Dat.

"We have a few more weddings comin' up in the next two weeks," Mamma said.

Joanna nodded. "Have ya decided which cousin's wedding to attend next Thursday?"

"Ach, two weddings in the family on the selfsame day," Mamma said, shaking her head. "Happens too often, jah? Lena and Ruthann—such a hard choice to make."

Cora Jane didn't bother to look up, and Dat would leave the decision to Mamma. *Poor Mamma,* thought Joanna.

"Which wedding will Salina go to?" Joanna asked. Salina was the only married daughter in the family and already a mother to three young children. The rest of Joanna and Cora Jane's siblings were boys, all married with youngsters of their own.

Mamma's face lit up. "Now, why didn't *I* think of that? I'll ask her this afternoon."

Joanna wasn't surprised. After all, Salina stopped in quite often. So then it was settled: They would go to whichever wedding Salina chose.

Weddings abound, thought Joanna, taking another bite of pie while avoiding Cora Jane's impudent stare.

When the clouds lowered during supper that evening and a tremendous wind came up, gusting snow, Joanna knew she was in for a challenge getting out to the phone shanty several acres away. The white-out conditions were hazardous—some farmers were known to tie a rope to the house and their own hand just to go out to the barn and back in such conditions.

She hoped the snowstorm was short-lived and done by the time she needed to get to the phone. How she yearned for the lovely months of summer, when their closest neighbors could easily wander over for some watermelon or homemade ice cream and a back porch visit, or the other way around. Mamma, for instance, hadn't been over to see Ella Mae Zook or even Rachel Stoltzfus, the bishop's mother-in-law, in weeks. Joanna missed all the impromptu conversation at the end of the long day, as well as the sight of green leaves and blossoming flowers.

Joanna had never quite forgotten the impression she'd had of Ella Mae when Mamma had taken her along for tea with the Wise Woman. It was years before Ella Mae's husband passed away, when Joanna was but four and Ella Mae was still living in the farmhouse a mile or so away. Joanna couldn't help but feel comfortable in the sun-drenched kitchen so similar to Mamma's own. She'd sat across from Mamma on a wooden chair with a mound of pillows tucked beneath her, a little yellow daisy teacup and saucer set before her filled with peppermint tea.

Mamma and Ella Mae sat sipping and chatting on the other side of the table while Joanna picked up her spoon and began to stir, looking at the murky hot water.

"Here, dearie," Ella Mae said, rising just then and going to her old icebox to get a jar of real whipped cream. "This'll make your first cup of tea extra yummy." With a twinkle in her eye, Ella Mae put a dollop of the sweet white cream atop Joanna's tea. Mamma's eyes widened when Ella Mae encouraged Joanna to stick her little pointer finger in the whipped cream and lick it off.

Even then, Joanna had wondered how a woman that old could have possibly known what a child was thinking. Then and there, she sensed something special about this lady the People called wise, whose sincere and welcoming manner—and specially brewed tea—drew people like bees to roses. Particularly women who needed a caring friend and a listening ear.

Joanna smiled with the dear memory as she drew hot water after supper dishes were cleared from the table. She squirted an ample amount of dish soap into the water and swished it around. Cora Jane came over, jerked the tea towel off the rack, and stood stiff and uncommunicative, waiting to dry the dishes. Joanna sighed inwardly and listened to see if the wind outdoors might be dying down some. Less than an hour and a half left before she needed to make her trek out to the phone shack for the seven o'clock call.

When the kitchen was all redd up, Mamma suggested the three of them make chocolate chip cookies for the upcoming weekend. Cora Jane brightened immediately, voting to make snickerdoodles, her very favorite. Joanna agreed to help, knowing she'd have to watch the clock, as well as find a way to leave gracefully without raising eyebrows.

Going over to preheat the gas oven, Joanna noticed Dat get up from his chair near the heat stove and wander out to the utility room. Mamma followed, asking where he was going in such weather.

"Want to check on the livestock . . . see how the newest calves are doin'."

Her father opened the back door, and Joanna could see that the wind was not as fierce as before. And when it was time to place the cookie sheets into the oven, Mamma slipped away to the sitting room and Cora Jane went upstairs. Joanna breathed a sigh of relief.

It's now or never! She made haste to don her warmest coat, boots, woolen scarf, and gloves. Then, lickety-split, she put on her black candlesnuffer-style outer bonnet and left the house.

Chapter 3

Eben Troyer headed through the cold toward Peaceful Acres Lane wearing his old work boots and black felt hat, as well as his father's dark blue muffler. The frosty air stung his cheeks and nose, and he could smell the smoke from the new woodstove he and *Daed* had installed in the barn just a few days ago. *In time for the turn in weather*. He'd spent a good part of the day stacking hay in the loft and, later, hooking up the horse's water tank to the generator to keep it from freezing.

The rickety phone hut was a half mile from his father's farmhouse, not far enough away to warrant hitching up the horse and carriage. He had been counting the days till he talked to Joanna, and judging from the way she'd responded in her letter about their conversation tonight, he presumed she was equally excited. A *phone date*, *of all things!*

As he approached the shanty, he noticed his father's older

brother, Solomon, standing inside and talking by lantern light. Sol's hands were moving to beat the band, which was the way he always talked.

Didn't expect this, Eben thought, searching for his pocket watch. Unable to see it, he pulled out his flashlight but then thought better of turning it on. He certainly didn't want to call attention to himself, not with talkative Uncle Solomon nearby.

So Eben hung back in the trees, waiting his turn and hearing the *clip-clop*ping of horses' hooves in the distance. Who would've guessed the weather would sour like this on the very night he'd chosen to phone Joanna. He could only imagine what it was like in Hickory Hollow.

Growing colder by the minute, he wondered how much longer his uncle would be and wished he'd worn heavier gloves. Even so, he'd wait all night if it meant hearing Joanna's sweet voice again.

He removed her letter, folded with the phone number face up. It was to some extent amusing that of all the girls he might have fallen for, Joanna Kurtz happened to live in another state. But there was no doubt in his mind she was worth any amount of distance. And as pretty and thoughtful as she was, it had initially puzzled him as to why Joanna was still single.

Has God kept her just for me? The thought was encouraging as Eben waited for Uncle Sol to complete his call, which it appeared he was doing just now. Sol hung up the receiver and opened the wooden door, then closed it right quick. But he'd forgotten his lantern and had to step back inside to retrieve it before leaving again.

I'll wait just a bit. Eben watched his uncle amble across the field toward his farmhouse. Then, lest someone else wander along to use the phone, Eben flicked on his flashlight and made his way into the shanty, his pulse quickening. After exchanging letters as their only means of communication since this past summer, he was certain this wintry night was about to warm up in a very big way.

Joanna shivered as she stood inside the narrow shed, holding her breath for the phone to ring. The light from her small flashlight began to dim, and she wished she'd put in new batteries before leaving the house.

Despite the weather, she'd arrived a few minutes before the designated time. After all, it would be a shame to have missed Eben's call. But now that she was here and the hour had passed, she wondered if something had come up on his end, maybe, to keep him from getting to the phone.

It was snowing harder, and the wind blew through the openings around the door. All the little cracks in the shanty that helped keep the place cool on the hottest days of summer made it downright frigid now.

Just when she was beginning to think he might not call after all, the phone rang. Joanna let it ring twice, so as not to appear too eager. "Hullo?" she answered, feeling terribly shy.

"Joanna?"

"Jah. Is this Eben?"

"It's so *gut* to hear your voice."

"Yours too."

"I'm sorry it's a little later than I'd planned, but it couldn't be helped." He explained that the phone had been tied up. "You just never know with these community telephones."

"That's all right." It was such fun hearing him, and he sounded so happy to talk to her. She wanted to flutter around; it was all she could do to stand still.

"Our neighbors to the north have a phone installed in their barn, but so far my father will have nothing to do with that."

She mentioned that some of the youth there in Hickory Hollow had cell phones. "And so do a few folk who work away from the farm."

"What do you think of that?" he asked.

"Ain't for me: I'm baptized."

He agreed, sounding somewhat relieved. "My bishop only permits them for business use," he said. "But how's it possible to enforce?"

She nodded, then laughed because he couldn't see her.

"Ach, you laugh just the way I remember," Eben said. "How've ya been, Joanna?"

"Real *gut*, and you?"

"Oh, just fine. Keepin' mighty busy here."

She loved listening to his voice, but was still curious as to why he'd wanted to call.

One thing led to another, and soon they fell easily into talking about their weeks. Then he surprised her by asking, "Would it suit for me to come visit, say, next week sometime?"

Joanna was elated. "Why, sure . . . what day are ya thinkin'?"

"Thursday or Friday, either one."

"Well, we have a wedding on Thursday, so Friday would be better."

"All right, then. I'll ride out with a Mennonite van driver who makes regular trips between here and Lancaster. I'll grab a cab from there. It'll be about ten hours to get to your place."

"Such a distance! How long can ya stay?" she asked, her heart thumping hard.

"Just overnight. Then I'll have to head back the next afternoon." He mentioned needing to get someone to cover his farm work.

"So do your parents know, then . . . 'bout us?"

"I plan to tell them in due time."

She smiled. "I haven't told anyone here, either. We still keep a bit quiet 'bout such things."

"We don't as much anymore here, but I wanted to wait to say anything till a few more things are worked out."

She wondered what things he meant. "You'll need a place to stay."

"If that's all right. Whatever's best for you and your family, Joanna."

Oh, she loved it when he said her name! "I'll see if you can stay with our neighbors, the Stoltzfuses. That is, if you're comfortable having the bishop's in-laws suspect you're here to see me."

He chuckled. "Sounds wonderful-*gut*." Pausing, he continued, "I'd like to meet your parents, too."

Her heart leaped at the thought. *Oh, praise be!* This was getting serious! "All right."

A gust of wind suddenly pounded against the door.

"Sounds like a windstorm there," Eben said.

"Practically a blizzard."

"Will you be all right getting back to the house?" There was concern in his voice.

"I haven't far to go and I'm all bundled up, so no worries."

"Well, don't get chilled."

"I'll be quite fine, Eben," she said, not wanting to hang up just yet.

"Can't have my girl catching her death of cold," he added softly.

My girl . . .

Oh, Eben, she thought, shivering now with something more pleasant than cold.

"Say, I have an idea. What if we talked by phone like this every so often? We could set a regular time. Would ya like that?"

Would she? "Sounds ever so nice," she said, hoping her voice sounded calmer than she felt. It was happening at last . . . and just as she'd hoped. Surely he was planning to court her in earnest!

Then they were discussing several things they might do together during his short visit, and Joanna said she hoped things might warm up. "But ya never know this time of year."

"True, but no matter what, we'll get better acquainted, which is why I'm comin'. That and to meet your family."

She smiled into the phone. "I look forward to it."

"Jah . . ."

She could tell Eben was every bit as reluctant to hang up

as she was. Eventually, though, she had to tell him she was afraid her flashlight was going to conk out.

"All right, then, I'll let you go." He said he'd write to let her know what time to expect him on Friday. "I hope to get an early enough start so I can arrive sometime in the afternoon."

"I'll see ya soon," she said.

"Until then," he said. "Good-bye, Joanna."

"Good-bye." Slowly she placed the receiver back in its cradle.

The flashlight dimmed, and she picked it up. She opened the shanty door and ran through the snow, hoping to get home before the light sputtered out completely. Still enraptured by the *wunnerbaar-gut* phone visit, Joanna scarcely minded the wind and cold.

Eben's coming to see me!

Chapter 4

The familiar smell of freshly baked cookies greeted Joanna when she returned to the house from the phone shanty.

"Where've *you* been?" Cora Jane asked, eyeing her sharply.

Joanna wasn't ready to reveal her news yet, not without Mamma around. "Oh, just outside."

"Well, that's obvious." Cora Jane reached for two cookies and sampled both kinds as she continued to watch her. "Well, aren't you the secret keeper!"

Joanna ignored that and took her time removing her boots and outerwear. She wanted to savor every moment of her phone chat. Nearly too good to be true!

The back door opened just then, and there was Dat, his boots tracking in snow. He wiped his feet on the rag rug near the door as usual, just as she had, and looked at her curiously as she hung up her coat and scarf. But he said nothing.

All during family worship, Cora Jane stared at Joanna, taking away some of her joy. The minute the silent prayers were finished, Joanna slipped upstairs to write in her diary, which she kept hidden between the mattress and the bedsprings.

"He's comin' to visit at long last!" Joanna whispered as she dressed for bed.

But it was hard to fall asleep, if not impossible, with Eben's voice still in her head. She cherished everything he'd said and was nearly as excited as the first time they met. Oh, she could scarcely wait to show him around Hickory Hollow!

The bitter cold and steady winds made delicate designs on the windowpanes the next morning. Joanna was captivated by the frosty patterns when she awakened just as the sun rose, spraying light on them. She'd overslept, and no wonder, having replayed Eben's phone call happily in her mind throughout the night.

When should I break the news about him—and his visit—to Dat and Mamma? She pondered this while getting ready for another day of chores prior to the Lord's Day tomorrow. She took extra care to inspect her best blue church dresses on wooden wall pegs over near the dresser, thinking she'd wear one of them next Friday when Eben arrived. She wanted to look her very *bescht* since he hadn't laid eyes on her all this time.

Breakfast was applesauce, bacon, and steel-cut oatmeal, which Mamma always said had a way of sticking to your gizzard. Cousin Lena Witmer stopped by right afterward. She didn't bother knocking, just rushed in, tossing off her boots at the back door. She made her entrance into the kitchen still wearing her outer clothes, her blue eyes aflutter.

Lena grabbed Joanna's hand and hurried her upstairs to her room, where she closed the door and fell into Joanna's arms, coat, mittens, and all. "Oh, cousin, I don't know what to do!" Lena cried. "I hope you can help me."

"What's happened?" Joanna tried to comfort her, suggesting Lena sit on the bed.

Lena carried on a bit longer, then managed to wipe her tears away, though she looked terribly forlorn as she sat down. "My sister Verna was going to be my first bridesmaid, but she's been called away to Wisconsin to help with our father's ailing sister." She sighed and seemed to gather herself. "With the wedding next Thursday, I'm out in the cold."

Joanna sat beside her. "Have ya thought of askin' one of your younger sisters?"

Cousin Lena removed her black outer bonnet and fiddled with the strings. "That's just the problem: They're both lined up to be bridesmaids on that day—for Ruthann's wedding, and our neighbor, Kate Elizabeth's."

Joanna hardly knew what to say. Or think.

Again, Lena sighed, her eyes tearing up once more. She searched Joanna's face, then looked away. "I know it's awful late, but I was wondering if, well, maybe you'd consider standing up with me. Along with my cousin Mary Ruth."

Joanna wondered if her surprise registered on her face.

"I really don't want to ask anyone but you, Joanna."

So she has no other options. . . .

It may have sounded presumptuous, coming from any other cousin, but Joanna could see poor Lena's dilemma.

"Well, it's nice of you to consider me, but have ya thought of Cora Jane? She's closer in age," Joanna suggested.

Lena wrinkled her nose, then shook her head. "Ach, not sayin' anything against your sister. It's just that, well, I much prefer you, Joanna."

Joanna wondered whether she'd even have time to sew a bridesmaid dress if she consented. "What color are ya planning?" As was the custom, the two female wedding attendants would dress to match the bride.

"Plum's what I chose for under my white cape apron, since nearly all the brides wear blue anymore."

"Well, I don't have a dress that color, but—"

"Oh, I'll give you money for the fabric and thread. I'd be ever so glad to."

"It's just that, well . . . I'd need time to sew it." With Eben's visit coming up, too, Joanna would be scrambling.

"I can hem or do whatever ya need." Cousin Lena smiled. "*Denki* ever so much, Joanna! You have no idea how grateful I am."

Based on Lena's jubilant reaction, Joanna certainly did understand. And just that quickly she was committed, without even really agreeing. She must try to dismiss the notion that this was to be her fourth time as a bridesmaid, of all things. Once Cora Jane heard this, she'd say Joanna was pushing it for sure. But Joanna felt more confident than ever now, because Eben Troyer was arriving the very day after Cousin

Lena's wedding. To think he was traveling nearly half a day just to see her!

What's it matter how many times I'm a bridesmaid? Joanna thought as she hugged Lena good-bye. "I'll get started with the dress first thing Monday, after the washing's hung on the line."

"Ach, I feel so much better." Lena kissed her cheek. "Denki, dearest cousin."

Joanna walked her downstairs and waited while she donned her black bonnet. Cousin Lena reached to give her another hug. "This means so much to me."

"Glad to help," Joanna said, aware that Cora Jane and Mamma were within earshot now. "I'll go and get the material and thread this afternoon yet."

Waving, Cousin Lena made her way over the snowy walkway to the waiting horse and buggy.

Just as Joanna thought she might, Cora Jane crept up behind her. "What on earth was that about?"

Joanna briefly described the pickle Cousin Lena was in.

Mamma kept silent, but Cora Jane pressed for more. "So she wants *you*, then?"

"Guess I know which wedding I'll be attending." Quickly changing the subject, Joanna asked to borrow the driving horse. But Mamma said to ask Dat, just in case he needed the mare for a trip of his own.

With Cora Jane's eyes boring into her, Joanna slipped on her winter things and headed out to the barn to talk to her father. Truth be known, she was relieved to exit the house. Glad, too, that she just might have an opportunity to talk privately with Dat about Eben's upcoming visit. Such a father-daughter chat she'd never undertaken before.

The field mules were dismantling several hay bales in the barnyard as Joanna made her way to the stable. Sliding open the door, she was greeted by the damp, earthy smell of animals and bedding straw.

She found her father freshening the foals' area. She stood back before making herself known, waiting for courage. Knowing how reserved her father was, Joanna felt tense about breaking this news.

She drew a breath, then stepped forward as Dat acknowledged her. "Can I have Krissy for an hour or so? I need to run an errand right quick."

Dat nodded his consent.

Then, while he was still forking straw from the bale, she ventured ahead and brought up Eben. "We met while at Great-Uncle Amos's funeral back last summer and have been writing since. He's from Indiana, Dat." She paused, aware that her hands were clammy inside her gloves. "And . . . somethin' else. Eben's comin' to visit next Friday."

When her father said nothing—didn't even make eye contact—Joanna tried not to make too much of it. After all, this was Dat's customary response to most things. "He wants to meet you and Mamma, if that's all right."

Her father stopped what he was doing and leaned on the pitchfork. "This is what you want, daughter?"

"I'm in agreement, jah."

Dat frowned. "Is he willing to move here and join our church?"

"I 'spect so."

Dat reached for the pitchfork and resumed his work. At last he said, "Then, jah, we'll meet him."

Joanna had to make herself be still, although she'd much rather have squealed her delight. For Dat's sake, she remained sedate and calm, at least on the outside. "Denki ever so much!"

The slightest hint of a smile crossed his face, warming her clear through. Then she turned toward the stall to get the driving horse. *A pleasant look is a good start*, she told herself.

So all was well.

Doubtless Dat would pass the word to Mamma later in the privacy of their room, so Joanna wouldn't have to go through this again with her. But as for Cora Jane . . . it would be best to tell her directly. "I'll wait till she's in a *gut* mood," Joanna murmured as she led her favorite mare out of the barn to hitch up. "Whenever that might be."

Chapter 5

In the middle of the night, Joanna dreamed she was running through a cornfield, chasing after Cora Jane, trying to catch her to tell about Eben. But in the dream, each time Joanna drew near enough, her sister darted ahead . . . relentlessly out of reach.

Joanna's heart pounded in her sleep. Oh, how she wanted to talk to Cora Jane once again, like sisters should, to say she'd never felt this way about a fellow. She tossed and turned, pulling the sheet like a rope.

Awaking with a start, Joanna was grateful to realize even in her clouded state that what she'd just experienced was not real. *Surely my sister will want to hear my news*, she thought, rising to greet the dawn.

It was the Lord's Day, and a Preaching Sunday at that. The sun's rays were just beginning to extend over the horizon, and Joanna went to raise the dark green shade at first one tall window, then the other. Instead of digging into her hope chest for her writing notebook as she liked to do, she instead felt compelled to read several psalms to start the day. Working on her story somehow didn't seem wise this morning.

Glancing across the hall at Cora Jane's partially closed bedroom door, Joanna contemplated what she ought to do. Surely by now Mamma knew about Eben's plan to visit. Dat would've told her without delay.

Joanna sighed and stared at the lineup of postcards on her dresser which she'd received from her Englischer friend, Amelia, presently in Europe. Such interesting sights and descriptions of London, Amsterdam, and Berlin—places Joanna would never see.

She reached for her Bible and read two psalms, then considered going over to awaken Cora Jane—tell her right away about Eben and be done with it. Yet with her sister so quick to find fault, news of an out-of-state beau had the potential to spoil the reverence of the day, and Joanna decided against it. *At least, not before church.*

Joanna ended up postponing her talk with Cora Jane even longer, as her sister seemed in no disposition for it. *Perhaps after the common meal?* she mused while waiting in the cold to go into church at Cousin Malinda's. Shivering, she stood with Mamma and Cora Jane and her maternal grandmother, *Mammi* Sadie, along with Salina and several of their sisters-in-law, all of them in line with the other womenfolk.

Everyone was bundled up, most of them waiting with their arms wrapped around themselves for warmth.

Up ahead, Joanna spotted Cousin Lena with her own mother and two younger sisters. Despite the frosty air, Lena was smiling.

Such a happy bride to be!

Later, after the Preaching service, Joanna sought Lena out, greeting her warmly. Lena clasped Joanna's gloved hands and insisted they walk around the barn until it was time for the second seating to be served.

In the chilly air, they strolled along together. What a difference a day had made for Lena. "You're simply beaming," Joanna remarked, her breath floating before her. "You actually seem relaxed."

"I surely am." Lena flashed a big smile. "Because of you."

"Ach, don't know 'bout that."

"Well, I do!" Cousin Lena squelched a giggle, then dug into her purse and handed some bills to Joanna. "Here's *Geld* for your dress fabric, before I forget."

Joanna thanked her as she accepted the money. Lena began to describe all of the extra-special treats her mother and many aunts had planned for the wedding feast at Lena's parents' home. Joanna wished she and Cora Jane could talk so easily like this again. What had happened to make Cora Jane so tetchy? Was it truly just about Joanna's being a bridesmaid?

When they rounded the barn for the second time, Joanna noticed Cora Jane walking with Cousin Ruthann, who was also scheduled to wed this week. It was clear the pair were having a confidential chat, so Joanna and Lena hurried back to the house, both of them offering to help Cousin Malinda even though neither had been assigned to kitchen duty.

"Next time," Malinda said, thanking them. "Now go *waerme*—warm up." She pointed to the heater stove, and Joanna willingly obliged.

Eventually, Lena wandered away to talk with her grandmother, who was enjoying the light meal, and Joanna headed to the glassed-in porch to visit with some younger cousins. She imagined how each girl she talked to might take the news of her Indiana beau. What might she say? But, of course, Joanna's parents were wiser than to tell it around, undoubtedly wanting to see how things went with the actual visit.

Will they like Eben?

She observed Cora Jane across the yard, still talking with Cousin Ruthann. Sighing, Joanna wondered whether her sister would mind her manners when Eben arrived. Or would Cora Jane just be Cora Jane and spoil things but *gut*?

Monday morning washday—*Weschdaag*—Joanna, Mamma, and Cora Jane worked together with Mammi Sadie in the cold yet sunny air to hang out all of the wet clothes by seven-thirty.

Once the chore was accomplished, Joanna hurried indoors to check on her bread dough. She planned to bake enough to share with her grandparents and Cousin Malinda, too. She ran tepid water over her nearly frostbitten hands to restore the feeling. The wet clothes would surely dry stiff as boards on such a day.

Once the bread was in the oven, Joanna began to pin her dress pattern to the plum-colored fabric on the kitchen table. She couldn't remember when she'd owned such a lovely dress. Despite the last-minute invitation, being one of Lena's bridesmaids was going to be right nice.

At that moment, Cora Jane wandered down the steps and offered to help cut out the pattern, surprising her. "I know you're in a hurry, jah?" she said.

Pleased as pie, Joanna smiled. "So nice of you. Denki." She glanced up at her sister. *Is now a good time to talk?*

"An unusual color for the bride and the attendants, ain't?" Cora Jane said, running her hand over the fabric.

"Cousin Lena wanted something different than most brides round here."

"I see that."

"She'll be a perty bride, I say."

"A nice color for you, too," Cora Jane replied. "With your blond hair and all."

Glad to work alongside her sister once again, Joanna pinned the seams, eager to sew them up on the treadle sewing machine. The neck facing wouldn't take long, nor would the hem. Lena had offered to help her mark the latter sometime this evening.

Cora Jane began pinning the tucks into the sleeves by hand, humming a hymn as she worked. Her sister's apparent cheerfulness gave Joanna the courage she required.

"I've been wanting to tell ya something," she began.

Cora Jane's head bobbed up. "Oh?"

"I've met someone."

"You've seemed awful preoccupied, so I wondered."

"He's not from round here, though."

Cora Jane frowned. "Isn't that risky?"

"Not really."

"Okay, then . . . tell me more."

Joanna smiled. "Well, he's from Indiana."

"Ach, so far away!"

"And he's comin' to visit this Friday."

"Honestly, now!"

"His name is Eben Troyer . . . and he wants to meet Dat and Mamma."

"And what about the rest of the family?" Cora Jane asked.

"No doubt he'll be happy to meet whoever is around that day."

Cora Jane fell silent. "You aren't thinkin' of going out there to live, are ya . . . if you marry?"

"I daresay he'll come here to court me, when the time comes."

"Well, I should hope so," Cora Jane said emphatically. Her forehead pinched up.

"Please, ya mustn't worry 'bout my promise to the Hickory Hollow church, if that's what you're thinkin'."

"Still, what if he wants you to go there, like some fellas in other districts? What then?" There was an edge of panic to her voice.

Joanna didn't want to get into this. Not when she and Eben hadn't really discussed it. "I'll take things as they come."

She sighed. "I just wanted you to know before he arrives." She didn't dare say, *"So you'll behave yourself."*

Cora Jane moved slowly to the windows and looked out. "Where'd ya meet this fella?"

"At the funeral last summer."

"Way back at Virginia Beach?"

"Jah."

Cora Jane turned to face her. "Where we'd planned to spend lots of time together."

"Please, Cora Jane . . ."

"I'd looked forward to it, ya know . . . but you kept disappearing." Cora Jane's expression turned accusing, her lips curved down. For the longest time, Cora Jane just stared at her. She looked almost stricken. Then her eyes became moist, which surprised Joanna no end. "Well, I'm not goin' to stick around and watch this fella steal you away."

Joanna was flabbergasted. "I never meant to upset you."

Cora Jane reached for the needle, thread, and sleeve once again. "I hope you know what you're doin' is all. I've seen the postcards from your fancy friend, traveling through Europe."

"Amelia has nothin' to do with my long-distance beau," Joanna assured her.

"It just wonders me if you're itchin' to move away from here. Maybe she's given ya a taste for the world."

Joanna didn't offer more to ease her sister's concerns—surely Cora Jane knew her better than that! Nor did she wish, worried and forlorn as Cora Jane looked, to say how wonderful it had been to receive Eben's letters for nearly five months now.

An uncomfortable silence fell between them. "So what's this fella look like?" Cora Jane finally prodded.

Eben was precious to Joanna. She couldn't bear to have her sister criticize anything about him. "I'm really not up to sharing much right now, if ya don't mind. If you stick around, you'll see him for yourself."

"Is he writing to you?"

Joanna said he was.

"But ya never breathed a word of it to me." Cora Jane grimaced. "This is nothin' like the way things used to be. I really don't know what to say."

"Why not just say you're happy for me?" Joanna's stomach was tied up in knots. "Weren't you afraid I'd never be more than a bridesmaid?"

"I *am* happy. How's that?"

Could've fooled me! Joanna looked at her. "What's happened to us, sister?" Her lower lip trembled.

"You tell me!" Cora Jane tossed the sleeve with the needle and thread stuck in it across the table, then abruptly exited the room.

Joanna could hardly believe her eyes. *Will my own sister interfere with my chance for love and marriage?*

Chapter 6

Today's the day, thought Eben, planning to talk with his parents during the noon meal. *Surely they suspect something's up . . . all the letters back and forth.*

He strode across the snowy yard toward the side door that led into the kitchen. Undoubtedly his father would enter the house by way of the utility room door, first stopping to take off his work boots so as not to dirty *Mamm*'s spotless kitchen. Eben was careful to scrutinize his boots, as well, before heading indoors, though today he did not dally long, eager for some black *Kaffi*. Eben removed his work gloves and pulled off his boots on the back porch, leaving them near the door. The appealing aroma of washday stew hit him and, stocking footed, he made a beeline into the warm and inviting kitchen.

The kettle was shrilling as he washed his hands and dried them on the old towel Mamm left out for him and Daed to use. He caught her smiling softly, as if she suspected his reason for taking the shortcut into the kitchen. Mamm nodded and poured boiling water into a coffee cup, then carried it to the table. Eben had never made a fuss over brewed coffee or instant—it made no difference to him. He was just glad for the hot pick-me-up on such a cold morning.

Once Daed appeared, Eben found his tongue. It was long past time to forge ahead and tell them about his sweetheart residing in Lancaster County. Pretty Joanna Kurtz was the dearest girl he'd ever known.

Daed eyed his chair at the head of the table and ambled over to sit down. Eben could hear his father's stomach growling even as they waited for dinner to be served. His mouth watered at the thought of the thick morsels of beef blended with potatoes, corn, and beans. Still, he sat with his hands folded under the table there in his younger brother's spot just to the left of their father. The wooden bench next to him had been scooted beneath the table, dutifully waiting for a larger family gathering. It had been Mamm's idea to offer Eben the solid chair, similar to Daed's own.

After Leroy left for the world.

Eben still recalled the emotional devastation his brother's rebellion had inflicted upon the entire family. And because Leroy's decision to leave remained mighty painful, Eben had waited this long to communicate his interest in Joanna of Hickory Hollow to his parents. Of course, it wouldn't be anywhere close to the same sort of leaving as Leroy had done. Despite that, Daed and Mamm would be greatly affected by Eben's announcement today.

"A girl in Pennsylvania, ya say?" his father replied, nearly sputtering as he set down his spoon.

Eben explained where and how they'd met. "Seemed providential."

Daed's brown eyes were suddenly serious. "I expect you'll want to bring her here to live, after you wed." He paused. "*If* ya do."

"Not sure how Joanna would feel about that." Eben had never brought up the idea to her, knowing how hard it had been on one of his girl cousins to move clear to Wisconsin a few years back. And it was plain from her letters, as well, that Joanna was quite attached to Hickory Hollow.

"We look forward to meeting her," Mamm said, and Daed agreed with a jerky bob of the head.

"You'll meet Joanna before we marry," he assured them, realizing his father's grave look of concern had everything to do with Eben's being his temporary partner in running the farm. "Of course, I'm prayin' Leroy will come back first."

"Jah, we're all still holding out hope for that," Daed said.

Daed gave Mamm a hard frown, then turned back to Eben. "I'm sure ya know, you and your bride will have to live here if Leroy doesn't return home. Your Mamm and I are dependin' on ya, son."

The very thing that kept Eben up at night returned to plague him anew, and he said no more as he pondered his father's declaration.

Joanna worked alongside Mammi Sadie to get the wash indoors and folded that afternoon. She also managed to finish the plum-colored dress, all but the hemming. Because of the latter, she wasn't available to help Mamma get an early start on supper like she usually did. Tonight's meal was an oven casserole of turkey, buttery egg noodles, and mushroom soup—one of her father and Cora Jane's favorites.

Grateful to have a short break in her routine, Joanna thought of running over to Rachel Stoltzfus's before returning to set the table for Mamma.

"Looks like Cora Jane's flown the coop," Mamma remarked with a peculiar look at Joanna when she came down to the kitchen after putting away the dress.

"Most likely upset with me."

"What now?"

"I told her 'bout Eben's visit."

Joanna knew by the glint of recognition on Mamma's face that Dat had filled her in.

"Well, I should think she'd be downright pleased for ya."

Joanna nodded. "If ya don't mind, I'm going to check with Rachel about Eben staying with them for one night. All right?"

"*Gut* a place as any, I 'spect."

"I'll be right back," Joanna said, going to put on her boots and coat for the trek across the snow-covered field.

"If ya see Cora Jane anywhere, tell her to come on home," Mamma said as she followed Joanna into the utility room. "She knows better than to throw a fit like this."

Mamma's fed up, too! Joanna thought as she picked her

way over the windblown snow. She wrapped her scarf more tightly to protect her face from the fierce cold. "How long before word gets out about Eben and me?" she whispered. Her precious secret had been safe for this long. She shuddered at the thought of most all the People knowing her business; the cocoon their love had grown in was dear to her. Yet that was the price of moving forward with a real-life romance. Nothing story-like about it! Of course, hard as it was to surrender their relationship to others' scrutiny, Joanna was thankful Eben was apparently ready to start seriously courting. *Just as I am . . .*

Blue patches of sky appeared through the high clouds, and she wished Eben were coming to see her when it was warmer. Certainly, there were still interesting things to do in November. Why, with all the cold they'd been having, they might even be able to go ice-skating on Samuel Lapp's pond.

She spotted the Stoltzfus farmhouse and hurried toward the driveway. Then, thinking it might be best if she didn't appear too eager when she greeted Rachel, Joanna quickly flattened her smile. No sense in Rachel's guessing right away who Eben was to her. She made her way around to the side door, turning her head away from the wind, and knocked.

"Well, goodness me! Hullo there," Rachel greeted her. "Won't ya come in?"

"Hullo, Rachel." Joanna followed her into the balmy kitchen, replete with a delicious aroma.

"What brings you out in this weather?" Rachel's face was cherry red from cooking over her woodstove. She was one of only a handful of women in the area who still cooked the old way.

"Sorry to barge in so close to supper," Joanna said. "Just wanted to ask a favor."

"Why, sure . . . anything a'tall."

"We're havin' out-of-town company this Friday . . . and, well, I wondered if you'd mind keepin' him overnight."

Rachel fixed her gaze on Joanna, a hint of a smile in the corners of her mouth. "Why sure, we'll put your guest up for ya, Joanna."

"Denki ever so much."

Rachel's curiosity was evident in the arch of her eyebrows. "Is this anyone we know?"

Joanna guessed she wouldn't be getting out of this without filling in a few details. So she did her best to satisfy Rachel and yet not come right out and say that Eben Troyer was her beau.

"Rest assured, we'll treat Eben real *gut*," Rachel said with a nod of her head.

"He'll take his meals with us, of course. You won't have to bother with that."

"Oh, 'tis no trouble—but as you wish." A smile spread across Rachel's face. "We'll look forward to meetin' your friend, for sure."

She saw right through it! Joanna thought as she turned to leave. *Just as everyone else will.* Even so, it was her job to trust that all would go well.

Still feeling hesitant, Joanna tightly pulled her old wool jacket around her and hurried back to her father's house.

Chapter 7

After supper, Cousin Lena arrived to mark the hem of the bridesmaid dress as she'd promised. Joanna stood like a statuette on a stool in the middle of the kitchen as Mamma observed merrily from the head of the table, where she rarely sat.

Meanwhile, Lena chattered nonstop about the many relatives coming to town for the wedding—some from the Somerset area, and others from upstate New York, near the Finger Lakes. All were first or second cousins of either Lena's mother or father and had received written invitations.

"It'll be nice to see some of my own second cousins, then, too," Mamma mentioned, putting the family tree in better perspective for Joanna.

"Which makes them Lena's second cousins once removed?"

Mamma agreed. "And yours, too."

Once the hem was precisely marked by many pins, Lena

insisted on sewing it up at home for Joanna, asking to take the dress with her. "I'll press it up real nice for ya, too." Her eyes twinkled gaily.

Joanna thought Lena might be overdoing it. "It's your wedding, for goodness' sake!"

Yet after a few more exchanges, Joanna realized she wasn't going to get Lena to change her mind; there was nothing to do but let her have her way. Joanna went into the bathroom to step carefully out of her new dress, then folded it neatly. She put on her work dress again and took the lovely plum one out to the kitchen, where she watched Lena tuck it into her wicker basket. "I'll come and pick it up Wednesday afternoon, then. All right with you?"

"Sure," Lena said before marching to the wooden pegs in the utility room, where she'd hung her coat and scarf. Then, just that quickly, she was ready to go. "Denki ever so much, Joanna!" And she was out the back door to the waiting horse and carriage.

"Well, I did my best to persuade her to let me finish the hem," Joanna said, joining Mamma at the table.

"That's one strong-willed bride, I'll say." Mamma laughed softly and glanced at Cora Jane, whose back was to theirs now, where she stood near the counter. "Such traits tend to run in the family."

Joanna caught her meaning and rolled her eyes.

"How'd it go over at Abe and Rachel's?" Mamma changed the subject.

"Everything's all set."

"Sure's nice of Rachel," Mamma said rather cryptically.

Smiling briefly, Joanna agreed. "She's doin' it for you, Mamma, ya know. For her *gut* friend."

Mamma said she supposed that could be. "But even so, Rachel must be awful happy for you . . . just as I am." Mamma eyed Cora Jane again, as if she almost expected her youngest to speak up now and say something kind.

"Well, I can't wait for you to meet him," replied Joanna.

At that, Cora Jane slipped out of the room.

Mamma waited till Cora Jane was gone a few moments before saying, "Someone's definitely sufferin'. Not sure just why."

"Maybe I shouldn't have waited so long to tell her about Eben."

Mamma shrugged. "I wouldn't blame yourself. Some folk are just afflicted with a grouchy disposition."

"Comes and goes like the wind, jah?"

Mamma sighed into her hands. "It might be best if your sister's gone on Friday, like she's threatened to be."

"She said that, too?"

Mamma nodded her head. "It'd be such a shame if her attitude spoiled things for ya."

"Well, Eben comes from a long line of siblings, so surely he's encountered a *schniekich*—persnickety—sister at some time or other."

"Just hope she grows out of whatever ails her," Mamma added.

Or just plain grows up, thought Joanna.

All day Wednesday, Joanna, her mother, and Cora Jane scoured the interior of the house as thoroughly as if they were planning to host Preaching service. They'd washed all the throw rugs the day before, having done up the rest of the laundry on washday.

Cora Jane's apparent disdain for the effort to make things spotless annoyed Joanna. She worked slowly and grudgingly; Mamma actually had her go back and redust or remop certain rooms. Although firm, Mamma was altogether patient, like a mother might be with a youngster. Joanna was grateful for her mother's example and resolved not to let her sister's sour attitude get the best of her, not with so much happiness just around the corner.

Joanna rose early the next day to arrive at Lena's in plenty of time to offer support to the bride. Joanna offered to brush Lena's long blond hair while the other attendant, Mary Ruth Beiler, pressed Lena's white organdy cape apron one last time.

Joanna recalled Cousin Malinda's emotional pre–wedding service breakdown and smiled to herself. There was no evidence of tears for *this* bride. No, Lena seemed impatient to get on with the wedding.

Out the window, Joanna spotted Salina arriving with her husband, Noah. She wondered if Salina would have chosen to come to Lena's wedding had Joanna not been one of the wedding attendants. Nevertheless, it was good to see her and

Noah looking so nicely dressed for the occasion. She loved the way they still glanced so fondly at each other.

Hours later, once the wedding feast was under way, Joanna noted which courting couples were in attendance. As beautiful as the wedding table was, she could hardly wait to get home, thinking of Eben's arrival tomorrow.

She was glad that Dat and Mamma had come, which meant Cora Jane was somewhere around the house. But because Gideon Zook evidently hadn't been invited, her sister must have had to resort to spending time upstairs talking with other girl cousins. Joanna hated to admit it, but she felt more comfortable with her sister in another room just now.

It wasn't till much later, after the evening Singing, that Joanna and Cora Jane walked home together. This was the first they'd been alone since Joanna had told her about Eben's visit, and Joanna was content to walk in silence for quite a ways.

Then, out of the blue, Cora Jane muttered something about Joanna's defying the odds. "You're pressin' your luck, sister."

"I don't see it that way."

"Well, how *do* you see it?"

Breathing deeply, Joanna felt the icy air cut into her lungs. "It's about believing, really."

"That someone's going to marry you?"

"Not just someone." She sighed. *Should I say it?*

"So your beau's comin' to propose marriage, is that what ya think?"

"That's what fellas usually do after writing to a girl so long." She'd divulged nothing more than the truth.

"Okay, so maybe he *is* going to . . . but don't forget he could take you away from Hickory Hollow forever!" Cora Jane sounded hurt. Really hurt. And Joanna didn't know what to say.

"After all, he's already taken you from me before: You never once explained your absence while we were in Virginia Beach, ya know." Her sister paused.

Joanna shook her head. "I didn't realize you were counting on me, Cora Jane—you seemed to be having plenty of fun with our cousins. Honestly, I didn't think I'd be missed."

"Well, now ya know."

Cora Jane's tone was bitter, and Joanna couldn't bring herself to apologize. Lots of older sisters kept romantic things to themselves until closer to an actual engagement. Just because Cora Jane herself had always been so open about fellows didn't mean Joanna was bound to be, as well . . . especially when she'd had so few fellows take an interest in her over the years. *And, too, I didn't want Cora Jane to ruin anything with Eben when we'd only just met,* she thought. Considering her sister's present concern about his being from Indiana, Joanna didn't think she'd been wrong in that.

Cora Jane sped up the pace a bit, not saying more. And Joanna fell in step with her once again.

Chapter 8

Joanna stirred until late that night, unable to sleep. She was excited about tomorrow, yet apprehensive, too. She offered a silent prayer to God, who alone saw her troubled heart. If only Cora Jane hadn't refused to understand the need to keep Eben's affection a secret. After all, this was Joanna's first and only love. *Why can't Cora Jane understand?*

The moonlight crept under the dark shades, playing across the wide plank floor. Was Cora Jane restless tonight, as well? Joanna was too drained to go across the hall to see.

Eventually, Joanna fell asleep, although her rest was fitful.

Hours later, when it was finally time to get up, she tiptoed to Cora Jane's room, expecting her to just be waking. But the bed was neatly made, with no sign of her. *What's this?* Joanna clenched her hands. Where had her sister disappeared to at this early hour? Had she already made good on her threat to leave?

Nor was Cora Jane present at the breakfast table. And when Joanna asked Mamma where she might've gone, her mother shook her head in dismay. Dat raised his eyes fleetingly to meet Mamma's, then resumed eating his eggs and bacon.

She'll return once Eben goes home, Joanna felt sure.

After dishes were done up and put away, Joanna dressed warmly and hurried outdoors to brush and curry both the driving horses, not knowing which one she and Eben might use later. She was anxious to show him around Hickory Hollow, hoping he, too, might fall for its winsome charms. She combed the horses' thick dark manes and tails till they were beautifully smooth.

When she was satisfied they looked exceptionally well groomed, she and her father oiled the harness, working together. While Dat remained mum on the subject of Eben's visit, she did catch him looking her way several times, wearing a thoughtful expression. He'd also taken time to clean up his work boots and was wearing one of his better black felt hats instead of the old gray knit one he usually wore around the farm this time of year.

Even though there was no way Eben would arrive before four o'clock, Joanna found herself keeping an eye out for him from midmorning on. She wanted to be completely prepared in every way. Once she was satisfied all was caught up, she went to bathe and dress in her best blue dress and matching cape apron. She dabbed some light perfume behind each ear and on each wrist. Then she went through the house, scrutinizing the downstairs rooms, trying to see them through Eben's eyes as best she could.

Mammi Sadie dropped in a few minutes later, mouth pursed. "It seems that Cora Jane's run away from home," she muttered.

"I know," Joanna said, offering her grandmother a chair near the heater stove. "She's peeved."

"Joanna's beau's comin' from Indiana," explained Mamma.

Mammi Sadie's eyes lit up. She looked quizzically at Joanna. "So then it's true, what Cora Jane said."

"Cora Jane told?"

"Oh . . . lots of sisters slip up and spill the beans, 'specially about such exciting news, honey-girl."

Joanna didn't know what to think.

Soon, Mammi Sadie had her talking again, and Joanna quickly filled her in about last summer at the beach.

"Well, praise be!" Mammi made over her like a mother cat tending to her kitten. "Today? Your beau's honestly comin' today?"

Joanna said he was, but she wanted to know more about Cora Jane. "Do you know where my sister's gone?"

"Why, sure I do. She's sittin' over in my kitchen eating me out of house and home."

"Ach, now." Mamma's shoulders visibly relaxed. "*Gut.*"

"Is she comin' back anytime soon?" Joanna asked.

"She's in a foul mood. So I didn't dare ask," said Mammi Sadie.

"Well, better keep her over there, then." Mamma gave Joanna a knowing look. "We sure don't want any fussing today."

Mamma doesn't want to run Eben off is what! Joanna had to

smile at how much his visit seemed to mean to her mother and grandmother.

"Tell Cora Jane she's welcome to have supper with us, if she'd like," Joanna offered.

Mamma shook her head. "Do ya really think that's a schmaert idea?"

Joanna wondered. "Well, I dislike excluding her."

"Looks to me like she's doin' that herself, ain't so?" Mammi Sadie said, accepting the hot coffee Mamma offered.

"Jah, 'tis best to leave her be," Mamma said firmly.

"All right, then." Joanna looked out the window from sheer habit. "Keep Cora Jane occupied."

"Oh, will I ever," Mammi Sadie agreed. "There's plenty of patching and whatnot that needs done."

Won't she just love that? Joanna grimaced for her sister, then poured herself some hot water for tea and wandered into the front room, letting Mammi and Mamma talk alone for now. She stood at the window facing the road and peered out. Heavy gray clouds had moved in, and delicate flakes drifted in the air like bits of onion skin. She hoped the snow slowed by the time Eben arrived so they could have a ride around Hickory Hollow, but she didn't want to dictate their activities. Whatever they did was up to him, even though he was their guest.

Now, if only Cora Jane would behave herself and quit causing a silent rumpus!

By five o'clock, Joanna had almost given up on Eben's arrival in time for her delicious meal. She was warming the potato rolls she and Mamma had taken great care to make when she heard her mother let out a little gasp.

Turning, Joanna saw a bright yellow cab pull up to the end of the lane. "Ach, he's here . . . Eben's here!"

Mamma rose and went to the window, smoothing her apron. "He certainly is."

"Are ya nervous, too, Mamma?"

They laughed, acknowledging their shared anxiety, and Joanna's eyes locked with hers.

"Oh, Mamma, pray nothin' goes awry." Joanna fussed with her hair, smoothing the middle part.

"*Puh*, what could go wrong?"

Joanna dared not ponder that. Instead, she asked, "Do I look presentable?"

"You're fine, dear. You look just fine." Her mother smiled and waved her toward the door. "Go on now. Meet your beau."

Reminding herself to breathe, Joanna went to the door, her heart beating double-time. Only in the pages of her stories had she ever experienced a moment like this before. Mere romantic imaginings . . .

Joanna spotted Eben strolling up the lane, carrying a dark duffel bag. He wore a black frock coat and black felt hat, as though for Sunday go-to-meeting. By all indications, he was coming around the back of the house, the way everyone else did in Hickory Hollow. And oh, did he ever look handsome!

Joanna made herself move slowly to greet him, glad to see

the lineup of coats and boots was still tidy from her morning redding up. A *marvel!* Now, standing a few feet from the closed door, she stared at it, nearly boring a hole with her anticipation as she waited for the knock to come.

A thickening band of clouds had blown in with the afternoon, depriving the area of color. The change in weather had occurred just since Eben had arrived in Lancaster city. Joanna's Hickory Hollow looked pale gray beneath the gloomy sky as he paid the cabbie, then walked toward the Kurtz home. He'd checked the address twice for good measure. At long last, the day he'd waited for had come.

Eben took note of the well-kept older farmhouse, similar to his own father's abode. The horse fences had been newly whitewashed, and someone had just recently swept off the long walkway around to the back door, where he assumed he ought to go and knock. Would Joanna herself open the door? If so, how would she greet him?

Relax, Eben told himself. *This is the girl who writes you every single week.*

The reminder was encouraging. And now the moment had come. He stood tall, pushed his feet together, and took a deep breath. *O Lord, bless this time with my sweetheart-girl*, he prayed.

He raised his hand and knocked on the back door with what sounded like confidence, even to him.

Chapter 9

Joanna opened the back door, and there stood her beau, a broad smile on his face.

"*Willkumm*, Eben." She'd never meant anything more.

"Hullo, Joanna . . . it's wonderful to see you again."

"You too." Her cheeks warmed at his words. "Come inside." She opened the door wider.

"Mighty cold here, ain't?" he commented as he removed his boots.

"Jah, 'tis," she said. "Was it this wintry in Shipshewana this morning?"

"Not nearly, and it was mighty early when I left." He shook his head, still smiling. "Driver said you might be getting a big snowstorm here."

Joanna led him through the outer room to the kitchen. Just seeing him again, sensing the lovely feeling of attachment between them, she wished he might get snowed in here for days on end.

Then, remembering her mother was sitting nearby, Joanna introduced her. "Eben, this is my mother, Rhoda Kurtz."

Eben set down his duffel bag and shook her hand. "Denki for allowing me to visit your daughter."

Mamma's eyes glinted her approval. "I daresay you've had yourself a long day." She rose and went to the stove. "Would ya like something hot to drink? Coffee, tea . . . some cocoa?"

Eben kindly accepted some coffee, and Joanna offered to take his coat and hat, which he gave her. She turned toward the utility room but thought better of it. Eben's outer clothes ought to be hung elsewhere. They looked so nice . . . and new. Surely he hadn't put himself out just for her!

Joanna slipped into the sitting room and hung Eben's coat in there, then, returning, she found Eben and Mamma talking quite freely, and she felt momentarily sad that Cora Jane wasn't around to meet him, too.

"My husband's still in the barn, but he'll be along soon," Mamma was saying.

Joanna eventually showed Eben into the sitting room, knowing Mamma wouldn't mind setting the table and putting supper on for the four of them. Joanna had so enjoyed preparing the special meal, delicious recipes in the family for generations: dinner in a dish and Hickory Hollow salad. Dessert was lemon sponge pie, which she dearly loved to make and eat.

"I'm eager for you to meet my father," Joanna said as they sat down. "Just a little warning, though—he's quiet. Rarely says much."

"Ah, I have uncles like that." He laughed a little. "You kinda get to know what they're thinkin' after a while."

"That's exactly right."

Eben smiled at her and leaned forward slightly. "You're even prettier than when I first met ya, Joanna."

She lowered her head. "Ach, Eben . . ."

"You truly are," he said, reaching for her hand. "After supper, I say we go riding . . . just the two of us."

She agreed, unable to pull her eyes away from his.

"We'll have us a nice time," he said.

She knew they would. Goodness, she knew it as well as her own name!

Then, hearing Mamma in the kitchen, she let go of his hand and settled back in the chair.

Eben winked at her before looking around, resting his hands on the upholstered arms of the chair—Mamma's favorite. "A pleasant spot, jah?" He glanced toward the corner windows.

"Mamma likes to read her devotional books and the Bible here where the light streams in."

He picked up a magazine with the title *Ladies Journal: Inspiration and Encouragement by Women of Faith*. He thumbed through and stopped at a particular page. "Well, look at this—an article on natural homesteading."

Joanna leaned over to see.

"It mentions the bugs folks need in a healthy garden. How 'bout that?"

This brought a fond chuckle; then he began to read from the article. "Listen to this: 'Hoverflies and chalcids will consume aphids, white flies, and stinkbugs' . . . oh, and even grasshoppers in alyssum." He looked at her. "Do you plant alyssum?"

"In the late spring, jah." She found it interesting how casual and familiar they were together. "May I see that article?"

He handed her the magazine, holding it open. "Looks like men might even enjoy some of these columns. My father would, I think," he added. "He's not much for reading, though. Mostly the Bible."

"Same with mine. But he does faithfully read *The Budget* and the *Farmers' Almanac*—just not in that order."

In a few minutes, Mamma softly called them for supper, though without coming into the room, honoring their privacy. They rose and walked into the kitchen just as Joanna's father was entering the back door.

May this supper go well, prayed Joanna.

She could hardly wait to share her meal with Eben. But then the back door opened once again, and Cora Jane stepped inside, as if she'd never gone anywhere at all.

Suddenly realizing that Mamma had set the table with only four plates, Joanna scrambled quickly to the cupboard and pulled out another for Cora Jane. It would never do for her sister to think she wasn't wanted, not after spending all day with Mammi Sadie next door, undoubtedly stewing.

But Cora Jane caught her eye just then and saw what Joanna was doing. She raised an eyebrow as Joanna placed the plate and an extra set of utensils on the table. *This is sure to set her off again!*

By the time Dat came into the kitchen after washing up,

Joanna didn't know whom to introduce to Eben first. But it was her sister who looked the most interested, standing in the middle of the room and trying not to be conspicuous in her scrutiny of Joanna's beau.

"Cora Jane, I'd like you to meet Eben Troyer from Shipshewana," Joanna said, finding her voice. "Eben, this is my sister Cora Jane."

"Hullo." Eben offered to shake her hand, which she did with a pleasant enough smile. "It's nice to finally meet you and your family . . . put faces to names, ya know."

"Willkumm to Hickory Hollow," Cora Jane said, eyeing the table again. She went to her regular spot to the left of Dat, who'd dried his hands and was moseying around Eben's duffel bag to the head of the table now without stopping to speak.

"Dat, this is my friend . . . Eben Troyer," Joanna said, holding her breath for what he might say.

Her father said hullo agreeably, then stuck out his hand to shake Eben's.

"Gut to meet ya."

"Please call me Nate," Dat said as he took his seat. "That'll be just fine."

Cora Jane attempted to squelch the smirk that appeared at this but failed. Joanna was on pins and needles as she went around the table to the right of Mamma, where she sat with Eben on her opposite side.

So the suppertime setting was lopsided, instead of the way Joanna had envisioned things earlier, without her sister present. At least Cora Jane had shown some respect and come home to meet Eben. Yet Joanna still wasn't convinced that was such a good thing.

Eben found the unspoken interplay between Joanna and her younger sister curious. There was certainly an undercurrent of tension between them, yet Joanna hadn't referred much in her letters to Cora Jane or to her older, married siblings, all of whom had two or more children of their own. She had written mostly about the sister named Salina and her *three* S's, as Joanna liked to call her young nephew and two nieces. And Joanna had also told of an English friend named Amelia, who played the fiddle, as well as an elderly woman nicknamed the Wise Woman and other folk who lived there in the hollow.

Eben listened as Rhoda Kurtz praised Joanna's cooking skills, finding it somewhat humorous. After all, his taste buds were definitely in the know, and right this very minute, too.

"Joanna cooks and bakes near everything from scratch," Rhoda added.

"'Cept for her pizzas," Cora Jane said, leaping into the conversation, her eyes sparkling mischief.

Eben felt Joanna stiffen on the wooden bench next to him.

"Oh jah, the store-bought tomato sauce," Rhoda defended Joanna. "Well, all the womenfolk use it."

Eben glanced at Nate Kurtz, a seeming caricature with a healthy appetite. His graying beard had somehow managed to grow in the shape of a V, something Eben hadn't seen before. It almost looked as though someone had taken a scissors and trimmed it, and in a droll way, it complemented the man's reserved demeanor.

"Is this your first visit to Lancaster County?" asked Joanna's mother, obviously changing the subject, and abruptly at that.

"Sure is," Eben said as he turned to smile at Joanna.

"Had ya thought of comin' sooner . . . to meet us, I mean?" Cora Jane said, her eyes fixed on her sister.

Eben had to laugh. "Oh, many times."

Dear Joanna fidgeted next to him.

"Couldn't get away before now," he explained. "Bein' my father's right hand, so to speak." He thought now was as good a time as any to let Joanna and her family know about his dilemma. "You see, my younger brother's away from the fold . . . left us two years ago. My father had him pegged to be his partner in running the farm, which hasn't happened. Not just yet."

Cora Jane's eyes widened, as did Nate's. Eben didn't look at Joanna or her mother just now.

"Is that why you didn't come to court my sister right away?" Cora Jane asked.

Her father looked at her, face vexed. "Daughter . . ." he said softly, though the warning in his tone was clear enough. Then, turning toward Eben, he said, "You do plan to move here in time, ain't?"

Eben nodded. "That's my intention." He drew a long breath. "Once my brother returns home."

Cora Jane was looking at Joanna now, no doubt sending messages with her big eyes. It reminded Eben of Leroy, who'd always sat across from him at the table, pulling faces.

"Well, you must know by now that Joanna's already made her baptismal vow to God and the church here," Rhoda remarked. "In accordance with *our* bishop."

"So how's this ever goin' to work, then?" Cora Jane blurted.

"Sister, please!" Joanna said, nearly coming up off the bench.

Cora Jane's head went down and Nate's shot up. Rhoda quickly rose and hurried to the stove, where she reached for the coffeepot. She returned to the table and began to pour it rather shakily into everyone's cups, whether they'd asked for more or not.

Eben felt it was on him to say something to calm things down. "All of my family, and many others in our community, are prayin' for my brother Leroy to return to his senses, to join church."

"The Lord God is sovereign," Rhoda said firmly, turning to carry the coffeepot back to the stove.

"He certainly is," agreed Eben.

"In all His ways," Nate Kurtz added.

Eben made a mental note to privately ask Joanna's father his permission to court her on Hickory Hollow soil. Given the concerned reaction at the table just now, that seemed like the wisest approach. *Best to stick with my original plan.*

Chapter 10

Joanna was surprised when Mamma let Cora Jane know that she alone was to be responsible for clearing the table and redding up the supper dishes.

Meanwhile, Joanna managed to keep her composure until Dat took Eben outside to the barn. "You had no right to speak up like that, Cora Jane! What were ya thinkin', for pity's sake?"

Cora Jane still sat at the table, leaning her head into her hands.

"Now, girls," Mamma said, getting up to look outside. "This'll never do. Let's make this a pleasant time."

"Well, Eben's trouble." Cora Jane rose from her seat. "He is . . . you'll see."

"Listen here, I'd never think of talkin' up to your beau like that."

"Well, don't ya think it's a *gut* thing I did?"

Joanna left the kitchen to go and sit where she and Eben had enjoyed a quiet and relaxed moment, prior to supper. *Before Cora Jane came home!* She sat there, not knowing what to do. Would Eben take the next van out of here tonight yet? She wouldn't blame him if he called for a driver immediately. What sort of hornet's nest had he walked into? *Ach, I hope he isn't thinking the selfsame thing!*

She folded her hands, trying to soothe herself by taking deep breaths. Sometimes it was a good idea to just breathe, especially when feeling fit to be tied. Joanna looked out the window at the rising moon. *Eben never told me about Leroy's role in all of this*, she thought, feeling sad.

Even so, Eben was here now, and she believed he'd meant business about courting her. He had also been honest enough to share his quandary. So shouldn't she simply make the best of their time together? Surely things would work out eventually.

Sighing, Joanna wished Cora Jane had just stayed put next door with *Dawdi* and Mammi for the day.

Eben came inside to warm his hands by the heater stove and urged Joanna to dress "extra warm tonight." Joanna layered up quickly, happy at the thought of going out. And then, with a word of good-bye to Mamma and Cora Jane, Eben picked up his duffel bag and they headed out together. Joanna was surprised to see the sleigh waiting and ready. Evidently, Dat and Eben had hitched Krissy up to the one-horse open sleigh as a treat.

"Thought it'd be fun to see the area while it's snowing," Eben said, guiding her by the elbow as they made their way over the slippery sidewalk and across the driveway.

Even though she was fully capable of getting into the sleigh on her own, Joanna accepted his help, a feeling of relief settling on her. *At least he's not ready to rush right home*, she thought.

Nightfall was approaching as they set out for the evening, turning west on Hickory Lane. Snow was falling more gently now.

She smiled at Eben and was surprised to see he was looking at her, his soft brown eyes seeking her out. "I want to apologize for my sister's impertinence at supper," she said, then paused. "I'm awful sorry."

"I didn't mind, really," he said kindly. "Maybe it's all for the best . . . getting things out in the open right away, ya know?"

"Well, I'm sure her outspokenness bothered my parents. And me."

Eben reached for her hand. He held it close against his chest. "I don't mind a plainspoken woman at all, 'specially when she's speakin' what she believes in."

Joanna couldn't imagine her father saying something like that. Most men she knew felt just the opposite—they wanted their women to be passive and obedient. And even though her own father was a man of little speech, he was most definitely the family patriarch. He made all of the big decisions. Mamma was fairly placid when it came to Dat.

They were coming up now on Samuel and Rebecca Lapp's

sandstone house. Seeing the downstairs windows glowing with old-fashioned amber light made her think of the Lapps' adopted daughter, Katie, who lived in the English world, not far from Hickory Hollow. Since she was shunned, Katie was still very much out of arm's reach of the People.

"There's a nice big pond out behind the Lapps' barn," she told Eben. "I've skated on it many times."

"Maybe we could go before my ride leaves tomorrow afternoon. Would ya like that?"

She smiled, delighted he was so accommodating. "That'd be wonderful-*gut*."

Riding a little ways beyond Samuel and Rebecca's home, Joanna pointed out their bishop's farmhouse. "John Beiler was a young widower, but eventually he remarried a much younger woman," Joanna mentioned. "You'll be stayin' at his wife's parents' house tonight—Abe and Rachel Stoltzfus are just across the field from us."

"Then I guess it might not be a *gut* idea to be out all hours, jah?" He winked and playfully pulled her closer.

"I didn't mean that," she chuckled, explaining that Rachel had said the back door would be unlocked. "You can sleep in the downstairs guest bedroom, just to the right of the kitchen. She'll keep a lantern lit for ya."

"So we *do* have all night, then." Eben kissed her gloved hand.

"If we don't mind getting frostbit."

His laughter filled the sky. "I won't let you get too cold, believe me," he said, pointing to the woolen lap blankets. "Your father saw to it that I was well supplied."

Which means Dat approves of Eben. "The two of you conspired, then?"

"In so many words."

Joanna caught his meaning and had to smile. He must not mind Dat's reticence, she decided.

"He wasn't reluctant to give his blessing when I asked," Eben surprised her by saying. "But I made it clear where the courting will take place. And now we must pray fervently for Leroy's return."

She wished things didn't depend upon his brother's actions. But she was hesitant to say so.

"Where to now?" he asked when they came to a crossroads.

"I know! The one-room schoolhouse is comin' up soon," she said, pointing with her free hand. "You'll see it in the moonlight."

"Did you ever teach school after eighth-grade graduation?" he said.

"I was never asked, but my sister Salina did for three years before she was engaged."

"What about Cora Jane?" he asked. "Did she?"

"There was some talk of it, but she was passed over for one of our cousins."

"And why was that?"

Joanna didn't want to shed more negative light on her sister. "Cora Jane just wasn't ready."

"Too blunt . . . is that it?"

"Maybe so."

Eben slowed the horse a bit. "If your school board's anything like ours, I understand. They tend to have rather inflexible expectations."

She agreed as they pulled into the school yard. Eben helped Joanna down from the sleigh, keeping her hand in his even after she was safely down.

Eben slipped his arm around Joanna while they peered into the windows of the little schoolhouse. She pointed to the large plaque on the wall, just over the chalkboard: *Trust in the Lord*.

"It's been there for as long as I can remember," she said. Joanna was talkative, even expressive, and he liked the way she strung her phrases together—made him think she was well read, although she never mentioned books. Certainly her letters were exceptional. She wrote in a manner he'd never encountered before, as if she were sharing her very heart on the page.

"Come, Eben, I want to show you where I used to sit and eat my snack during afternoon recess." She tugged on his hand, and he loved that she seemed so comfortable with him.

He followed her around to the front of the school, near the steps. "Were you a shy girl?"

"Well, I still am . . . sometimes." She smiled up at him, blinking her eyes.

"*Most* of the time, right?"

"S'pose so." She led him to the swing on the far left. "Right here. This was always my spot," she told him. "I liked to swing as hard as I could, sometimes leaning back and lookin' down at the ground almost upside down, just a-yearnin' for that giddy feeling in my stomach. Know what I mean?"

Did he ever! "I did that hundreds of times." He paused. "So you took your snacks to the swing?"

"I put my lunchbox on the ground until I got tired of swinging fast; then I dillydallied and ate my snacks later, dragging my feet in the dirt."

"Ah, but only after you tired yourself out."

"My classmates didn't call me *schpassich* for nothin'." Her laugh was delicate in the cold air.

"I don't find you peculiar at all, Joanna."

"Well, you're still getting to know me, jah?"

Eben stepped near, reaching for her again and catching the scent of her perfume. "I can't wait till we have more time for that. And . . . I'm thinkin' our courtship shouldn't last too long." Looking into Joanna's eyes, he was incredibly drawn to her. He wanted to take her in his arms right then and there. He had to purposely force away the thought of kissing her parted lips.

"We best be goin'," she said, apparently sensing what he was feeling. "There's so much more to see."

Sighing inwardly, he agreed. There was plenty of time to demonstrate his affection for her—a whole lifetime ahead. *Lord willing*.

Snow was falling harder now, and it made him remember the woolen blankets, which he unfolded and placed over her once Joanna was settled back in the sleigh. "Let me know if you're still chilly. All right?" he said, loving the sweet, reserved way she had about her.

Joanna nodded without speaking, and he wondered if she, too, had yearned for him to hold her close back at the schoolhouse.

They made a complete circle of Hickory Hollow, and Joanna pointed out one fond landmark after another. She told interesting stories, too, about her many kinfolk, her interactions with Englischers at market . . . and a beautifully secluded spot called Weaver's Creek, set back from the road. She said she hoped they'd have time to at least drive by there before he left tomorrow. The way she talked, there was no doubt in his mind she was extremely attached to this small speck on the map. No, a girl like Joanna wouldn't think of leaving her home. She shouldn't have to.

Our very future lies in my brother's hands. . . .

Chapter 11

Along about eleven o'clock that night, Joanna realized she had very little sensation in her fingers and toes. She and Eben had gotten caught up in conversation about his hope to move to Hickory Hollow to live and work. He had a real interest in becoming an apprentice for a smithy, and he wanted to meet the local blacksmith tomorrow. Of course, farming was definitely in Eben's blood, so that was also an option, if they could just find a parcel of land. But considering the lack of available farmland, it was unlikely.

Just then he leaned his face against hers. "Time to get you home," he said. "I'll unhitch while you get warmed up."

"Don't ya want to go directly to Abe Stoltzfus's place? It's on the way back to Dat's." She was thinking of him.

"But then you'll be stuck unhitching by yourself," he said, clearly unhappy about that.

"Won't take much, really. Maybe I'll get Cora Jane to help me."

He chuckled. "You wouldn't."

"No," she said, smiling. "I'm not that brave."

"I really hate to leave ya with that chore on such a cold night." He paused. "Why don't we just head back to your house?" he suggested. "And I'll unhitch while you warm up indoors. Then, once the horse is stabled, I'll come inside for a while."

She touched his arm. "And I'll make ya some hot cocoa."

"We'll sit in your mother's kitchen and talk a bit longer, jah?"

Joanna could tell he liked this idea. "*Gut*, then."

Eben unhitched the mare faster than Joanna expected—surely his fingers were as stiff and numb as her own, and gloves made it even harder to maneuver. Yet presently she could see him leading Krissy back to the barn.

She paced in front of the heater stove, remembering what Eben had said about appreciating a frank woman. His response still surprised her. Evidently Joanna had worried about Cora Jane's candor for nothing.

Looking across the field, she wondered if Rachel Stoltzfus had remembered to light the lantern in the kitchen. She strained to see, and sure enough, it looked like she had. Joanna could just make out the kitchen windows from where she stood. She might simply point Eben in the right direction and let him walk over there on his own, once he'd had a good chance to thaw out. It wouldn't do for them to say their farewell for the night outside Abe's farmhouse anyway, for goodness' sake. Nor would it do for them to get too cozy here in Mamma's kitchen. The way Eben was talking, he might be stuck in Shipshewana working with his father for who knew how much longer yet.

So I mustn't let him kiss me. Joanna didn't want to be sorry later, if for some reason Leroy Troyer didn't return home to partner with his father. *In case Eben can't leave there. . . .*

No, she didn't want to risk giving away her first kiss.

There had been many moments in Eben's life when his head had ruled his emotions, but tonight hadn't been one of them. Eager to get back to Joanna, he pushed hard against the barn door, closing it soundly. He was grateful for the time he'd spent earlier with Nate Kurtz. *My future father-in-law, if all goes well*.

Glancing toward the house, he could see movement through the back door window—was Joanna standing there, waiting? Poor thing, if she was even half as frozen as he was. He tramped through the fresh snow as he made his way back to the house, ready for the hot chocolate. And a few more precious moments with Joanna, as well. He needed to slow down, he thought, lest they spend all their time cuddling. Much as he longed to hold her close, they had so little time together; he wanted to learn as much about her as possible—keep her talking. And, if he wasn't mistaken, there seemed to be something she was holding back from him, something she was hiding, though he couldn't put his finger on it.

Eben thanked Joanna for the large mug of cocoa and plate of cookies. She'd lit the gas lamp over the table so that the light spread across the room and poured into part of the small sitting area where they'd first sat when he arrived. Seeing her again now, in this place, he marveled at how dear she'd become to him since that first evening by the ocean. He realized anew how fortunate he was that she was still single, not snatched up and married years ago.

Joanna came over to the table and sat next to him on the bench. She smiled without speaking as she began to sip her own cocoa, but her eyes danced in the warmth of the kitchen.

"I enjoyed seein' Hickory Hollow," he said.

"Would be nice if you could see it in the daytime, too."

He agreed. Then he thought to ask the name of their blacksmith. "I'd like to talk to him right quick tomorrow, if you don't mind."

"I'm sure Smithy Riehl would be happy to meet you and talk shop."

"Of course I'd like to work in some fun for us, too," he went on. "I've been wondering . . . do you have an extra pair of skates big enough for my feet?" he asked, wishing he didn't have to leave so soon.

"I'm sure we do somewhere."

He nodded. "How well do you skate?"

She ducked her head, shy again. "Salina says I'm perty *gut*."

"I'll bet you are." Eben reached for a chocolate chip cookie. "So we'll go skating bright and early tomorrow."

"After a nice hot breakfast, jah?"

"If you're cooking, it'll be delicious."

She blushed and nodded. "What's your mother usually make for breakfast?" she asked.

He realized just then that, other than Leroy, he hadn't talked much about his own family. "Anything from oatmeal to chicken and waffles and gravy. Sometimes scrambled eggs with ham."

"Sounds filling."

"I'd like you to meet Mamm sometime . . . and Daed, too."

"That'd be real nice."

"I hope it can be soon." He sensed her sudden hesitance. Who could blame her, after what he'd revealed at supper? "Don't worry. Something will work out, Joanna." He reached for her hand. "I believe God has a plan for our lives . . . yours and mine—together."

Slowly, she smiled. "I've felt that way, too."

"So we'll just trust in that, jah?" He leaned near. "All right?"

After a time she asked if he'd like more cocoa, but because it was growing late and he was mindful of the Stoltzfuses' kindly gesture for the night, he said he should head over there.

Quickly, Joanna offered him a flashlight from the lowest cupboard. "This'll help ya see your way."

They walked hand in hand out to the utility room, where he turned and thanked her again for the delicious drink and the evening. "I'll see ya tomorrow." He paused. "My sweetheart," he added in a whisper, reaching for her.

"*Gut Nacht*, Eben." She stepped back ever so slightly, and he knew right then that he didn't dare stay any longer. He picked up his duffel bag.

"*Da Herr sei mit du*—God be with you, Joanna." With that, he reached for his black felt hat from the nearest wooden peg, then pushed open the back door and stepped out into the frosty night.

Chapter 12

The moment Eben left, Joanna went upstairs to find Cora Jane near the doorway to her bedroom. "You're wasting your time with Eben," she declared.

Joanna walked past her sister, letting it go—she wasn't about to allow anyone to spoil her lovely evening.

"I'm serious. How can ya go out ridin' when he basically told you he's uncertain he can ever move here?"

Hearing her own fears verbalized, Joanna shuddered.

"*How*, Joanna?"

Turning slowly, she measured what she ought to say. "Why are you makin' this your business, sister?"

"I hate to see you get hurt . . . and you will."

"You seem so sure," Joanna said.

"I'm just good at tellin' the truth."

Suddenly exhausted, Joanna motioned toward her room. "Good night, Cora Jane. *Ich geh noch em Bett*—I'm goin' to bed."

Her sister was big-eyed but mum as Joanna closed her door and leaned hard against it in the darkness.

"I hate to see you get hurt," Cora Jane had said.

Oh, what Joanna wouldn't give to erase those words.

But how, when her sister's fears were her very own?

Eben made his way over the snow-covered ground to the Stoltzfus house, glad for the flashlight. He flicked it off and moved quietly into the dimly lit kitchen, still carrying his duffel bag. There, he found a lantern and a welcoming note, which reminded him of his own mother's hospitality.

Recalling where Joanna had said he was to sleep, Eben carried the lantern through the kitchen and toward the front room, into the guest bedroom on the right. Then, raising the wick a bit, he sat on the bed and opened his Bible to Matthew's gospel and began to read as he did each night.

After several chapters, his eyes felt scratchy, and he closed them. He recalled a long-ago afternoon. He and young Leroy had been in charge of bringing home the herd for milking. Leroy had carried a long stick, shaking it back and forth over the emerald-green pastureland as they headed toward Daed's big bank barn.

Eben had seen it first: a single-engine plane buzzing overhead. But it was Leroy whose wide eyes were filled with craving as he stopped suddenly to raise his stick and trace the plane's path across the sky, like an artist's brush on a vast blue canvas. Then and there, he stated, "*Mark my words, Eben. One day I'm goin' to fly like a bird.*"

At the time, Eben had thought his brother meant he wanted to be a passenger on a flight someday. But no, even then Leroy's heart must have been set on being a pilot.

Years later, in the wee hours one night, the distinct sound of Leroy's tennis shoes squeaking in the upstairs hallway would record itself in Eben's brain. Stiffening under the covers, Eben had heard Leroy descend the stairs and knew better than to rush after him or attempt to call out to stop him. Eben hadn't even considered alerting their parents. No, when morning came, they all knew Leroy was gone.

Shaking off the miserable recollection, Eben began to pray the prayer he'd offered up ever since Leroy jumped the fence. But this night, he did so more earnestly than ever before: *O Lord, hear my prayer for my brother. Lead him back to us in your will and time, for your sake.*

Eben paused, thinking how to phrase what he wanted to add.

And for Leroy's sake, too . . . as well as Joanna's and mine. Amen.

Joanna awakened full of anticipation the next morning. She slipped on her white cotton bathrobe, then raised the shade to peer out, welcoming the rosy daybreak. Another inch of snow had fallen in the night, making a soft covering over yesterday's accumulation. The beauty made her think of

Eben, just a field away. Was he also up early, contemplating their day together?

Looking down, Joanna saw where a small fox, or perhaps a young deer, had cut across the newly fallen snow toward the pastureland, its tracks meandering around a walnut tree in the side yard. This time of year had always been bittersweet for her—the year had matured to its eleventh month, and wedding season was in full swing. The season brought joy to most families, but melancholy to the women who'd been passed over . . . another reminder of romantic rejection.

She moved from the window and returned to the small table next to her unmade bed. *Have I grown this year in the fear and admonition of the Lord?* She prayed so, and sat next to the window to read a single psalm before asking for a blessing on the day.

Joanna began to make a nice hot breakfast to start things off, even though Cora Jane's eyes were sending a silent message that Joanna was merely endeavoring to impress Eben.

Then, of all things, Cora Jane hurried off to cook breakfast next door, first making a mumbled effort to say where she'd be before leaving by way of the back door.

"You know your little sister," Mamma said, excusing her to Joanna.

Joanna tried not to pay attention to the slight, keeping her focus on Eben's imminent arrival. With a fork, she lifted a slice of bacon in the pan to make sure it was perfectly crisp.

When Eben arrived and the food was ready, she and Mamma worked quickly to get everything on the table nice and hot. Then, eager to dig in, Dat led the silent prayer before the four of them enjoyed the tasty spread.

Surprisingly, Eben and Dat had plenty to say to each other during the breakfast of fruit, sticky buns, fried eggs, bacon, and blueberry pancakes. They discussed not just the weather, but the upcoming farm auctions, which made Joanna smile.

Dat likes him!

Mamma was also relaxed compared to last evening and seemed to know without being told that Joanna and Eben had plans for the remainder of his visit. In fact, Mamma practically shooed them out the door, saying she'd do the dishes alone. "Have yourselves a real nice time."

"Denki. We will, Mamma," Joanna said before settling into the sleigh amidst many warm lap robes, thanks once again to Dat. She was thrilled to be alone again with Eben—she'd never felt so comfortable with anyone.

Not far up the road, Joanna finally decided to reveal her love for writing. She'd wanted to wait for the ideal time.

"Stories? Really?" He was all smiles.

"And some poetry, too."

"Well, I'm not surprised, given your letters—they're always so interesting. I really look forward to them."

She didn't mention that other people—especially her circle letter pen pals—had told her they also enjoyed her descriptive letters. "But my stories are just for fun, kinda like your picture taking. I don't share them with anyone."

"So . . . a secret writer." He appeared to mull that over,

then asked, "Do you ever write anyone you know into your stories? Me, for instance?"

She flirted back. "As a matter of fact . . ."

"Well, now I'm going to have to read them for certain."

"Oh, you think so?" She laughed, but truly she was delighted.

"What's to hide?"

"No secrets," Joanna said, more thankful than ever for her wonderful beau, someone with whom she could share all of her heart.

Their first stop was Smithy Riehl's blacksmith shop. Joanna was happy to see the stocky middle-aged man grip Eben's hand in a friendly handshake as he offered to show him around. Not wanting to listen in, she walked to the house and visited the smithy's wife, Leah, who was busy mending a pair of her husband's pants. Joanna sat and kept her company, all the while hoping Eben's visit here might bring a promise of work from the highly respected blacksmith.

"That's a fine young man you've got there," Leah said, eyes smiling. "From round here?"

"Indiana," Joanna was quick to say.

"Oh, is that right?"

She nodded, knowing the grapevine would be swinging soon. "I can help ya mend while I wait."

Leah gave her some socks to darn, and the two women

sat silently working, although Joanna couldn't help noticing Leah's frequent glances at her.

Later, when Joanna and Eben were on their way to the pond behind Samuel Lapp's barn, Eben volunteered some of what he and the smithy had discussed, including the fact that Eben was encouraged to do some apprentice work with the blacksmith back home.

"Have you been interested in blacksmithing for long?" Joanna asked.

"Well, I learned a few things from our smithy back home one summer, during my teens." Eben explained that his father had urged him and his brothers to learn a trade, along with farming. "Daed always said, 'Ya just never know when it might come in handy.'"

Joanna felt reassured by the fact that her beau was planning ahead for their future as a married couple. As they rode along the familiar back roads, she realized just how wonderful life in Hickory Hollow would be with Eben by her side.

When they came upon Weaver's Creek, Joanna pointed out the lovely spot, so pretty with the dusting of snow on the boulder in the middle of the creek. "Once you're settled here, I'll show you round the whole area," she said. "It's a little too cold today."

"I'll get myself back here the minute I can," Eben promised, reaching for her gloved hand. "Do you trust me, Joanna?" His eyes searched hers.

She nodded her head, relishing his nearness, already dreading his departure. *How I'll miss him!*

⁂

Eben was relieved to busy himself with parking the horse and sleigh while Joanna dashed to the Lapps' big house to ask permission to skate out back. He wasn't so keen on riding around in an open sleigh, letting the People here see Joanna with a virtual stranger. The last thing Eben wanted was to have folk murmuring about Joanna's romance with an out-of-state boy. *Hopefully I won't be one for long*, he told himself.

Waiting near the horse, he eyed the two-story bank barn over yonder. The more time he spent with Joanna, the more he knew they were meant to be together. Surely the wedge that was keeping them apart for now would vanish in good time, leaving Eben free to depart Shipshewana.

The Lapps' pond belonged entirely to Joanna and Eben, a novelty for Joanna, who had never skated there without at least a dozen or more other youth sharing the patch of ice. The sun rose higher in the sky, and she enjoyed the warmth on her back as she and Eben couple-skated, flying over the frozen surface together. But what she liked most was his strong arm around her waist, guiding her, supporting her as they went . . . connecting them as a unit. It was as if he had always been there for her.

What'll I do when he leaves?

She made herself reject the miserable thought, wishing the sun might slow its steady climb.

After the noon meal of hearty chicken corn soup, Eben suggested they go walking around her father's property. He said it with a wink that told Joanna there was more on his mind than merely seeing Dat's farmland.

She liked his more casual appearance today, his combed hair free of its more formal black felt hat, and a warm jacket instead of the dressier frock coat he'd arrived in yesterday. Oh, to think of all they had seen and done in the space of not even twenty-four hours! She doubted she'd sleep tonight with thoughts of Eben rushing over her. How could she turn off such strong feelings, just because he was gone from sight? He'd managed to impress himself upon her heart, and there wasn't anything she could do about it.

They walked leisurely, dawdling as they picked their way over the field lane that ran along the perimeter of Dat's vast acreage. Eben held her hand like he might never let it go, and more times than she could count, their arms touched, sending shivers down her spine.

"There's where I got your phone call." She pointed to the old shanty to the left, clear out in the silver field.

He smiled down at her, reminding her that he would always call her every other Friday at seven o'clock.

"Guess I'd better make sure my flashlight has plenty of fresh batteries," she said.

He laughed lightly, and when they looked at each other, neither seemed to want to turn away.

"Will ya wait for me, Joanna?" he asked, serious but hopeful.

"Jah," she said softly, knowing his words were more of a promise than a question.

"For certain?"

She assured him with her smile.

And when it came time to part, Eben took her tenderly into his arms. For the sweetest moment ever, she felt the beating of his heart.

"I'll write to you, my darling," he whispered.

Much as she loved writing, she dreaded the thought of returning to that way of communicating when his nearness was just so lovely, the very answer to her heart's cry. And when he said her name, she raised her face to his, still wrapped in his strong arms.

"Oh, Joanna, I'll miss ya so."

Tears sprang to her eyes as he searched her face, lingering over her brow, her eyes . . . and then her lips. She couldn't help it; her resolve flew far away, and she longed for his kiss.

A crow cawed loudly over their heads, and just that quick, Joanna shifted slightly, offering her cheek instead of what he'd surely prefer. And what she, too, so yearned for. Oh, to know the feel of his lips on her own! *When Eben's my husband, I'll know*, she reminded herself. *We must wait. . . .*

She slipped gently out of his arms, smiling to comfort him. And he followed her, reaching again for her hand as they walked more quickly now to the phone shack, where Eben made his call for the cab. Too soon he'd be taken away from her, all the way to Indiana.

Chapter 13

That night, Joanna put pen to paper, writing the story of her heart. She included every emotion she'd felt during Eben's wonderful visit, and after she outened the lamp, she could scarcely sleep, reliving again and again how he'd held her . . . and the sweet desire she saw so vividly in his eyes.

As days passed, she attended still more weddings, assisting in the kitchen at several, and looked forward to the weekly quilting circle at Mary Beiler's. Joanna's older brothers and Dat worked to shred cornstalks for bedding and attended packed-out farm sales as far away as the eastern county line and into Honey Brook. Other older Amish farmers, weary of the cold, headed south to places like Pinecraft, Florida, and other sunny climes, once wedding season was past.

Joanna and Cora Jane said precious little to each other all the while. Joanna had learned soon enough that things went more smoothly that way. She enjoyed going next door to sit with Dawdi Joseph twice a week, giving Mammi Sadie time to run errands or just to have a slice of pie and a quiet afternoon with her older sisters or Mamma. Joanna cherished the time with her Dawdi, though his memory seemed to be weakening. His recollection of Bible verses was perfect, but he was often hard-pressed to remember where Mammi had gone off to, or what they'd been up to just a day before. *How long before he won't recognize me anymore?* she sometimes wondered.

Besides time with her *Grosseldre*, Joanna also anticipated her occasional visits to see Cousin Malinda. And every other Friday evening a few minutes before seven o'clock, she dashed off to the phone shack to receive Eben's calls, ignoring the looks Cora Jane sent her way.

Yet as wonderful as the phone calls were, Joanna pined for Eben. Joanna recalled his suggestion that they trust God for their future. So much hinged on a day too far ahead . . . at least for her liking. How she longed to hear the three words he hadn't said. Was he waiting for just the right moment to say "I love you"?

Upon his return from visiting Joanna, Eben had been pleasantly surprised when his father agreed to let him take a day off from farm duties each week to work as an apprentice with the local smithy.

The area blacksmith shop where Amish farmers came to

have their horses newly shod was set back a ways from the main farmhouse, with its own lane. In just a short time, Eben had discovered how much he liked the work—everything about it from trimming and filing horses' hooves with clippers and rasp, to measuring the new shoe against the hoof, and then heating it on the blazing anvil. Eben worked mighty hard, too—an experienced smithy could shoe a horse in less than an hour, shoeing anywhere between six and eight horses during the space of a typical day. Eben was determined to learn the particular skills involved, anxious to move forward with the hope of working alongside the Hickory Hollow smithy one day.

Yet as Eben joked with customers and busily went about his duties, he couldn't quash the concern that ever hovered in the back of his mind: His splendid plans for the future were for naught if Leroy did not return.

Joanna fretted as the months dragged on without another visit from Eben. Winter melted into spring, and still he stayed away. Was he stepping back? To his credit, he continued to call her, and his letters arrived with the same frequency. He wrote of working with his father to run their big dairy operation, and also told about his apprenticeship with the smithy. Promising as that was, nothing further was said about Leroy or any type of backup plan if his brother didn't come home.

Joanna assumed that with so much responsibility resting on his shoulders, Eben was sacrificing any free time to write to her, and she was grateful. She did wonder if her worries were the fault of her active imagination. Or was she actually reading between the lines? Surely his thinking hadn't changed. Surely the hope of leaving Shipshewana still remained strong.

Trying not to lose heart, she occupied her time by making quilted potholders and embroidered pillowcases for market, as well as helping around the house and next door, too, at the *Dawdi Haus*. She was thankful for the opportunity to earn extra money at the Bird-in-Hand Farmers Market.

As for her sister, when Cora Jane wasn't sewing market goods with Joanna, she was still accepting buggy rides from the same fellow—Gideon Zook. Joanna envied the frequency of their outings under the stars, remembering that one sweet November evening in the sleigh with Eben Troyer. Oh, she hoped Eben still felt the same way about her! With all of her heart, she did.

One March day, Joanna was delighted to receive a letter from her English friend, Amelia Devries. Not wanting to alert—or alarm—Cora Jane, she took the letter to her bedroom and closed the door, settling onto the chair next to the window. Feeling secure there, she began to read.

Dear Joanna,

Thanks so much for your recent correspondence!

I hope you're doing well . . . and still writing your wonderful stories. You might be surprised, but I often think about the one you shared with me when I was there visiting last summer. It was quite compelling—your characters seemed so very real!

Have you ever thought of getting your stories published? If so, I would be the first to encourage you to do whatever it takes.

Just recently, my own mother received a book-publishing contract. Mom jokingly says that if she can do it, anyone can. Of course—like you—she has been writing secretly for quite some time. So this is by no means a sudden success. . . .

Joanna smiled at Amelia's enthusiasm but was also cautious not to let the remarks go to her head. And she wasn't about to get herself an agent or move heaven and earth to get published, not when seeking publication was frowned on by many Plain communities. It was the farthest thing from Joanna's mind.

Yet there were times when she privately considered what it might be like for other people to read her work . . . but precisely what form that might take, she really had no idea.

It was April now—ten months since Joanna had first met her beau—and the flowering shrubs were starting to burst forth alongside Hickory Lane. A horse's neigh caught Joanna's attention where she sat at Mamma's table beneath the gaslight, writing yet another letter to Eben. She was glad to have the house to herself this evening. Thankful, too, that Cora Jane had followed Mamma out the back door after supper dishes were put away, to hurry over the dirt field road to visit Mattie Beiler, longtime Amish midwife.

Joanna smiled as she signed off: *Yours always, Joanna.* It was a good thing her nosy sister couldn't be here to peer over her shoulder! Cora Jane had made it clear over the past months that she still frowned on Joanna's Indiana beau. It didn't help Eben's case when he was still stuck in Shipshewana.

Barefoot, Joanna rose and made her way to the rear screen door, where she looked out at the hazy sky, the humidity obscuring the sunset. Over in the pasture, eight mules meandered toward the barn—dark, lumbering figures against the coming twilight.

She stared at them, sighing. It was such a long time since she'd delighted in snuggling with Eben, his smile ever so dear in her memory. More and more like just a pleasant dream. Her heart had never ached for someone like this. They were supposedly a couple. Yet at such lonely times, Joanna feared that nothing more might come of their long-distance courtship. After all, Eben had made only that one visit.

If we could just have more time together!

Their days at the beach and last November's visit and their phone calls were hardly enough to sustain a near engagement. Their relationship needed a shot in the arm—they needed to see each other again, face-to-face. And more frequently, too.

Surely Eben also feels this way.

Joanna noticed a golden barn cat squeezing beneath the newly painted white porch banister. All the while her father and his two older brothers discussed feed prices in their lineup of hickory rocking chairs. They also speculated who might get the most cuttings of alfalfa come summer.

Leaning her head against the doorjamb, she enjoyed the sweet fragrance of Uncle Ervin's pipe tobacco, though neither her father nor Uncle Gideon had ever taken up the habit. *Bishop John disapproves.*

Joanna sometimes wondered about Eben's bishop. Her beau rarely mentioned these kinds of things in his letters. Was their man of God patient and measured . . . kind? Or unyielding and stern, as she knew some to be—like their own bishop, John Beiler? Would it be difficult for Eben to transfer his church membership here, to relocate to Hickory Hollow at the appropriate time?

Joanna didn't see Mamma and Cora Jane anywhere just yet. Mattie's husband had recently remodeled the kitchens in both the main house and the Dawdi Haus, and Mattie wanted to show them to Mamma. Nearly all the Amishwomen nearby had beautiful kitchens resembling most any modern one—except, of course, the stove and refrigerator ran on propane gas. Mattie had gone on about the "perty oak woodwork" this morning while having coffee here, and that had apparently sent Joanna's mother running over there. The two friends were known to work well together, putting up jellies or jams in the space of a few hours, even after the day's chores were done. And oh, the stories that flew from their lips . . . especially from Mattie's, telling all about the many babies she'd caught through the years.

Heading back indoors, Joanna gathered up her letter to Eben and went to her room, placing it in the middle dresser drawer for now. Her heart beat faster at the thought of his reading it in just a few days.

Smoothing her hair bun, Joanna headed back downstairs and exited by way of the front door so as not to interrupt her father and uncles. She skirted the main house to visit her grandparents in the adjoining Dawdi Haus. Mammi Sadie often baked sweet cherry desserts—a favorite fruit of Joanna's—and thinking of warm cherry cobbler with a dollop of vanilla ice cream on top made her quicken her steps.

There was no need to knock on the back door—she'd been told for years by Mammi to "chust come in," which she did, pushing on the screen door and stepping inside.

Sure enough, Dawdi and Mammi were seated at their kitchen table having dessert—still like best friends after all these years. "Hullo," Joanna said softly. "Thought I'd drop by . . . see how you're doin'."

"Oh, fine . . . fine," Dawdi said, a bit droopy eyed as he forked up another bite. "Pull up a chair, won't ya?"

"Denki." She did just that as her grandmother dished up an ample portion of cherry cobbler and placed it on one of several dessert plates nearby on the table, just waiting for company. *The best baker round Hickory Hollow, hands down.*

Mammi Sadie looked flushed and reached into her dress sleeve to produce a white hankie, fanning herself with it. "A *gut* strong breeze would help to blow this humidity out of here, jah?"

Joanna agreed as she took another forkful of the dessert, glad she'd come over. "Have yous had evening prayer and Bible reading yet?" she asked.

Dawdi Joseph smacked his lips. "*Gut* thinkin'. Sadie, where's the old *Biewel?*" He winked at Joanna. "Might as well let our young whippersnapper here do the readin'."

"Well, my German's not so *gut*," Joanna warned.

"Mine ain't much to boast about, neither." Dawdi motioned toward the bookcase. "Look for the bookmark," he added.

Joanna rose and went to the shelf where the Bible for daily use was stored, as well as the old family Biewel with tattered edges. She lightly touched the latter, recalling that it had possibly come over in 1737 from Switzerland with some of their ancestors on the *Charming Nancy*. The Lancaster Mennonite Historical Society would love to have it for their secured archives, if they knew.

Picking up the newer Bible, she found the spot in Psalms and returned to the table. She wished her grandparents used the English Bible so they could more easily understand the verses, like Eben said he did. Some of the young people around here did the same.

"'O Lord God of my salvation, I have cried day and night before thee: Let my prayer come before thee: incline thine ear unto my cry. . . .'"

When she'd finished, she closed the Bible reverently, finding it curious that the reading was so fitting for her tonight. How good of the Lord God to be mindful of her sadness. Silently, Joanna breathed a thankful prayer.

"Nice of ya to read for us," Mammi Sadie said, scooping more ice cream and plopping another spoonful on Joanna's plate without asking.

She knows I crave homemade ice cream!

Dawdi Joseph peered over his glasses. "Better save some for Reuben, or he'll be disappointed when he gets here."

Mammi's mouth dropped open. "Joseph, dear, your brother passed away nearly two years ago."

"What're ya talking 'bout, Sadie Mae?"

Mammi gave Joanna a quick frown, her cloudy blue eyes dim with concern.

"I just talked to Reuben—yesterday, in fact. Why, sure I did." Dawdi shook his head repeatedly, his face perspiring. "You keep gettin' things mixed up." He continued mumbling. "You were off somewheres baking pies and whatnot."

Wisely, Mammi Sadie said no more, her lips tightly pressed. Joanna had seen her handle worse things before, sometimes talking gently to Dawdi when he was disturbed or confused due to memory issues. Things like *"I know it's hard, Joseph,"* or *"I'll stay right here till you feel better."*

Mammi Sadie was as kind as Ella Mae Zook, and Joanna was glad she and Dawdi lived so close in their final years.

Later on, after Dawdi Joseph wandered into the sitting room and Joanna was alone with Mammi, she asked about Dawdi's fixation on the past. "His memory is so sharp 'bout the olden days, ain't?"

"Seems to be the way of aging," Mammi replied. "For some of us, at least."

Joanna felt sorry for her grandfather but knew he was in the best of care with Mammi Sadie, whose mind was as clear as a bell. "You let me know when you'd like some time off, jah?" Joanna offered. "I'm happy to sit with him more than a couple times a week."

"I'm all right, really."

"Well, ya need to get out, too, don't forget."

Mammi reached across the table and touched her hand. "I daresay it's you, Joanna, who needs to get out more often, dear."

She nodded, guessing her grandmother had heard it from Mamma. "S'posin' you're right."

"Which reminds me, your cousin Malinda asked 'bout you the other day."

"Oh?" Joanna perked up. "Is she all right?"

"I think so, but she misses her family at times, like some young brides do."

"I should go see her more often." Joanna finished up her dessert.

"Jah, I think she'd like that."

Joanna pushed her chair back and thanked her grandmother for the tasty dessert. Then, making her way toward the back door, she called "Gut Nacht" to Dawdi and decided to go see Cousin Malinda tomorrow. Malinda's parents and younger siblings lived clear over on the other side of the hollow, so no wonder she sometimes seemed lonely.

Might cheer us both up.

Chapter 14

"Well, lookee here!" Malinda said, smiling after supper the next evening as she opened the back door and met Joanna on the porch. Her blond hair was parted perfectly in the middle and neatly pinned into a thick bun at the base of her slender neck. Beads of perspiration glistened on her temples.

"I've been missin' ya." Joanna kissed her cousin's moist cheek.

"Everything all right?"

"Oh jah . . . just keepin' busy with planting the family vegetable garden and whatnot." Joanna followed Malinda around to the potting shed in the side yard. *"The heart of my garden,"* Malinda liked to say. In the summer, it was a cool spot to relax or pray amidst stacked pots, drawers filled with seed packets, and book-sized shelves ideal for storing gardening magazines and guides. There were snips, pruners, and trowels in an old clay pot. Birdseed, sprayers, several spare buckets, hoes, rakes, and shovels, as well as kneeling pads, were well organized in many nooks and crannies. And along one windowless wall, Malinda had a pegboard where she stored garden shears, scissors, and a hammer for small repairs. She even had a comfortable old rocker in the corner.

Joanna's cousin lit a small lantern and pulled out two wooden stools, and they settled in for a heart-to-heart talk beside the wheelbarrows and a push mower.

"Are ya goin' to the quilting bee tomorrow?" Joanna asked, noticing the way fair Malinda beamed in the lantern's light.

"Maybe next time. I'm helpin' my neighbor with spring house cleaning."

"We're hopin' to finish up one real perty friendship quilt," Joanna added.

Malinda continued to smile.

Looking at her, Joanna sensed she had something on her mind. "You want to tell me something?"

Malinda glanced over her shoulder, toward the barn. "Honestly, you might not be surprised at all." She paused a second, her eyes twinkling. "So far I've only told Andy."

Joanna's heart leaped up. "Oh, I think I can guess."

"Can ya, now?"

Nodding, Joanna said, "Are you expecting a baby?"

Malinda clapped her hands and laughed softly. "Well, aren't you the schmaert one."

"Oh, such wonderful-*gut* news!" Joanna nearly toppled the stool in her hurry to embrace her cousin. "I'm so happy for ya."

Malinda's face radiated joy. "Just think . . . our first little one, comin' in early November."

Tears sprang to Joanna's eyes. Oh, to be married like Malinda and starting a family! She could just picture herself confiding the same sort of lovely news to her cousin, once she was wed to Eben.

Returning to her stool, Joanna ventured a quick look at Malinda's middle, which as of yet showed no signs of the wondrous news. She imagined how it might feel to have her own tiny babe growing so close to her heart.

Malinda continued talking. "I suppose it's much too early to be makin' cradle afghans and other baby things. Even so, I've already started jotting down names."

"I'd be doin' the same thing if I was in your shoes." Just that quick, Joanna noticed they were both barefoot, and they laughed heartily.

"Dare I ask how things are progressing with your beau?" Malinda's expression turned quite sober.

The question was certainly warranted, but Joanna was caught off guard. She shrugged, feeling the need to keep mum.

"Ah, now, there must be *something*." Malinda leaned forward, clearly wanting to coax it out of her. Joanna recognized that look as one she'd seen on Mamma's face, as well. "I'll keep quiet, promise," Malinda assured her.

"There's nothin' much to tell."

Malinda frowned, her gaze more scrutinizing. "Aw, cousin."

"No, really."

Malinda relented. "All right, then. But I'll keep you in my prayers."

Joanna forced a smile. She disliked pushing her cousin away, but what could she say?

Darkness began to settle in. "No one knows I'm gone from the house," she said. "Might I borrow a flashlight to head back?"

"Of course." Malinda rose and motioned for Joanna to follow her. "But before ya go, I want to show you something I found in the attic during my recent airing of some stored items. This find was quite unexpected, I'll say."

"What is it?"

"Ach, you'll see." Malinda's smile was mysterious. "I'm just sure you'll be delighted . . . 'specially once you're engaged to your young man."

"Ya mean, it's for me?"

"Oh, Mammi Kurtz insists."

"You've talked to our grandmother 'bout this?"

Malinda nodded as they walked through the yard. "It'll make you ever so happy, believe me."

Joanna followed behind her cousin, thinking she should ask the question she'd already posed to several family members in a sort of poll. She wanted to include some of the responses in the story she was writing, the longest one to date. She enjoyed observing people—*real* people—storing away the images in her mind. This had been a hobby since childhood, when she watched others wherever she went, be it the one-room Amish schoolhouse, Sunday Preaching, or at the roadside vegetable stand where Englischers stopped by. Only later had Joanna started recasting these remembrances into fiction on the pages of her notebook.

Joanna and Malinda strolled back to the house, and Joanna was aware of the stars appearing one by one. Insects fluttered against the screen door, hungry for the light. She recalled the small bees she'd seen curled up, asleep, the other day inside the creamy-yellow rose petals along the side of the house. *The wonders of spring . . .*

Joanna paused on the back porch, leaning on the railing. "Have ya ever considered what's been the happiest time of your life, so far?"

Malinda wrapped her arm around a porch post and closed her eyes for a moment. Then, laughing softly, she opened them. "Frankly, I don't have to think hard 'bout that. It's the day I married Andy."

Joanna was mighty happy to hear it, particularly considering how very emotional Malinda had been. Goodness, to think she'd misread her cousin so completely! "Several of the womenfolk have said their happiest moment was becoming a mother for the first time," Joanna told her.

"I guess I'll know that soon enough."

Joanna hugged her. "It does me *gut* seein' ya so contented."

Malinda studied her for a moment. "Why did ya ask, Joanna?"

"Oh, just something I'm curious about." She pressed forward. "I like to know what others think . . . maybe because I like to write stories."

"Stories?"

"Jah . . . it's a secret I've kept from nearly everyone. Well, 'cept Eben and my friend Amelia." Pausing now, Joanna hoped she wasn't making a mistake by revealing this to her cousin. Yet Malinda had always been one to keep a confidence.

"I daresay you've been a curious sort since you were born."

"Guess you're right. But now I'm starting to wonder if I should've kept it to myself and not told Eben at all."

Malinda bit her lip thoughtfully. "Well, I've never heard of a fiction writer amongst the People."

"Me neither. Well, least not in Lancaster County so much."

"Bishop John doesn't want us to think too highly of ourselves, ya know—Scripture has a lot to say on that."

"Jah, 'tis best to stay humble."

"S'pose if you wrote stories to help others . . ."

"That's an idea," Joanna agreed. "But so far they're really only for me." She was quite relieved Malinda didn't seem to think any less of her for her confession. "Truth be told, I'm concerned my beau might be backin' away from me a bit."

"Whatever do ya mean?"

Joanna didn't know if she should say more.

"If anything, at least from what I've heard, the Indiana Amish are less strict in some ways than we are." Malinda smiled endearingly. "Are ya sure he's become aloof?"

Joanna shook her head. "Just a feeling."

"Maybe you're worrying too much."

Her cousin had a point. "Maybe so."

Together, they made their way indoors, through the kitchen, then upstairs to one of the guest bedrooms. Malinda moved to a lovely oak blanket chest just beyond the footboard of a double bed. Carefully, she lifted several blankets and other linens off the top and placed them on a nearby chair. Then, smiling, she raised up the prettiest double wedding ring quilt Joanna had ever seen, all done in reds, purples, and blues. "Just look at this."

"For goodness' sake!" Joanna peered at the exquisite work of art. "It's breathtaking." She reached to hold one end, and Malinda held the other as she inched back to exhibit the entire length of the beautiful quilt.

"Mammi Kurtz says it's a family heirloom."

"And in perfect condition—must not have been used as a covering at night."

"That's exactly what I thought," Malinda said. "But it was somehow misplaced for forty years."

Joanna stared appreciatively at the large interlocking circles. "Such a wonderful-*gut* discovery you've made."

"Well, I don't plan to keep it," Malinda said.

"Oh, but you must!"

"Remember what I told ya?" Malinda's eyes were soft. "Mammi insists that it goes to you."

"*You're* the newlywed in the family," Joanna protested.

"That's kind of you, but I already have plenty of quilts."

Joanna studied her cousin. "Are ya sure?"

"There's no arguing with our grandmother."

"Or you either, ain't so?" Joanna was delighted.

"Besides, there's an interesting story behind this quilt."

"They say every quilt has one."

Malinda nodded her head slowly, eyes twinkling. "It's not just any story, mind you."

Joanna was all ears. "Well, no wonder. Just look at it."

"I don't mean the colors or the stitchin'."

"Oh?"

"Mammi Kurtz says it has a spiritual legacy. And," she said more softly, "there's something of a mystery about it."

"Did Mammi tell you?"

"She said it was a known secret many years ago, but it was forgotten when the quilt disappeared."

"Now you've got me wondering." She searched the quilt for any initials. "Mammi must know who made it, jah?"

"She says it was made in the late 1920s by one of our great-great-aunts."

"That long ago?"

Malinda laid it out on the bed, and Joanna knelt to trace her finger over the familiar pattern, marveling at the choice of such a bold combination of colors. "It's really not much different from our present-day double wedding ring pattern, jah?"

Malinda agreed and knelt on the other side of the bed. "And just look how straight the stitches are. I'm told it was done by only one quilter, if you can imagine that."

"What an enormous undertaking," whispered Joanna.

They fell silent for a time, admiring the family treasure. Joanna let herself imagine the woman, their talented ancestor, who'd lovingly taken the time to make this quilt. To think Malinda had rescued this heirloom from the attic. And, even better yet, Mammi Kurtz wanted Joanna to have it!

Her cousin's and grandmother's sentiments touched Joanna deeply. "Denki," she managed to say. "Thank you ever so much." Did this mean they no longer believed she was destined to be a Maidel?

Her cousin offered to keep the quilt until Joanna could retrieve it in the buggy another day, and Joanna thanked her as they walked downstairs and then out to the porch. A loud chorus of crickets and the scent of honeysuckle filled the air. They spotted Andy coming out of the stable.

Malinda gave her a sweet hug and a flashlight. "Don't wait so long to visit again, all right?"

Joanna said she'd stop by tomorrow, after the quilting bee. She waved, then made her way down the porch steps. She felt nearly giddy, not only about Malinda's pregnancy, but the special quilt. Such a wonderful gift! Indeed, the idea of placing it in her very own hope chest did much to renew Joanna's hope.

She looked forward to hearing what Mammi Kurtz knew about the tale behind such a quilt. *Soon, very soon.*

Chapter 15

Driving horses trotted up and down Peaceful Acres Lane, the thuds of their hooves accentuated by the evening's quiet. Eben wiped his forehead on the back of his shirt sleeve before he opened the mailbox on the front porch of his father's white clapboard farmhouse. Hoping for a letter from Joanna, he was surprised to find a mighty big stack and wondered why Mamm hadn't come out to check for mail before supper.

A single letter caught his glance as he thumbed through the ads and bills. Looking closer, Eben could hardly believe his eyes. *Leroy's handwriting—and a letter addressed to me?*

Quickly, he opened it, holding his breath. How long had it been since he'd heard from Leroy? As best as he could recall, it had been a good six months since his twenty-four-year-old brother had written.

Not wasting a second, Eben walked around the side of the

house, peering closer in the dim light of dusk to read the short letter. He felt a surge of excitement at the final lines. *I'll be home a day or so after you get this, and not anytime too soon. I'll look forward to seeing you and Mamm and Daed, too. We'll have a fine reunion. Best regards, your little brother, Leroy.*

Eben refolded the letter and squinted toward the barn and the outbuildings, including the woodshed, where he and his brother-in-law had spent several hours chopping wood this morning. "Glory be! A reunion, then?" Eben muttered aloud, making his way around the side of the house, toward the door. "What's on his mind?"

Set back on the narrow country lane and surrounded by two hundred acres of farm and grazing land, the Troyer house was grand and welcoming. His parents and two generations of paternal grandparents before them had built the place up from scratch, tilling and cultivating the soil, raising pigs and chickens, and milking a small herd of cows to provide for the family and to make a living. The house itself was over a hundred years old, and Eben knew first-hand what that meant, having helped with the constant repairs through the years.

He reached for the door leading to the combination screened-in porch and catch-all utility room. The mud room, Mamm called it.

"Is Leroy comin' to claim his rightful place?" Eben wondered aloud as he stepped inside. If so, what an answer to his prayers of the two and a half years since Leroy forsook his upbringing, yearning for higher education. The bishop had preached about advanced learning in a sermon not long afterward, urging young people to avoid it like the plague.

"There's a reason why college is called 'higher education,'" the minister had declared. To him the word *higher* indicated a desire for self-advancement and disobedience to God. As if high school and college weren't enough, Leroy had even learned to fly a plane, far and free.

Free . . .

Leroy was apparently that—liberated and modern—to the detriment of his own family and close friends. And to Leroy himself. Initial word had spread right quick through their community: Will Troyer's youngest boy had finally gone fancy.

Still gripping the letter, Eben considered the wisdom of revealing this news to his parents. Twice now Leroy had mentioned returning for a visit, but something had come up each time to postpone it. Eben certainly didn't relish putting his mother through the heartache again, not the way she'd gone around nearly holding her breath, for pity's sake. And it had been just as tough for Daed, poor man. No, it was best to simply wait and see what happened. See if fancy-pants Leroy followed through this time.

Eben pushed the letter into his pocket and tore the envelope in half, placing it in the trash receptacle under the kitchen sink. His dear mother sat in the small room adjacent to the kitchen, her nose in a book—an Amish love story, it looked to be. She said nary a word over there in the corner, all snug in her overstuffed chair, surrounded by devotional magazines and the weekly newspaper, *Die Botschaft*.

Eben headed to his bedroom upstairs at the end of the long hall. It was still early enough this evening to write to

Joanna. What he wouldn't give to tell her this news—was the dreadful holdup on their formal courtship finally at an end?

Goodness, if any girl deserved a proper one, it was Joanna, sweet as a honeycomb. And with each month that drifted by and with every letter he wrote, Eben felt downright aggravated at not being able to give his girl so much as an update. There simply had been no word from Leroy . . . till now.

When Joanna arrived home from Cousin Malinda's, she rushed upstairs and noticed Cora Jane lingering near her doorway, looking rather sheepish. "What're ya doin'," she asked, her suspicions rising.

"Just thinkin' is all."

Joanna excused herself and slipped past her sister. Closing her door, she immediately went to her hope chest to see if her binder of story notebooks was still safely concealed.

Satisfied nothing was amiss, she shook off the prickles of concern and headed downstairs in time for family worship.

Cora Jane had already gathered with their parents in the front room as Joanna came in and sat in her usual chair near the windows. Cora Jane was scrunched up nearly in a ball over in the far chair, her head turned toward the window. Was she thinking about her beau, just maybe?

Settling in across from Mamma, Joanna envisioned each spot where their older siblings had always sat around the front room for morning and evening family worship. Having five older brothers and two sisters, Joanna knew plenty about siblings and their personality clashes, but she also knew that no two siblings were ever alike. Again, she glanced at Cora Jane, wondering how *she* might react to hearing about the heirloom quilt.

Joanna tried to picture Eben and his family beginning their evening prayers, too. And his siblings—six in all, he'd told her—a mixture of sisters and brothers. Did they read and pray every morning and evening as her family did? Except for Eben, all but his younger brother were married. And also like Joanna, he was the next to youngest. *Another common bond between us*.

As for herself, for now, Joanna was quite content to be one of the last two children living at home. She had it worked so she was the sole person getting the mail every afternoon, for one thing. Surprisingly, that had helped to keep questions about Eben's plight to a minimum. *Thus far, anyway . . .*

Presently, Daed began to read the old Biewel in the firm voice he always used for reading God's Word. He placed his callused hands just so on the thin pages. Mamma sat humbly with her pink hands folded in her lap as Joanna listened, watching her sister fidget.

The Good Book had always held an important place in her parents' hearts, and in Joanna's, too. Dat had shared the Scriptures in this manner with the family from their earliest childhood on, starting and ending each day with prayer and Bible reading.

Someday Eben will want to share the Word of God with our children. In her mind's eye, Joanna saw herself sitting next to Eben as he read to the family—how many children? Oh, she longed to move ahead, to be done with her single and sometimes lonely life. She longed to be loved.

Later, when it was time to kneel for prayer, Joanna offered silent thanks for Cousin Malinda's fun discovery of the quilt, and she also prayed for Eben's wayward brother, Leroy.

After Dat said amen, Mamma headed to the kitchen, and Dat shuffled out to the barn one last time.

Joanna said good-night to Cora Jane and hurried upstairs to her own bedroom. *If only tomorrow had wings*, she thought, eager to get her hands on the stunning wedding quilt.

Carefully, she lit the gas lamp in her room and went to the window that faced west, toward Indiana. *I miss you, Eben. . . .* For the longest time, she stood there, looking out.

Then, perceiving someone else in the room, she turned to see Cora Jane in the doorway, her golden hair cascading over both shoulders, a brush in her hand. "May I come in?"

"Sure," Joanna replied. "Want me to brush your hair?"

"Would ya?" Cora Jane's face lit up momentarily.

Joanna motioned for her to sit on the sturdy cane chair near the window. "It's been a long time," she said quietly. *Too long . . .*

Cora Jane sat nice and still, saying no more. Looking at her sister just then, Joanna felt cheerless to think the two of them had been at something of a standstill since Joanna met Eben in Virginia. She tried to make small talk as she brushed Cora Jane's beautiful hair, mentioning things like the next trip to the bakery and wanting to go and see Mammi Kurtz sometime soon. Things that didn't hold a candle to what they'd shared before, sometimes late into the night, lying on each other's beds.

But Cora Jane didn't speak at all.

Joanna shaped the words in her mind: *I'm sorry we're at odds*, she thought sadly. But tonight Joanna believed she could not bridge the gap if she'd wanted to. Cora Jane knew how she felt. Her sister was immovable in her thinking that Eben would never come here to live . . . that he was being less than forthright with Joanna.

Holding Cora Jane's heavy hair in her left hand, Joanna brushed with long, sweeping strokes, again and again. *We've fallen apart*, she mused, hoping this gesture might somehow demonstrate her care for Cora Jane.

And because her sister remained silent, Joanna let her mind wander back to Eben as she continued to brush. Long as it had been since she'd seen him, she wished she had just one picture of Eben. But in keeping with their strict *Ordnung*—the church ordinance—she had none.

I scarcely remember what you look like, my love. . . .

Chapter 16

After Cora Jane left the room, Joanna raised the lid on her hope chest—there was scarcely enough room inside for the heirloom quilt. "I'll make a place somewhere," she whispered, eager to have the wonderful handiwork in her possession.

Then, digging deeper, she carefully removed a wooden letter box, a gift on her twenty-first birthday from Salina. Every letter Eben had ever sent was safely concealed inside.

She found her favorite—one he'd written in early winter—intending to read it for the hundredth time. She'd marked it with a pink heart on the envelope, so when she missed him the most she could always find it amongst his many letters.

Dearest Joanna,

How are you?

You might laugh at this, but I can hardly wait to see if there's a letter from you every other day or so. Denki for writing as often as you do . . . it's always wonderful-good to hear from you!

Here lately I've been getting up earlier than usual, going with my father to nearby farm sales. But even though I'm fairly busy this winter, I'm never too busy to write to you at night, my sweetheart.

I love being with you! And I wish I could see you again . . . soon.

She stopped reading and held the letter close, pondering his final words. "That's the closest he's ever come to sayin' 'I love you,'" she said softly, wishing with all of her heart he'd tell her so in person. *Oh, to have that as a memory!*

She slipped the stationery back into the envelope and found its spot again, then closed the pretty letter box, slipping it under two knotted comforters and other linens. Joanna then took out the large three-ring binder where she kept her many writings and removed her blue notebook. She carried it to her bed, eager to reread the scenes she'd written yesterday. It hadn't taken long to learn that what seemed good on a particular day often read much differently the next. So she spent time reworking her sentences and paragraphs many times over—*a rewriter*, she liked to call herself.

Joanna tucked her feet beneath the long dress and apron, wishing her church district wasn't so strict. However much some might frown on her spending hours each week bent over her notebook, she loved to express herself that way and couldn't see anything wrong with it. What was she to do? She knew of only one Amish church district, one not far from

Harrisburg, whose bishop had given a baptized Amishwoman permission to publish her novels, but they were based on the Plain life, so Joanna guessed that made them all right.

Writing had always been something she did just for herself, but since Amelia's suggestion, the desire to be published sometimes tugged at Joanna during the day when she helped Mamma bake bread or sew. And at night, too, when it poked at her . . . in her dreams. Truth be known, if she could have anything at all, she longed to see something meaningful come from her writing. That, and to marry Eben Troyer.

When she wasn't writing an actual story, she loved jotting down character traits and descriptions of people. Also ideas, things that popped into her head, including questions to explore, like the one she'd asked Cousin Malinda earlier today.

Just yesterday she'd asked Mamma's opinion about the happiest time of *her* life, too, but the question was met with raised eyebrows, as if her mother were saying, "*Think about something useful, child.*"

Joanna's oldest brother, Hank, married for some time, had given her a ragged frown when she'd asked him the same thing. He'd spouted his response all too quickly. "*That's easy enough! Courting age*," he'd said, perhaps implying that marrieds were strapped with responsibilities.

But it was the Wise Woman, Ella Mae Zook, who gave the most profound answer of all. "*For me, right now—this moment—is the very best time.*" She'd spoken with a faltering smile. "*At my advanced age, I've already learned the hardest lessons, or should have, anyway. Everything we learn when we're young is useful for the years ahead. Unfortunately, sometimes we never really learn the life lessons we're supposed to. Sad but all too true, don't you agree?"*

Frail Ella Mae hadn't spelled out what those lessons were, but Joanna understood her well enough to know she meant the gifts of the Spirit found in Scripture: love, joy, peace, longsuffering, gentleness, goodness, and faith. Some folk called them the simple gifts.

Joanna whispered to herself, "Cherish each and every moment. That's what Ella Mae meant."

She took up her pen, continuing to work on her longest story to date, about an Amish couple deeply in love and separated by several states: *At their first reunion, they talked long into the night, sharing their truest hearts.*

Hearing a sudden creak behind her, she turned and saw Cora Jane standing on this side of the doorway, inching away.

Quickly, Joanna closed her notebook. "How long have you been there?" she asked, her voice quivering.

"Sounds like ya have a guilty conscience." Cora Jane was staring at the notebook.

"Oh, sister . . ."

Cora Jane folded her arms. "Just take what I'm about to say as a warning."

Joanna shifted forward on the bed. "You really can't go through life bossing and judging everyone in sight. It's not your place."

"I've seen you filling pages and pages, sister. Sure doesn't look like a letter to me . . . nor a diary. Who exactly are these people—and places—you're writing about? Did ya make them up?"

Joanna blushed; she'd been caught. "So you're sneaking round, snooping over my shoulder?"

"Then it *is* a story, jah?"

"Writing stories doesn't hurt anyone!" Joanna justified her secret passion to Cora Jane, just as she'd always done to herself. Beyond flustered, she locked eyes with her sister. "I must answer to the Lord God and no one else for what I do. And I don't believe writing the stories in my heart and mind is wrong, not really."

"Have it your way," Cora Jane said. "It sure seems you're bent on that. But what I don't understand is why you've kept this secret from me all this time. You shut me out of your life even before Eben came along, ain't?"

Joanna groaned but said nothing more.

"Why, Joanna? 'Specially if there's nothin' wrong with it, as you say?" Cora Jane demanded. "First your worldly friend, Amelia, then a faraway beau, and now this fiction writing! Next thing, you'll be slippin' away from the People and running off to the fancy English world. It's like I scarcely know you anymore." With that, she turned and fled the room.

Joanna moved to the door and closed it soundly. Her sister was absolutely wrong to lump Amelia and Eben together with her love for writing. *Oh, if only I'd been more careful!*

A torrent of emotions plagued Joanna as she returned to her cozy nest on the bed. She found her place and tried to begin again. But her sister's critical words echoed in her mind, clamoring for consideration until Joanna put her pen down and leaned back on the pillow, tears spilling down her cheeks.

Chapter 17

Joanna was startled awake the next morning at her mother's call up the stairs. "*Kumme* now, Joanna, and help make breakfast!"

"All right, Mamma." Joanna stretched, yawned, and got out of bed, still feeling groggy. She stepped across the hall to peek in at her sister, who was still in bed. "Cora Jane, time to wake up. Mamma needs us."

"I heard her," Cora Jane said sleepily, rolling over, her golden hair sprawled out all over the pillow. "She called for *you*!"

With a sigh, Joanna hurried to wash up. She recognized that Cora Jane was still rather young and in the process of maturing. But sometimes her prickly edges were hard to overlook, especially when she confronted others as she had Joanna last night.

Choosing to wear her gray choring dress, Joanna then quickly brushed her long hair and wove it into a tight bun, pinning it securely. No sense risking getting hair in the scrambled eggs!

Peering into her dresser mirror, she noticed how bright her eyes looked after a night's sweet dreams of Eben. *Closer in my dreams than in reality.*

Suddenly it occurred to her that Ella Mae Zook might be someone she ought to consider talking to about her beau. After all, the Wise Woman lived just over the cornfield, so it was easy to visit without having to bother hitching up the horse and buggy.

Even though Ella Mae was one of her mother's dearest friends, Joanna believed the older woman kept all shared confidences—she was a trustworthy soul. And ever so forthright, too, freely speaking her mind . . . even to the point of being downright *batzich*—spunky. So interesting, because the woman was nothing like Joanna's own mother, nor any of the other respected womenfolk in Hickory Hollow. Joanna privately wondered if the Wise Woman managed to get by with her plucky nature because she was much too old to be put off church.

"'Tis a *gut* thing," Joanna whispered as she set the white organdy Kapp on her head.

Dare I tell her about Eben's predicament?

Perhaps Ella Mae might have some advice to give about their long-distance romance. Might it help to simply voice her sheer frustration?

Joanna decided to test the waters later this week and see what wisdom Ella Mae might offer her . . . over peppermint tea. At this point, any counsel would be welcome!

...⊱⊰...

Cora Jane conspicuously picked at her bacon and eggs at the breakfast table, apparently also lacking any appetite for Mamma's homemade sticky buns. Joanna wondered what ailed her. Was she still upset over last night, or was she dreading the quilting bee today over at Mary Beiler's? Last Thursday one of Mary's Ohio cousins, Linda Jean, had showed up wearing a bright pink dress, unlike any color ever seen round Lancaster County. Cora Jane brought attention to it in a most critical way, causing a stir at the quilting frame.

Chagrined, Joanna had felt for her sister and wished Cora Jane might show more kindness. *"What if we simply made it our heart's work to pray more and judge less?"* Ella Mae had once said, years ago. And Joanna had never forgotten.

"I think I'll stay home today," Cora Jane announced across the table from Joanna. "Dat could use some help outside, ain't?" She looked at their father, who wiped his mouth with the back of his sleeve.

"Well, now," Dat said, "I thought you were headin' to the bishop's for the quilting bee." He glanced first at Mamma, then back at Cora Jane. "All of yous."

"That's right, Cora Jane. We're going to help finish the friendship quilt we started last week. And we need you." Mamma meant business. But so did Cora Jane, her eyes widening even as she sat there.

"But I ain't feelin' so *gut*," Cora Jane replied, sighing dramatically and placing both hands on her cheeks.

"Just that quick, you're sick?" Mamma shook her head; she

knew Cora Jane all too well. "If you're under the weather, I know just the thing to get ya feelin' up to snuff. A big tablespoon of cod liver oil should cure that in short order."

Cora Jane pulled a hard frown. The matter was quite settled.

"The boys and I will finish planting Elam Lapp's potato field by suppertime," Dat said casually, obviously attempting to squash any more tetchiness from Cora Jane.

"Next comes the cultivating," Mamma added, eyes still fixed on Cora Jane, who had managed to sit up tall and straight, the mere threat of fish oil lingering in the air. "You'll be mighty busy, too, with spreading manure on the vegetable gardens," she said to Dat, the ordeal of breakfast clearly behind them.

Joanna smiled as she listened to her parents' everyday small talk. A kindly person was a content one. Sooner or later, Cora Jane would understand that, too.

Eben sat down to breakfast, waiting for Mamm to take her seat near Daed. There was much on his mind, not the least of which was Leroy's letter. Keeping the news to himself was exhausting. It was as if the secret were weighing him down . . . refusing to be disregarded.

Glancing up, he saw his mother shaking her head. Then, slowly, she waved two pieces of paper, one in each hand. "What's this here, Eben?" she asked, frowning as she came to the table. "Did Leroy write to you?"

Eben recognized the envelope he'd ripped in half last night. He had no choice but to fess up. "Ach, Mamm, I didn't want to get your hopes up." He glanced at his father, sitting squarely at the head of the table.

"Oh?" Daed said, his brow creasing into a hard line. "What're ya talking 'bout?"

"Leroy says he's comin' home . . . maybe as soon as today."

Mamm's face broke into a smile. "Well, praise be!"

"I don't know much else. He really didn't say a lot."

"'Tis best not to jump to conclusions, Mamma," his father urged.

"It's been a long time comin'," Eben added. "Not to mention all the prayin'."

"That's the truth." Daed motioned for Mamm to take her place so he could offer the silent prayer.

She quickly slipped onto the bench, and Daed folded his hands and bowed his head low. Eben did the same, heart beating fast. He'd hurt his mother, and just when he'd tried to spare her further pain. During the silent table blessing, he prayed that Leroy's visit would be providential.

After the amen, Eben reached for the nearest platter and offered it to his father, then helped himself. He was grateful for the exceptionally hearty breakfast of cornmeal mush and sausage Mamm had taken the time to make.

He wondered how long it had been since Leroy had enjoyed such a breakfast but didn't feel sorry for him. After all, Leroy had pushed the boundaries even as a youngster; it was his own unwise decision to leave the People.

Even so, Eben hoped his brother had reconsidered all the

time he'd spent rubbing shoulders with the world. Might he be ready to settle down at last and assume his expected place on the farm?

What I wouldn't give for that! Eben thought, assuming such a thing was highly unlikely. No, something else had to be up with Leroy. Why *was* he coming?

Chapter 18

Joanna's mother breezed through the back door and began gathering up her basket of quilting supplies. "'Bout ready?"

"Perty soon, jah." Joanna wiped off the counter and turned to the table, where she had her own quilting needles and thimble in a little box, ready to tuck into her sewing bag.

"Don't want to be late," Mamma replied.

Cora Jane was the one dawdling, still in her room. "I'll see what's keepin' my sister." Joanna hurried to the bottom of the stairs. "We're hitched and ready to go," she called up.

Joanna waited a moment, giving Cora Jane time to respond. She heard only the creak of footsteps, but they weren't moving toward the stairs, so she called again, "Are ya comin', sister?"

A long silence.

At last, her sister replied, "I'll be right down."

"We'll be waiting." Turning, Joanna headed back through the kitchen, her navy blue canvas sewing bag slung over her shoulder and her writing notebook tucked safely inside. The notebook was her "insurance," in case of a lull in activity. That way, Joanna could go somewhere alone and write if she wanted to, and no one would be the wiser.

Hurrying out the back door, Joanna could hardly wait to get to Beilers'. Bishop John and Mary seemed to go out of their way to make the quilters feel welcome every week. And Joanna loved seeing their darling children, especially making over the younger ones.

The day was already quite warm as Joanna walked across the yard, taking in the sweep of land in all directions. Spring had its own unique smell, a freshness and earthiness found in no other season.

Joanna stepped into the carriage and sat beside Mamma. "Cora Jane says she's comin'."

"She'd better make it snappy. We're running behind." Mamma smoothed her cape apron over her long dress. "You're lookin' perky, Joanna."

For many reasons, she certainly felt good. "I'm eager to see how the friendship quilt turned out—all pieced together." Joanna thought, too, of Mary's ailing grandfather. "And it'll be *gut* to hear how Abram Stoltzfus is doin' this week."

"Sadly, word has it he's declining quickly . . . awful confused these days." Mamma glanced at the house, a glint of frustration in her eyes. No question Cora Jane was a slowpoke today. "Mary says her Dawdi clearly remembers what he did years ago as a youngster, but he can't recall his own grandchildren's names." She sighed loudly. "'Tis the saddest thing."

"Jah." Joanna thought of her own Dawdi Joseph. "Old folk tend to live in the past, ain't so?"

Her mother gave a sudden frown, leaning around Joanna to stare at the house again. "For pity's sake, where's Cora Jane? Slow as molasses in January!"

"She might be feelin' embarrassed 'bout last week."

"Well, we're not leaving here without her," Mamma declared.

Joanna resumed talking about Mamma's ailing father, saying he seemed to need more rest than ever before. "Mammi says he takes two or more naps a day."

"And the older he gets, the more he'll want to doze," Mamma agreed. "Seems elderly folk and wee tykes require more sleep than the rest of us."

Just then, Mamma brightened as Cora Jane burst out the back door and sped across the yard, her skirt tail flying.

"Ach, I'm ready!" Cora Jane called, nearly leaping into the carriage. She sat down with a thump, taking more than her share of space. Then she leaned back dramatically. "I shouldn't have rushed so!"

Joanna sputtered at that. Did she really have to make a spectacle of herself?

"Cora Jane, we've been sitting out here waitin' for ya," Mamma rebuked. "You best be more considerate in the future, hear?"

Cora Jane nodded slowly.

"I mean it," Mamma added, the reins taut in her hands.

Cora Jane gave Joanna a quick look.

Joanna hoped things would go well *this* quilting frolic. Far as she could tell, Cora Jane had gone from being rather lethargic at the breakfast table to just a mite too spunky now.

Hickory Lane was busier than usual with horses and carriages. Amish neighbors waved as they passed, and here and there small children ran barefoot after the carriage. Others skipped rope beneath shade trees or played jacks on the front porch, where it was still cool. And all the while, Joanna felt she was holding her breath, wondering how Cora Jane might behave today.

Yet neither her mother nor her sister made a peep, and the sound of the horse's *clip-clop*ping helped relax Joanna somewhat. She particularly enjoyed the sight of little red squirrels climbing trees along the roadside. Cows roamed the grazing land, and mule teams worked the soil, plowing and chasing sunshine.

The day was going to be unusually warm. Joanna was glad she'd thought to bring along her bandana for the ride home later this afternoon. She might even loosen her hair bun, although she'd never think of undoing it entirely in public. Looking at the sky, she hoped for the possibility of a rain shower. *Just maybe*, she thought, feeling terribly cramped with three in the seat.

Then, quite unexpectedly, Cora Jane folded her hands and looked at their mother. "Ach, Mamma . . . I'm real sorry for makin' a scene last week over Linda Jean," she said humbly. "Honestly."

A sweet smile spread across Mamma's face. "Well, dear,

maybe ya didn't realize that pink is an approved color for Amish dresses in some areas of Ohio."

Cora Jane hung her head. "It just looked so awful worldly," she replied, staring at her lap, her tone softer now. "Such a loud color."

Joanna wasn't sure she ought to put her nose into the conversation. She waited for a moment, then quietly suggested that there were many different church ordinances, even within a five-mile radius in Lancaster County. Maybe Cora Jane wasn't too aware of this, not being baptized yet.

"Just none that permits pink for courting-age girls, jah?" replied Cora Jane, raising her eyes.

"That's absolutely right," Mamma said.

The discussion triggered a curiosity in Joanna. What color dresses did Eben's mother and sisters wear in Shipshewana? Oh, she'd love to know more about his family and their church ordinances, too. Then she scolded herself, knowing she had no need to consider any of that, at least not for herself.

Yet, what if Eben *did* ask her to come to live in Shipshewana after all? What would she say to that?

Chapter 19

Joanna was pleasantly surprised by Cora Jane's change in attitude as she worked cheerfully with the other women amidst the chatter, using her tiny quilting needle at the frame. Cora Jane also went out of her way to show extra patience when Mary Beiler's youngest children were a bit rambunctious under the table during the noon meal. She got down on the floor, where she reached around the little girl and whispered something. Whatever Cora Jane said made the child's face light up like a lantern, and the child settled right down and played with her rag dolls more calmly from then on.

When no one was paying much attention, Joanna slipped outside with her sewing bag to the family carriage to write a few things in her notebook. She could get inspiration at the oddest times and was ever so glad she'd thought to bring the notebook and a pen along today.

Stepping into the buggy, she sat and opened her canvas sewing bag—but the notebook was gone. "*Wu is es?*—Where is it?" she whispered, looking behind the seat. Had it somehow fallen out of the bag? She peered into the rear section of the carriage.

Joanna's heart flickered. Her writing notebook was nowhere to be seen! Wracking her brain, she wondered if she'd dropped it back home, perhaps when getting into the buggy. Could that be? But no, she'd had it with her when they arrived here and when she helped Mamma carry her quilting basket into the bishop's house. She was fairly certain of that.

Her mind in a whirl, Joanna searched every inch of the carriage, then got out and hurried down the driveway leading to Hickory Lane. And as she went, she lamented ever bringing the notebook at all, especially when it contained a love story. Besides that, it was unwise to have brought it to the bishop's own house, of all places! *Why didn't I think of that?*

She fumed at herself and fretted, her head hurting as she stood at the edge of the road. And a dreadful thought came to her: Maybe she hadn't lost it after all.

"Did someone purposely take my notebook?" Joanna whispered, remembering Cora Jane's warning last night.

It was difficult to concentrate the rest of the afternoon. Joanna dropped stitches and was so distracted at one point, she even pricked her finger, causing a drop of blood to fall onto the quilt. Mary Beiler hopped out of her chair like she'd been stung by a wasp, her prayer cap strings flying, and went to get a cold washrag to dab at the spot.

"I'm awful sorry," Joanna apologized. "I truly am."

"Don't worry," Mary assured her as she worked feverishly on the stain, though eventually she gave up on getting it out completely. "This could happen to anyone."

Joanna groaned. "I've ruined the quilt," she said, worrying a thread loose.

"No, no. Ain't the worst thing, really," Mary insisted as she leaned down to nearly touch her forehead to Joanna's.

Mamma spoke up from farther down the frame. "The spot will come out, dear," and several heads popped up, nodding. "You'll see," Mamma added, her brow wrinkling with empathy.

Cora Jane averted her gaze and pressed her lips together in a flat line, appearing as concerned as Joanna felt.

Joanna looked once more to her mother for support, glad for Mamm's merciful expression, although still painfully aware of the all-too-noticeable blemish on the quilt. Right in front of Joanna's nose, too!

Alas, she had no one to blame but herself. She'd been a *Dummkopp* to bring her story notebook along. Yet never before had anything disappeared from her bag, for pity's sake!

Pondering the whole situation again, Joanna felt even more mortified.

Ach, I should've known better!

The ride home seemed considerably longer than usual as Joanna squinted into the late-afternoon sun. She could hardly wait to get home to see if she'd dropped her notebook in the yard or left it on the kitchen table. But although she didn't dare ask to look inside Cora Jane's own sewing bag, she was certain it looked more rigid than when her sister had climbed into the carriage that morning. In fact, Joanna was sure she could see the outline of her notebook tucked inside.

She chided herself—Joanna had never been one to falsely accuse someone. Yet who else was nosy enough to take it?

Thank goodness there was not a speck of conversation in the carriage as they rode. Joanna was so worked up, she was intentionally drawing slow, deep breaths, lest she spout off. She glanced again at Cora Jane, who looked at her quizzically but still said nothing.

Finally, when they pulled into the lane leading to the house, Joanna remembered the quilt waiting for her at Cousin Malinda's. "Mamma, would ya mind leaving the horse and carriage hitched up?" she asked. At this, both Cora Jane and Mamma looked surprised. "I need to go to Malinda's right quick," Joanna explained, not wanting to say why.

"But *I* need to go somewhere, too," Cora Jane piped up. "Why can't ya just walk over to Malinda's?"

"Well, I have to bring something back with me," Joanna said. "Something too heavy to carry."

"All right, then," Mamma said, appearing weary from the long day. "Make it quick so Cora Jane can get her errand run, too."

"Where are you headed?" Joanna asked her sister, wondering if perhaps she'd simply asked for the carriage to be difficult.

"Oh, you'll see," Cora Jane said mysteriously. "In due time."

Not interested in playing along, Joanna shook her head. "I shouldn't be long" was all she said.

Mamma, who'd surely detected the tension between them, asked Cora Jane, "Did ya enjoy yourself more so today, dear?"

"It was nice seein' everyone again," Cora Jane replied. "And we finished up the friendship quilt, 'cept for the hem, ain't so?"

"That we did," said Mamma, letting go of the reins as she eyed Cora Jane. "I'm sure you'll want to host some quilting frolics of your own one day."

"When I'm married?" Cora Jane said, a smile playing on her lips.

"From what I've heard, a wedding might not be too far off," Mamma replied with a sly look.

"Now, Mamma!" Cora Jane laughed, which solidified what Joanna—and obviously their mother, too—had strongly suspected: Cora Jane was planning to be a bride, maybe as soon as this fall.

Before me, Joanna thought with a sinking feeling.

While Cora Jane tied the horse to the hitching post, Joanna retraced her steps into the house, trying not to be conspicuous. The notebook was not on the back walkway or on the lawn, so she made her way inside and looked all over the kitchen, the table and counters, and even under the wooden benches, trembling now. *All the hours of writing, for naught!* She peeked out the window and saw Cora Jane standing near the horse, her own sewing bag over her shoulder.

Crestfallen, Joanna snatched up the flashlight she'd borrowed from Cousin Malinda last evening and headed back outside. She saw Cora Jane running to catch up with Mamma, who was walking to the stable, most likely to let Dat know they were back. Since Joanna had already asked Mamma for the buggy, she went out and untied the horse, then got back inside the carriage, sitting on the far right side this time as she picked up the reins. Her emotions were all jumbled up between the regretful loss of her notebook and the anticipation of bringing the wedding quilt home. *I shouldn't accept it*, she thought as she drove to Malinda's, *not if Cora Jane's getting married this fall*.

Even if Eben were to move to Hickory Hollow tomorrow, Joanna wondered if he could get established in a job quickly enough for them to wed come November.

Thinking then of her plan to seek some perspective from Ella Mae, Joanna continued on to her cousin's house. Soon, the lovely heirloom quilt would be in her possession.

My beautiful wedding quilt . . .

Chapter 20

Eben and his father were shoveling out the dung in the stable when a white Mustang convertible with black stripes along the side whooshed into the lane. Taken off guard, Eben realized Leroy had just arrived.

"Well, what do ya know?" Daed said, going to stand in the doorway of the barn.

"Looks like he's got himself a girlfriend," Eben muttered next to Daed. "Guess we should go and wash up, jah?"

"For certain!" His father fell into step right behind him, pulling his gloves off and tossing them on the lawn near the well pump.

Eben waved at Leroy. "Willkumm home, *Bruder*!" he called, motioning for Leroy and the pretty redhead to go inside. Eben waited his turn as Daed lathered his hands at the pump. "Been muckin' out the barn, so need to wash up *gut* before we shake hands."

Leroy's face broke into a frown, and he exchanged glances with the petite young woman. Eben took his turn with a bar of soap at the well pump before hurrying indoors to alert his mother to their company. "Leroy's back—has a lady friend along."

"Leroy's *here*?" Mamm's eyes grew big as she ran her hands over her Kapp and bodice.

"Comin' up the porch steps."

"Hullo, son. Good to have ya home," Daed said as he pushed his big hand into Leroy's.

Eben didn't want to gawk, but his brother looked taller than he remembered, broader shoulders, too. Was it the petite young woman at his side? He went over to shake Leroy's hand while Mamm hovered near, smiling like she didn't know what else to do or say . . . tears springing to her eyes.

"Daed . . . Mamm, I want you to meet Debbie," said Leroy, slipping his arm around her. "Mrs. Debbie Troyer."

Mrs. Troyer? Eben's heart sank at Leroy's news.

"You're married?" Mamm blurted.

"Two weeks tomorrow." Leroy grinned down at his bride, who had the thickest, darkest eyelashes Eben had ever seen.

"This is . . . well, a surprise," Daed said, managing a smile and shaking Debbie's hand.

Polite though his father was, Eben could tell he was masking his disappointment.

Debbie offered a warm smile of her own. "I'm real pleased to meet you, sir. I wanted to before the wedding, but it was so difficult for Leroy to get away."

Mamm intervened somewhat by directing them into the kitchen, waving Leroy toward the bench. Then, her face mighty pink, she offered a seat to Debbie, as well, and something to eat. "We can't have our new daughter-in-law goin' hungry, now, can we?" Like Daed, she was clearly flustered.

They sat around the table, except for Mamm, who made her way to the gas-powered refrigerator to pull out a pitcher of lemonade and some apples to slice. Freshly baked bread, butter, and several choices of jams were next, Eben guessed. And a pie, too, soon enough.

In the meantime, Leroy was talking a mile a minute, now that the ice was broken. But when Eben looked at Leroy and his bride and how very happy they seemed together, it made him think of Joanna's dress brushing against him as they strolled along the beach, hand in hand . . . and of reaching to hold her tenderly on her father's field road.

Any hope he'd had for marrying her in Pennsylvania and living there was gone. His father needed him here, working the farm. There was no one else to rely upon. And as much as Joanna loved Hickory Hollow, he couldn't think of asking her to leave to settle down and marry out here. Could he?

I'm locked in!

Discouraged, Eben looked down the table at Leroy, clean-shaven and wearing pressed navy slacks and a pale yellow shirt. Daed needed *someone*, and it sure wasn't going to be Leroy.

Never was, thought Eben miserably.

... ⁓ ...

When Joanna arrived at Malinda's, she found her pressing two Kapps in the kitchen, humming a song from the old Ausbund.

"Knock, knock," Joanna called to her.

Malinda looked up and quickly put the iron back on the stove. "Was wondering if you were goin' to make it yet today."

"Wouldn't've missed coming."

"I wrapped your quilt in brown paper," Malinda told her, going to the sitting room around the corner to retrieve it. "You can store it as is, if you want."

"Denki."

Malinda leaned down to set the wrapped quilt on the kitchen table. "Would ya like some meadow tea or lemonade?"

"I really can't stay long. Cora Jane's waiting for me to return with the horse and buggy."

"How's she doin' these days?"

Joanna considered what to say. "Well enough, I daresay . . . though the reason for that ain't common knowledge, so keep it under your bonnet for now."

"A wedding, maybe?"

Sighing, Joanna forced a smile, then looked away. "You didn't hear it from me."

Malinda tilted her head, eyeing her. "You look sad 'bout it, Joanna. Are ya?"

"Oh, not so much sad as concerned." She bit her lip.

"Do ya know Cora Jane's fella?"

"I do, but honestly her beau ain't the worry." She paused and looked down at the quilt. "That's all I best be sayin'."

"I won't press, but I'm here if you need to talk more."

Joanna was grateful but didn't know where she'd even begin. "I appreciate that . . . really, I do." All of a sudden, she could no longer restrain her emotions. Sobbing like her heart might break, she flew into her cousin's open arms.

A young elk grazed just beyond the woodshed, out near a stand of trees as Eben dutifully followed along with Leroy and his fancy wife on a tour of the farm. It was surprising how Daed was going overboard in his hospitality. He'd insisted on showing his new daughter-in-law around, leaving Eben in the dust and practically doting on Leroy and his bride. In fact, Eben felt more like the visitor than his father's dependable right-hand man.

He had long guessed that Daed preferred Leroy, not only as a son but as a potential business partner. Yet Eben had diligently worked to do Daed's bidding while ticking off the days, weeks, and months until he could see Joanna again. Their inferior approach to courtship had become wearisome, although he had attempted to hold his own with letter writing, eager to keep Joanna happy. She'd never complained, and he knew she was patiently waiting for him. He looked forward to their phone chats every other week.

Sadly, in the space of a few short minutes, the miles between them had grown to an impossible distance with the knowledge that Leroy wasn't coming home to stay.

The foursome headed into the birthing area to see the new calves, but Eben's attention wandered as he thought of the difficult letter he must write to his sweetheart-girl. However would he break the terrible news? He could visualize starting one letter after another, only to crumple them up. Was there any way to let Joanna down gently, so as not to break her heart?

She doesn't deserve this, he told himself while Daed showed Leroy and his wife the birthing stall. Daed thought of their dairy cattle as his pets; the whole family did—except Leroy. No, it was apparent that farming had never clicked with his brother.

Eben shook with anger that had simmered for months now. He'd marked time, waited for Leroy to decide to be Amish or not—working himself to the bone. And for what? Only to learn he was going nowhere, and least of all to Hickory Hollow.

Eben forced air through his lips. Let his father finish up the ridiculous tour. Let his brother show his bride the very farm he'd rejected!

A letter won't do—I have to explain things to Joanna in person! The realization burst into his head as he made a detour out of the barn to head to the house, swatting away mosquitoes as he went. Joanna would have to leave the community she so dearly loved to come here and marry him . . . *if* she was even willing to do so.

Inside the house, Eben dashed through the kitchen to his room. How fast could he get to Hickory Hollow and back? He wished he hadn't wasted any time trailing behind his father, brother, and new wife out there. Then he chuckled bitterly. Why, Leroy could fly him to Lancaster County in nothing flat!

What *would* it be like to arrive at Joanna's side in such a short amount of time? But air travel was forbidden by the bishop—Eben would travel as other Plain people did over long distances, by taxi-van or bus. First, though, he would have to line up someone to cover his farm work.

Letting his imagination run away, he envisioned showing up at the Kurtz farm once again and taking Joanna into his arms, holding her ever so close. And this time, he'd never let her go.

Knowing how impatient Cora Jane could be, Joanna quickly dried her eyes and thanked Malinda for a shoulder to cry on. She bade farewell to her cousin, whose eyes shone with concern as Joanna stepped out the door with the large quilt in her arms. With the greatest care, Joanna placed it in the back of the buggy. *The prettiest quilt I've ever seen*, she thought, glancing back toward the house with a wave at Cousin Malinda. She went around the buggy to untie the horse.

"Come again soon!" Malinda called, her hand held high.

"I surely will," Joanna said as she climbed into the enclosed carriage. She reached for the reins and clicked her tongue to get the horse moving. Oh, if only she'd held back her tears for dear Malinda's sake! The poor thing didn't need any stress now. Joanna promised herself to keep in touch with Malinda through the next months of waiting for the baby's arrival. And with the thought of a sweet infant, Joanna imagined a narrative that featured a brand-new baby. Ah, she'd love to write such a story . . . but her notebook had vanished. Such a dreadful loss!

When she arrived home, Cora Jane was standing in the lane, wearing a displeased expression, her large tan sewing bag draped over her shoulder. Joanna got out without offering a civility, and her sister got in without saying a word.

Upset, Joanna hurried to the house and went inside to start supper. And just that minute, it dawned on her: *Ach, no! I left the heirloom quilt in the back of the buggy!*

Without a second thought, she dashed outside, running down the long lane to the road, calling for Cora Jane to stop. "Come back, sister!" But the horse was nearly galloping as the carriage sped away.

Chapter 21

Joanna returned to the house, crestfallen and out of sorts. So ferhoodled she was today! She joined her mother at the kitchen table to peel a pile of potatoes.

"Where's Cora Jane headed?" she asked Mamma.

Mamma looked up, her eyes questioning. "Why do you ask?"

"She was in such a big hurry."

"As *you* were earlier."

Mamma's reply caught her off guard. "I just went to Cousin Malinda's is all," Joanna said. "I said I'd be by today after the quilting."

"Well, I have no idea what Cora Jane has in mind."

Joanna told about the old family quilt Cousin Malinda had discovered. "I went there to pick it up." She paused. "Evidently Mammi Kurtz wants me to have it."

A quick smile spread across Mamma's face. "That's awful

nice." Mamma peered around the kitchen, as if expecting to see the quilt nearby. "Where're ya keepin' it?"

"I accidentally left it in the back of the buggy."

Mamma's expression was inquisitive. "Have ya told Cora Jane yet?"

Shaking her head, Joanna continued to scrape out the eyes of the potatoes. Did Mamma think her sister should have the quilt instead?

Mamma placed her freshly peeled potatoes in her apron to carry them to the sink to rinse. "I'm sure curious 'bout that quilt."

Joanna repeated what Malinda had said regarding how old it might be, though she didn't say a word about how special it was, nor that Malinda had suggested it had something of a story.

Mamma inquired about the pattern and the color scheme, and Joanna was happy to share all of that.

"Where do ya plan to put it?" Mamma asked.

"Oh, prob'ly in my hope chest."

"Well, why not use it?" Mamma looked surprisingly serious.

"I don't . . . I mean, I'm thinkin' I'll just wait awhile." Something seemed off beam about having a wedding ring quilt spread across her bed, especially when things with Eben seemed at a standstill.

"Till you're wed, ya mean?"

Joanna didn't look up, for fear she might see reservation, even doubt, in Mamma's eyes. "It's been a while, for sure, but I can still hope things work out, ain't?"

"One can always hope." The halting way her mother said

it left Joanna believing her mother had lost faith in her beau. Had Cora Jane swayed Mamma to her thinking? Certainly now at twenty-five, most young Amishwomen would have accepted their singleness.

But Eben loves me, Joanna reminded herself.

The late-afternoon sun was still bright when Cora Jane returned home. Joanna spotted her from the kitchen window, where she was still working with Mamma. "I'll help her unhitch the horse," she told Mamma right quick. "And I'll bring in that quilt, too." She wanted to talk to her sister without Mamma or anyone else overhearing.

Cora Jane looked surprised as Joanna approached.

"Where'd ya go in such a hurry?" asked Joanna, wasting no time.

Cora Jane kept mum as she unhooked the back hold strap on her side of the horse.

Joanna unfastened the tugs, her jaw clenched. "I asked you a question."

Cora Jane shrugged, shifting her feet. "Guess you'll know soon enough."

"For pity's sake, Cora Jane, what's gotten into you?"

"I'd say pity's a *gut* way to put it."

"Why on earth can't ya say where you've been?" Joanna demanded, her stomach in nervous knots.

There was a long pause in which Cora Jane's face turned pale. "To see the deacon," she finally admitted.

"Whatever for?" asked Joanna.

"With proof. I think you know what I mean."

Joanna could scarcely speak for lack of air. She struggled with what to say—how to say it. "You didn't!"

Cora Jane nodded slowly. "You're a baptized church member, expected to follow the rules. Ain't so?"

"You honestly didn't take my notebook over there, did ya?"

Together, they held the shafts, and Cora Jane led the horse out, away from the carriage.

How could she? Joanna stared at her sister.

Soon misery began to overtake Cora Jane's countenance. Still standing next to the horse, she said, "I had no choice." Her voice was a near whisper. "Under the Lord God, ya know."

You little snitch!

"Is it really your job to judge—to help the Lord out?" Joanna thought of poor Mary's Ohio cousin and her pink dress. Where would Cora Jane's self-righteousness end?

"It's just one more sign, sister."

"A sign . . . of what?"

"I fear you're walkin' the fence." Cora Jane frowned sadly.

Breathing a prayer for patience, Joanna shook her head. "No, Cora Jane. There's no need to worry 'bout any of that," she said, tears welling up. "You betrayed me, and you know it!"

Cora Jane dodged Joanna's glare and looked toward the house with a sigh. "Preacher Yoder will drop by sometime this week to speak with you on behalf of the ailing deacon."

"You have no idea what you've done. How could a sister do this to a sister?" Joanna fought back tears. "*How?*"

"What about the ministerial brethren?" Cora Jane said quietly. "How could you transgress against *them*?" With that, she led the horse up toward the stable.

Joanna's chest felt tight as she walked back to the buggy, to the front seat, where she snatched up Cora Jane's entire sewing bag, the story notebook tucked inside. Then, with a huff, she moved outside to the very back of the buggy and retrieved the old quilt. She made the effort to carry both the large quilt and Cora Jane's bag across the yard.

Inside, Joanna couldn't bring herself to make eye contact with Mamma when she hurried through the kitchen. The pain in her heart knew no bounds as she made her way upstairs, to the privacy of her room.

The bedroom was strewn with sunlight, a contrast to Joanna's despondent mood. Tenderly, she unwrapped the quilt and placed it on her bed. Then she promptly emptied the contents of Cora Jane's sewing bag beside it. Sure enough: There lay her treasured notebook. She opened it and was stunned to see the first pages gone.

The start of my best and longest story!

She wanted to weep and wail. But she was not a child; she shouldn't let her emotions get the best of her. The truth was, she'd gotten caught at last, and at the hands of her own sister, which hurt worst of all.

"Everything all right in here?" Mamma asked, standing primly in the doorway. She frowned into the room.

Joanna sighed. Dare she spill out her woes to Mamma? She simply wasn't one to share much with her mother, maybe because of her own need for privacy . . . particularly when it came to her writing. "Just upset, I guess."

Mamma stepped into the bedroom and wiped her hands on her long black apron. "Your face is nearly purple." Mamma looked curiously at the sewing notions strewn on the bed, and at Cora Jane's bag lying there, too.

"I'll be fine, honest."

"Jah?"

Although devastated at the thought of anyone unsympathetic reading her stories, Joanna was also relieved Mamma wouldn't press for answers. She motioned to her bed. "Here's the wedding quilt I was tellin' about."

Her mother moved closer and sat on the bed to inspect not only its pattern, but the stitching on both sides. Eyes wide, she searched the top and bottom bordered hems for any indication of its maker, much as Joanna first had at Cousin Malinda's. "It's special, all right," Mamma said at last, eyes glistening. "An enduring connection to our relatives of yore."

"I felt that way, too, when Malinda first showed it to me."

They nodded in unison. And, in that strangely sweet moment, Joanna almost had the courage to open her heart to let the anguish of Cora Jane's disloyalty overflow.

Then, thinking better of it, she said only, "I'd rather Cora Jane not see this just yet. Not today, anyway."

Mamma grimaced but didn't ask why. Silently, she rose. "I'm happy for you . . . being able to call this quilt your own."

Joanna gave a tentative smile, thankful Cora Jane had kept herself outside—away from the house for this long. It was the very least she could do.

Chapter 22

The next morning was cooler, with wispy clouds hugging the sky.

"*A fine fishing day*," Joanna's Dat might say, if he wasn't all tied up this Friday with field work, as all the local farmers were.

Joanna was also occupied, rolling out pie dough with Mamma at the kitchen table while Cora Jane organized the sewing room upstairs.

From where she sat, Joanna could see clear out to the road and beyond, past the neighbor to the south, who was repairing the roof of their springhouse. She gazed over at the expanse of acreage to the edge of her newlywed cousin's freshly plowed cornfield. Maybe she'd go over there and help once the baby arrived. Such a special time that would be this fall, caring for a brand-new infant. Of course, Malinda would have plenty of help from the rest of her family, too.

Joanna let herself imagine other people's lives, as she often did when doing menial tasks. Why did Malinda seem so lonely when she'd married her best friend and sweetheart? That was one thing Joanna didn't quite understand.

Raising her eyes again to the window, she was jolted back to reality. Her breath caught in her throat. *No!* Preacher Yoder had just turned into the lane.

"Well, what's this?" Mamma sputtered, getting up to go to the back door.

Joanna's heart beat ever so hard as she remembered Cora Jane's declaration. *Preacher didn't waste any time!*

Soon their tall minister was standing on the back stoop, his bearded face looking mighty grim as he asked to speak to Joanna.

Mamma's cheerful expression changed quickly to shock; nevertheless, she motioned calmly to her.

Never had a minister come to call on account of Joanna. Anxious, she stood and walked to the screen door, wishing she could hide in the cold cellar below the house.

"*Guder Mariye*," Preacher Yoder said. Then, just as quickly, he asked her to walk to the well pump with him, in plain view, as was customary.

She nodded respectfully, her hands clammy. Mindful to walk slightly behind him, she willed herself to breathe.

"It's come to my attention that you're writing make-believe stories." The minister got right to the point. "And thanks to your notebook, I've seen it with my own eyes."

"'Tis true." She nodded.

"And . . . seems to me you're putting yourself into one

of them, jah?" He didn't let her answer but continued on. "That Troyer boy from Indiana is in there, too. Not hard to see that, even when the names are different."

She didn't know how to respond, or if she should.

"I wouldn't get any ideas, now, about asking permission to transfer your church membership out there, not with this secret ambition you're hiding." Preacher Yoder's eyes penetrated hers.

She lowered her eyes; he certainly wasn't finished.

"Do you understand why I've come here, Joanna?"

She raised her head and saw how solemn his expression was. With his black coat and trousers, he looked ready to conduct a funeral.

"Nee, not entirely," she said softly. Since her baptism, Joanna had been careful to follow the Old Ways in everything but this. Even so, writing her stories was one thing; sharing them in print was quite another. Yet hadn't she been tempted to do that very thing?

Preacher paused, then after a great, deep breath, he went on. "Writing such stories is a waste of time, but it also appears that you're a-hankerin' to get them published."

Joanna trembled under his stern gaze. "So far, I've written them only for myself."

"Well, that may be, but there is more than one note about possible publishers written in the margins of your notebook." He paused. "Is your fancy English friend, Amelia, encouraging you to seek publication?"

"She has." Joanna's heart wavered. "But I've yet to look into it."

"Far better for you to keep in mind your vow to God and

the Hickory Hollow church. No need letting an outsider influence you toward the world. And no need getting puffed up about your writing, neither."

"Is it considered a sin to put stories down on paper, then?" She looked over her shoulder, back toward the house. "I know such creativity is frowned upon . . . but not forbidden, jah?"

Preacher Yoder's responding frown was so harsh it enveloped his whole face. "Your attitude concerns me. I see rebellion in you, Joanna—the worst sin of all. The origin of all wickedness."

She was stunned. Did an innocent question make her rebellious? "I didn't mean to come across as—"

"You're a baptized child of God, are you not?"

"Jah." She bowed her head. "Forgive me for speaking out of turn, Preacher."

"It's been some time since I've encountered an attempt at compliance and stubborn insistence in the selfsame breath. Joanna, you must never talk back to a man of God," he stated firmly. "Doing so could eventually get ya shunned."

Despite her shock at this, another question sprang to mind: Was there a difference between telling a story out loud and putting it down on paper? How many storytellers did she know in the hollow? Yet they had not been silenced for sharing interesting tales at quilting bees and work frolics and such. Nor had they been threatened with excommunication.

Joanna pondered whether or not to voice her question. Certainly she did not want to push things, like Rebecca Lapp's adopted daughter, Katie, had some years ago. Katie was still under the *Bann*.

"Is tellin' stories out loud also considered a sin, then?" she asked in what she hoped was a meek tone, looking at him again.

He pursed his lips, deep furrows still evident in his brow. The preacher seemed more frustrated than indignant now that she had the gall to continue to speak up. But he did not pacify her by saying her writings were either forbidden or a sin. "If this type of questioning continues, you will be called upon to repent before the church membership."

Do I sound defiant? Joanna honestly wondered—she'd been too perplexed to remain silent.

Preacher Yoder gave a swift jerk of his head, signaling the end of the conversation. Then, without another word, he marched to his waiting horse and carriage, a profile in black except for his straw hat.

In a daze, Joanna tried to sort out what he'd actually said. She was fairly sure she was expected to stop writing her stories, yet he hadn't specifically said it was against the church ordinance. Nor had he declared it a sin. But getting published: The preacher had been mighty clear on *that* point.

Ach, I've never been so embarrassed in my life!

Trying to calm down from the upsetting visit, she looked up and noticed Cora Jane standing at an open upstairs window. Joanna was shocked to think she might have listened in on the private conversation. Reddening, Cora Jane inched back, away from sight.

What's come over her?

With a moan, Joanna turned away from the house. She stared at the clouds toward the northeast. Never before had she felt so alone.

So it's come to this. Joanna reached for the hem of her apron to dry her tears. The emptiness in her heart needed to be filled, and she yearned for Eben's loving arms, imagining what it would be like to have him with her now, walking together once again.

She poured out her heart in prayer. *O Lord, how can I give up what brings me such enjoyment?*

Chapter 23

Still shaky from her meeting with Preacher Yoder, Joanna darted into the small bathroom off the kitchen, where she washed her face. She stood at the sink and stared into the modest cabinet mirror, letting water drip off her chin. Her distress threatened even more tears, but she set her jaw and splashed cold water on her eyes and forehead.

She was thankful for indoor plumbing on such a day. Four decades ago, her family was using the wooden outhouse, which still stood a ways from the barn. Ah, the wonderful-good conveniences the ministerial brethren had permitted back then. Considering that, she wondered when individual creativity might be allowed. Would story writing—and music, like Katie's guitar playing—always be frowned upon? Now, sadly, her story would languish, forever unfinished. *Ironic.* She hoped that wouldn't be the case with her real-life love story.

She hadn't received a letter from Eben in the past couple days, and the knowledge compounded her misery.

After drying her face, Joanna turned to the window and moved the plain white curtains aside to look at the lush green lawn, carefully tended each week by her and Cora Jane. They'd also planted the brightly colored petunias along the walkway and around the well pump on the eastern edge. Alas, the old pump would always be a reminder now of Preacher Yoder's stern admonition.

Evidently, she was considered a transgressor in his eyes. Yet Joanna wasn't herself convinced. And she wished with all her heart that the minister would've answered her questions—now she was so confused. Did he think Joanna was merely a ferhoodled female? She'd sometimes overheard other men in authority talk so about their womenfolk, which had privately triggered her resentment, though she hadn't "given place to the devil" and acted on it. Still, she couldn't imagine Eben referring to her that way . . . nor her own father.

Joanna rushed through her indoor chores, avoiding Mamma as best she could. She simply could not reveal what had happened today, not the way she felt. But she needed comfort terribly, and thankfully she knew where to seek it. As miserable as Joanna felt, she could hardly wait to leave the house, to escape both her mother's questioning eyes and her sister's pained expression. She detested what Cora Jane had done. Yet she also knew that pursuing revenge was not the way of forgiveness.

Joanna headed on foot around the barn after the noon meal and cut through the field lane that bordered her father's cornfield. She relived Preacher Yoder's awful visit as she trudged over the lengthy pasture to the other side of their property.

How could she ever forgive Cora Jane? Yet she must.

Birds gathered in masses in the trees, calling back and forth, then flew together in a great gray cloud against the sky. They seemed to mock her.

When Joanna finally arrived at Ella Mae Zook's little house, she spotted the white-haired woman on the back porch, watering her potted red geraniums with a galvanized watering can. Several years had come and gone since many pretty annuals blossomed in the beds along the walkway and porch. But Ella Mae's knee joints could no longer tolerate bending to weed a garden.

Ella Mae looked up and gave a smile as Joanna made her way across the backyard. "Well, now, I *thought* that was you." She looked neat and proper in her green dress and black apron, graying hair in a low bun and her crisp white organdy Kapp over the widening middle part. "Nice to see ya, dearie. Come sit with me on the porch."

"Hullo, Ella Mae," Joanna said as she approached the elderly woman. "I've been wantin' to visit you."

"Glad ya dropped by, then." Ella Mae led the way up the steps, going to her own rocking chair near the far end of the white banister. "You're lookin' a bit *schlimm*, dear girl." Gingerly, she eased herself into the rocker.

"Do I?"

"Serious as ever I've seen ya."

Joanna took her seat on the only other rocker. Leaning back, she sighed, glad for the quiet and the peaceful landscape beyond the barn. "Honestly, I scarcely know where to start."

"Well, the beginning's always a *gut* place, ain't?"

Joanna crossed her legs and glanced at her dusty bare feet. She felt so comfortable with Ella Mae, who was certainly the best listener Joanna had ever known. "All right," she said, glad they were alone. "When you were a girl, did ya ever love someone who lived outside the community?"

"I never cared two cents for any Englischer boys, if that's what ya mean."

Joanna waved her hand. "No, no . . . I didn't mean to imply that." She scooted forward a bit. "What I meant was, did ya ever care for an *Amish* fella who lived in a different church district . . . maybe even in another state?"

"Can't say that I did." Ella Mae shook her head. "Never met any young fellas outside this community back in my own courting days."

Forging ahead, Joanna confided about Eben Troyer and all of the important details surrounding their long-distance courtship since their meeting on the beach and his visit last November. "Even though he wants to move here, things just aren't movin' forward like I thought . . . actually, they don't seem to be moving at all."

"Ain't surprising, really," Ella Mae said softly, blue eyes peering over her glasses.

Disheartened, Joanna hoped she might explain.

"Problems can arise in a long-distance courtship," Ella Mae said, no longer rocking. "Misunderstandings, for one thing. And sometimes a couple doesn't always mesh because of the different church ordinances, for another. What one bishop allows, the other doesn't—so there's some fittin' in that must happen over time."

Joanna wondered if Eben's bishop considered writing fiction a problem, but she quickly dismissed that.

"And there can be certain challenges to face by havin' to move far away from family and friends, too."

Joanna knew this—why, even Cousin Malinda seemed lonesome at times.

"What *I'm* wonderin' is, aren't there any nice fellas in Hickory Hollow?" Ella Mae asked, chuckling a little, her dimples showing.

"That's a *gut* question."

"Well, then?"

Joanna considered that. "But what if you've already fallen in love with someone else?" There. She'd said it.

"Guess it's just as easy to fall for a young man right here at home as anywhere, jah?"

Joanna felt discouraged. Ella Mae didn't seem to understand—the young men around here had had their chance, but none of them had shown much interest. No one had, in fact, till Eben. Yet the Wise Woman's questions lodged in Joanna's mind. Truth was, there would be no such difficulties for her and Eben . . . at least not once he finally arrived to court her. He'd never hinted at any worries about what the move would mean for him, or any concerns related to the Ordnung there in the hollow. On the other hand, he had never really written about anything controversial. Maybe he simply took things as they came.

"Problems can arise in a long-distance courtship. . . ."

Ella Mae's words continued to resonate in Joanna's mind later, as she walked back through the cornfield toward home, feeling worse for the visit. She glanced over at the top of the phone shack where she and Eben secretly talked.

Will he call again tonight?

"Oh, *gut*, you're home," Mamma said the minute Joanna walked in the back door. "I need ya to take a casserole and some fresh bread over to Mammi Kurtz right quick. Your father's already hitched up the team."

"I'll be glad to," Joanna replied, noting that Cora Jane was down on all fours, washing the kitchen floor. *Truly glad . . .*

"I would go, but Rachel Stoltzfus is comin' over any minute now, bringing ideas for the school's benefit auction next month." Mamma bustled around, gathering up the long loaf of bread, some strawberry jam, and the hot dish, putting everything in a large basket. "Hope it's not too heavy." She handed it to Joanna.

"No . . . I can manage."

"Just so ya know, your Mammi Kurtz ain't feelin' well," Mamma added. "Might not be a *gut* idea to stay long, ya hear?"

Joanna nodded, promising not to tire Mammi out. She did wish she could ask about the story behind the double wedding ring quilt, but it sounded like that would have to wait.

She glanced at her sister before leaving the kitchen with the food basket. Cora Jane kept scrubbing all the while, never once looking up, like she was taking out some frustration on the wood floor.

Joanna's Mammi Kurtz was the topping on any cake. She wasn't just dear, she was considerate, too. And beautiful for her age. Her skin was fair and unflawed, except for the wrinkles, and she wore her prayer cap pushed toward the back of her graying head.

"Well, aren't you nice, Joanna." Her grandmother got up from her comfortable chair in the tidy corner of the small kitchen, setting *The Budget* aside.

"No need to cook tonight," Joanna said.

Mammi shuffled over and touched her arm. "How'd your Mamma know I was under the weather?"

"Let's see." Joanna glanced at the ceiling. "From that trusty ol' grapevine, perhaps?"

Her grandmother gave a little laugh, then teetered a bit. Right quick, Joanna helped her back to her chair. "Maybe I should stay awhile and help ya serve supper," Joanna offered. "If ya would like."

"Ain't necessary, really. Fannie will be checkin' up, like always." Her daughter-in-law Fannie lived in the main farmhouse with her husband and children.

"If you're sure, then."

"Oh jah . . . ever so sure." Mammi nodded, though she looked pale. "But before ya leave, I wondered what ya thought of the wedding quilt Malinda found."

"It's astonishingly perty. I love havin' it, Mammi."

"Didja know your name's the same as the great-great-aunt who made it?"

"Really?"

"'Tis true . . . and Joanna wasn't a typical Amish name in those days." Mammi crossed her hands over her bosom. "That's why I thought you should have the quilt."

Not because she thought I'd be marrying anytime soon. . . .

"It's beautifully made," Joanna said.

"Oh, it's just the most wonderful quilt . . . for more than one important reason."

"Sometime, I'd like to hear more 'bout it," she ventured, heeding Mamma's wishes about staying too long.

"We'll need some time alone for that," Mammi said, her eyes flashing a secret. "Just the two of us."

"I'll look forward to it." Joanna set the hot dish on the back burner for warming later. "You sure it's all right for me to leave?"

"*Abseelutt.*" Despite her ashen face, Mammi was emphatic. "Come by anytime, dear."

Joanna went to give her a kiss on the cheek. "Be sure to

tell Dawdi or Fannie to bring ya over to see Mammi Sadie sometime, all right?"

"That I will." Mammi's smile was precious. "And you tell your Mamma that Dawdi and I are grateful for the delicious supper. Smells awful *gut*."

"I will." With that, Joanna headed for the back door. Knowing her name was the same as the quilt maker's tickled her no end. Moreover, considering the preacher's visit—and Ella Mae's depressing remarks about long-distance romances—it was the nicest thing Joanna had heard all day.

Now, what else did Mammi know about that extra-special quilt?

Chapter 24

One after another, cars with impatient drivers rushed past the horse and carriage as Joanna reined the mare closer to the safety of the shoulder. Yet she didn't hurry the horse whatsoever. She needed this time to contemplate all the many events of this Friday.

Ella Mae's words continued to turn in Joanna's head, begging for attention, even though Joanna wished to push them aside. She turned her thoughts back to the quilt. It was odd, but she wondered if the wedding quilt was somehow destined to have been passed along through the family to her . . . if for no other reason than to offset her doubts. She honestly didn't know what to think about the young man who loved her but who seemingly had no plan of action that would permit them to marry anytime soon. Even so, the quilt from the past encouraged her.

She tried to picture her great-great-aunt—surely as

resourceful and diligent as Joanna's own mother and grandmothers—sewing and humming as she worked . . . perhaps praying? Oh, she felt so reassured by the thought. It was almost as if the Lord was whispering in her ear, *All is well, my child.*

Her soul had to be silenced so Joanna could hear the still, small voice of God. Only then could she relinquish the reins of her life to her heavenly Father . . . and breathe a grateful prayer.

Joanna had just rounded the bend leading toward the fork in the road—the left side headed to Hickory Lane—when she noticed a young man walking on the other side, going in the same direction she was. He turned slightly, and she realized it was Freckles Jake.

Well, of all things!

He smiled and waved, and without a smidgen of hesitation, he called to her, "Joanna! Would ya mind giving me a lift?"

"Any other time, but I need to get home quickly."

His face fell. "All right, then."

Immediately, she felt guilty. Would it really be so bad to take him home or wherever he was headed? She thought better of it. "Well, if you're not goin' too far out of my way," she said, slowing the horse.

"Mighty kind of you," he said and thanked her.

She veered the horse off the road and stopped so Jake could hop in on the left. She hoped he'd stay put over there and not slide toward her for any funny business. Though for all the rumors, she'd never encountered anything out of the ordinary with him.

"Where're ya goin'?" she asked, suddenly feeling shy with him sharing the seat.

"Over yonder, past your father's farm—to Ella Mae's."

She was shocked, because she didn't know a young man would admit to going to see the Wise Woman. "Interesting," she replied, unable to keep her smile in check.

"Why's that?" The late-afternoon sun poured in on him, making his hair look redder than usual.

"Ach, I don't know," she said, embarrassed.

"Well, I think you do." He was grinning.

"Ella Mae's one terrific listener, for sure." *We all need to talk to someone*, she thought.

He shrugged.

"I can take you there, if you'd like."

"No, that's all right. I'll just get out at your place and go through the cornfield, if ya don't mind." He removed his straw hat, running his hand across the top of it. Then, glancing at her, he said, "I appreciate the ride."

"Don't mind at all."

He started to say something, then stopped and donned his hat. She was relieved. What if he asked if she was going to the next Singing? She didn't want to hurt him.

Besides, I belong to someone else, she thought. *Don't I?*

Her visit to Ella Mae's had certainly stirred up some issues. That and meeting with Jake on the road today—it was almost as if he'd turned up to reinforce the Wise Woman's remarks about local boys.

A few minutes later, they turned into her father's lane. "Here we are," she said, amazed how quickly Jake bounded out of the buggy, like he wanted to impress her. Then, before saying another word, he tied up the horse.

She turned to thank Jake for this small and unexpected favor and found him right behind her. His hazel eyes sparkled as he grinned at her. "Pleased to help . . . anytime, really." Then, crossing the barnyard, he turned to wave—twice.

Laughing a little at Jake's eagerness, Joanna headed around the side of the house and was completely astonished to see someone sitting on the back porch steps. There, looking altogether handsome, was none other than Eben Troyer!

Chapter 25

Hullo, Joanna." Eben remained seated for a moment, reconsidering his visit in the awkwardness of the moment. Had he done the right thing showing up unannounced?

But Joanna's contagious smile lifted the roof right off his heart, and he rose to meet her. "Ach, Eben . . . I . . . when did ya get here?" she stuttered, searching his face.

"A few minutes ago."

She was staring with disbelief, and if he wasn't mistaken, there were silent tears in her pretty eyes. "Ach, it's so *gut* to see you again! Does anyone know you're here?" She looked about her.

"I knocked, but no one came to the door. So I sat myself down to wait, and now you're here." He wanted to pull her into his arms and kiss her right there in broad daylight, but that wasn't called for. For one thing, he'd come bearing bad news. And for another, he couldn't easily dismiss the jovial fellow who had been riding with Joanna. Eben had never seen someone so smitten. He wondered why she hadn't introduced him before he ran off.

"Care to go walkin'?" he said.

"Or we could take the carriage." Joanna's eyes sparkled, and he saw again how exceptionally pretty she was. "We could walk along Weaver's Creek, if you'd like."

He didn't have the heart to tell her there was no time for riding like last time. Besides, lingering at the creek would simply prolong things. "I really can't stay," he said, pushing the words out.

Her face turned pale. "Why not?"

"I have a round-trip bus ticket. Gotta leave today." He couldn't bear her disappointed expression.

"I don't understand."

"We need to talk over some important things." He motioned toward the field lane on this side of the cornfield, where they'd walked in the cold and snow last November. Now that he was here, seeing her . . . he wanted to reach for her hand and feel it nestled in his, the way they'd walked before. Eben found it hard to voice what he'd come to say. Not hard, no—nearly impossible.

Joanna looked up at him as they headed across the driveway, a frown piercing her lovely face. And it was then he realized he was walking much too fast. He must slow down, slow everything down and take his time—*their time*—so he wouldn't regret it later. He had to first muster the courage to tell her how disappointed he was, soothe her with his own sadness, somehow.

He forged ahead. "My plans have suddenly changed, Joanna. Things are out of my control." He felt her stiffen as they walked beside each other, the electricity still evident between them.

"What do you mean?"

"You know I'd hoped to court you here." Eben drew a breath. Could he get the words out without making a fool of himself? "But circumstances have gotten in the way." His voice sounded foreign even to him. "It's become impossible for me to move to Hickory Hollow, after all."

Her eyes widened. "What's happened?"

He had to make her understand, so he tried again. "Leroy has thrown a wrench into everything. He got himself married to an outsider—brought her home to meet the family just yesterday."

"So . . . he's not comin' back, then?"

He shook his head. "I prayed he would get fed up with English life and come home to work with our father—and take my place."

She nodded her head slowly. "And there's no other choice but for you to stay put there?"

"My father can't manage on his own."

She fell silent as they walked farther away from the house.

After a time, he felt compelled to answer the unspoken question hanging between them. "I just had to come see ya, Joanna. I couldn't put this to you in a letter." If only she hadn't written so often about her great fondness for Hickory Hollow, this whole thing would've been much easier! "You deserved better, so I wanted to come here, to tell you in person."

"I don't know what to say." She stared at the ground for the longest time.

"What if you could move to Shipshewana?"

She immediately looked horrified, as if it was unthinkable. "I've never really considered it, Eben." She sighed audibly. "Thought you wanted to—"

"I know it's a lot to ask."

She shook her head, eyes glistening.

"You all right?" he asked, touching her elbow.

She flinched slightly. Then, raising her head to the sky, she pursed her lips and glanced toward a farm in the near distance . . . then smiled faintly.

What was this expression? Was she actually relieved they were parting ways?

He waited for her to say more, but when she continued in her silence, he remembered the auburn-haired young man who'd enthusiastically waved good-bye to her. No question, that fellow was sweet on Joanna.

Understandably so . . .

Somehow he found the courage to ask, "What is your bishop's stance on transferring church membership?" He hadn't wanted to broach this topic, didn't want to put her on the spot. He did recall her mother's pointed response to this during the last visit, but he needed to hear directly from Joanna.

"Bishop John's mighty strict," she stated, then paused like she was struggling terribly. "No, I doubt I'd be permitted to leave . . . now."

Eben wished he hadn't asked.

Joanna was so stunned she could scarcely speak. *He came all this way just to say good-bye?* She could not grasp this terrible turn of events. Truth was, Eben seemed at a loss to say more about his dilemma, simply blaming his brother Leroy for this mess. And the fact that Eben had asked, nearly out of the blue, if she'd move to Shipshewana . . . *What timing!* She was too embarrassed to tell him about the preacher's warning, especially now, when Eben seemed to be breaking up with her. Oh, how she loved him! How could she let him just give up on their relationship—everything they'd meant to each other?

Even so, she'd made a vow to God and to *this* church district, so there was no considering a move away to Indiana. Certainly not when Preacher Yoder's counsel burned in her ears.

Considering everything, it didn't make a whit of sense to keep walking like this, dragging out the inevitable. Her heart was being torn further with every step.

"I'm truly sorry it's come to this, Joanna," Eben said quietly. "I just see no way out . . . not anymore."

Because I'm not able to move to Indiana, she thought, knowing she'd pushed herself into a corner because of her love for writing. No, Leroy wasn't the only one who'd created this problem.

Joanna couldn't look at Eben for fear he might see her dismay.

They walked another few minutes without talking. She felt like Mamma's pressure cooker as the chasm between them grew by the second.

"I kept hopin' to see us together somehow," he said glumly. "I can't say enough how sorry I am."

"I'm sorry, too," she said, hoping he'd understand how much she cared for him. But she didn't dare ask anything more . . . she felt she was being as pushy as Jake was said to be. If only she could erase all the months of their separation and turn the clock back to the evening they'd first met in Virginia. When the world seemed to tilt as the sun fell into the ocean. When he'd whispered into her hair . . .

They were approaching the far perimeter of her father's field, where the grazing land bordered Ella Mae's son-in-law's property. Feeling forlorn and terribly helpless, Joanna looked toward the Wise Woman's Dawdi Haus again and remembered her pointed caution. True to form, she had not minced words. "*Complications*," Ella Mae had said about long-distance relationships.

Joanna wanted to turn around and hurry back to the house, put this painful visit behind her. But in that moment, she spotted Jake Lantz sitting with Ella Mae under a shade tree on a double glider. *Can he see us out here?* she wondered, hoping not. As it was, Eben might very well be peeved at her being with Jake earlier. She almost wondered if she ought to say something, clarify that Jake had asked *her* for a ride—that he was nothing but a casual friend, if that. But might that only draw attention to Jake? Oh, she didn't know what to do!

"We should prob'ly head back," Eben said. "I need to call for a cab soon."

Her heart sank as she pointed to the telephone shanty in

the next field over. The very spot where she'd looked forward to going to hear his voice. She sighed, choking back tears.

Eben offered a nod, then headed off in that direction.

Observing him walk, his posture so straight, his black suspenders perfectly crisscrossed against his white short-sleeved shirt—*he wore his for-*gut *clothes again*—Joanna refused to cry. "*Either a fella wants ya or he doesn't,*" she'd heard Ella Mae say some years ago. "*No sense in pleading for what's goin' to fizzle anyways.*"

No, Joanna wouldn't fight for what could not be, and she wouldn't fret over him, not in his presence, anyhow.

She would sorely miss his calls and the many letters postmarked from Shipshewana. They had become such an important part of her weeks . . . her life.

In the depths of her heart, Joanna knew this parting meant much more than losing a beau. Joanna felt her last chance to marry for love slipping away.

Brokenhearted, she watched Eben open the wooden door to the shanty and reach for the telephone.

Chapter 26

Eben's hand shook as he pulled the number for the cab company out of his pocket and attempted to dial the phone. *Worst day of my life.*

He stopped and hung up, still gripping the receiver as he stared out the lone window. If he did succeed in acquiring transportation back to the bus depot, he would sit there for a couple of hours until time to board for the overnight return trip—squander his precious time with Joanna. Yet there was nothing more to say; she seemed upset by his presence . . . even put out with him. It had been so long since he'd seen her, he wasn't sure he was reading her correctly. Was she sad he was calling off their plans? Angry?

We're almost like strangers.

He prayed for wisdom. Life had come crashing down indeed. And here he was, muddling through when he ought to be moving heaven and earth to win Joanna's heart and make her his bride.

Lifting the receiver again, he managed to dial this time. He went through the motions of speaking to someone at the dispatch office, asking for a ride within the hour, hoping that might give him a bit more time here—to make sure Joanna was all right. Although at the rate he was going, he wasn't certain she wanted him around at all. And who could blame her? He'd written her love letters, promising things based on mere hope . . . things he now knew he couldn't fulfill. "*Ich hab en Hutsch draus gemacht*," he whispered, glancing at his watch. There was no doubt in Eben's mind: He *had* made a mess of it.

Joanna was in such a bad way, she couldn't bring herself to stand there and wait for Eben to finish up his call. To preserve her sense of propriety, she walked back to the house and began to unhitch the horse, wondering where her parents and Cora Jane were keeping themselves.

She forced her thoughts away from the ragged ache that hadn't let up since she realized Eben was returning to Indiana, taking back his promise of love and a future together. Why hadn't she told on herself about the visit from Preacher Yoder . . . the complication *she'd* caused by not explaining herself? Why not, when their courtship was already coming to a painful end?

In a few minutes, Jake appeared again on this side of the barnyard, having returned through Dat's field. As before, his face glowed at seeing her. "Say, let me help ya, Joanna." And before she could politely refuse, he began to assist with the heavy harness. She hoped Eben wouldn't get the wrong idea, if he were to spot them working together. But then, realizing that was a ridiculous worry now, she dismissed it. After all, Eben had just let her go, so why should she fret? It might even be providential for Eben to see her with Jake.

Just that quickly, Joanna felt chagrined. No way did she wish jealousy on Eben. But she did wish she could erase his words and return to the days of their romance, however stalled. At least then the sting in her heart would not be so sharp.

In that moment, Cousin Malinda's husband, Andy, came rumbling down the road in his hay wagon. He slowed at the end of the lane, then called to her. "Joanna, come *schnell*! Hop aboard!" Something was obviously wrong. And without hesitation, she dashed to the road, leaving Jake behind.

Andy was hatless, his blond hair sticking out every which way like he'd run his hands through it.

"*Was fehlt?*" she asked.

"Mammi Kurtz collapsed in the kitchen . . . seriously injured her hip," Andy explained.

"Ach, no!" Joanna had seen how unsteady her grandmother had been earlier. *I should've stayed with her!* "Are my parents and Cora Jane over there already?"

"Jah, and your mother needs help with Dawdi, 'specially once the ambulance arrives."

Joanna felt terrible for not making sure her grandmother was all right. For more reasons than one, she should not have come home.

However anxious she was to be with her family, she also didn't want to leave just yet . . . not without saying goodbye to Eben.

Looking back, she saw him heading toward the house, within a few yards of Jake and the horse and carriage. She groaned inwardly, knowing Jake was a talkative sort. It was anyone's guess what he'd chew the fat about . . . and what Eben might say to him.

She asked Andy to wait a minute, then hurried to Eben. "My grandmother's fallen—might have a broken bone," she said. "I'm needed over there."

Disappointment seemed to cloud his countenance as she offered a quick farewell.

Unexpectedly, he reached for her hand and gave it a quick squeeze. "*Gott* be with you, Joanna," he said simply.

She tried to give him a smile in return, then, knowing it was best not to linger, headed back to Andy, who hoisted her up and into the wagon.

The horse moved forward, and Joanna looked back to Eben . . . just in time to see him shake Jake's hand. The two of them turned and were standing shoulder to shoulder, looking altogether befuddled as she rode away. If Joanna hadn't felt so miserable right then, seeing Jake and Eben together like that might've struck her as almost comical.

"Looks like it's just us," Jake said after introducing himself, helping Eben lead the horse to the stable. "Most folk call me Freckles Jake . . . guess you can, too."

Eben, still reeling with emotion, felt momentarily thankful Jake was being so down-home and relaxed. *Like Leroy always was . . .*

"*Gut* to meet ya, Freckles Jake. I'm Eben Troyer."

Jake removed his straw hat and scratched his head. "That's a family name we don't hear much round here."

Eben nodded. "I'm from Indiana . . . Shipshewana, to be exact."

"Ah, so you're the fella who visited last year." Jake grinned now, planting his hat back on. "Nice to put a name to a face."

"Have you lived here your whole life?" Eben asked.

"Born and bred." Jake straightened and pushed out his chest. "We here in Hickory Hollow are mighty proud—well, in a *gut* sort of way—of our secluded little spot, hidden away from the English world. 'Tis hard to find, if you don't know where you're goin'."

Eben could vouch for that. The cab driver today had never even heard of Hickory Lane and didn't know it was east of Intercourse Village—*a strange name for a town*, Eben thought. *Thank goodness for the cabbie's* GPS.

"Well, what do ya think of our hollow?" Jake asked, looking him over but good as they walked out of the stable.

"I see why folk like it." *Joanna especially*.

"Looks like you've got some time on your hands, what with Joanna carted off and all."

If Eben had been in a better mood, he would have chuckled. "Not much time, actually."

"All right, then. You gonna spend it standing lookin' like you're lost?"

Something about this young man demanded his attention. "I like you, Jake. I truly do." He clapped his hand on Jake's shoulder, feeling the muscles there. No question this was a hardworking, responsible fellow. "What can ya tell me about your Ordnung here? How strict is your bishop, for starters?"

A frown appeared on Jake's face. "Oh, now, you don't want to fool with the likes of Bishop John Beiler."

"So . . . mighty strict, then?"

Jake bobbed his head. "Imposed the harshest shunning anywhere some years ago. A young girl wouldn't submit to the church over her music."

Eben's ears perked up. "Really, now?"

"She ended up leavin'—took her guitar with her."

Eben didn't need to hear how harsh they'd treated her, but he did wonder about the types of vows required at church baptism. "Some churches want their members to stay put in the same district their whole life."

"Jah, that's pretty much what we've got right here."

Eben considered that, his mind going a hundred miles an hour. "Ever know anyone who managed to get permission to move to another Amish church?" No doubt the reason for his questions was apparent to Jake, but Eben couldn't help asking.

"Well, a few . . . sure. But they were members in good standing." Jake studied him hard. "Why do ya ask?"

"Curious is all." Eben couldn't help but wonder why Joanna had said so emphatically otherwise. Had she purposely misrepresented the bishop? Surely not. And he couldn't imagine a girl like Joanna not being highly regarded in the church.

No, Eben knew the real truth. She simply was not interested in leaving her beloved home . . . not even to marry him.

Chapter 27

As she rode to her grandparents' house, Joanna could still picture Eben with Jake, standing at the end of the lane. She squelched the urge to cry, knowing she must be strong for her mother . . . and for poor Dawdi, who would surely want to go along in the ambulance with Mammi. That's just how he was these days—hardly let her out of his sight.

I'll be the one to stay home with him.

Tears sprang to her eyes as she considered both the unforeseen breakup with Eben and now Mammi's terrible fall. Truly, Joanna could hardly hold herself together.

Eben spotted the yellow cab coming this way and immediately regretted having to leave. If only he could have come here under much different circumstances. Like his visit last wedding season. Yet, knowing what he did now, he could see she was not willing to commit, not when it meant a move.

Otherwise, why would she not say there were exceptions to membership transfers? She'd lost interest in him . . . perhaps in part because of the friendly fellow beside him.

"Mighty nice talkin' with ya," Jake said, moseying onto the road with a wave as he headed toward home.

"You too." The encounter with Jake had seemed meant to be.

Eben opened the back door of the cab and got in, watching Joanna's house fade from sight as they sped away. He took in the springtime views, especially noticing the well-tended lawns and surrounding flower gardens—every farmhouse here was pristine and tidy, too. Not that his community back home wasn't as well cared for, of course . . . it just struck him that each and every property here was remarkably maintained.

No wonder Joanna adores the area.

With a glance into the rearview mirror, the cabbie asked if he had kinfolk here.

"No."

"Ah . . . a girlfriend, maybe?"

"Not anymore." Eben shrugged. "It didn't work out."

"Sorry, man."

No more than I am, Eben thought. *My whole future was bound up in Joanna Kurtz.*

"Remember, there are lots of other good fish in the sea," the driver said with another glance over his shoulder and a sympathetic smile.

Eben considered that. Meeting Joanna had seemed providential—so much that he had trusted in it completely.

As they drove a bit farther, he noticed a large farmhouse where an ambulance was parked in the lane, as well as several gray buggies, a van, and the same hay wagon that had come for Joanna.

He caught sight of Joanna herself standing on the front porch, opening her arms to an older man. Was it her Dawdi? Watching her comfort him, Eben swallowed the lump in his throat, touched by her compassion.

Oh, dear Joanna, he thought sadly. *What have I done, letting you go?*

Just as Joanna had guessed, she was left in charge of her grandfather as a vanload of various relatives, including her parents and Cora Jane, followed the ambulance with Mammi inside to the hospital. She helped get Dawdi settled in a rocker on the front porch, where he'd insisted on being positioned facing west, in the direction the ambulance had gone.

"Would ya like something cold to drink?" She concentrated on doting on her grandfather, glad to have something to occupy her mind.

Dawdi smiled a little, his blue-gray eyes still moist from weeping. She supposed, as tenderhearted as he was, he might sit out here and cry some more. "There's a pitcher of lemonade in there," he said.

"I'll get some for ya."

"You're as thoughtful as your Mammi, ya know?" he surprised her by saying.

"That's awful nice." Joanna remembered again Eben's disheartening visit. Lots of girls would've questioned him even further—talked up to him, perhaps. Cora Jane would have!

While Dawdi drank his lemonade and kept cool outdoors, Joanna put the casserole she'd delivered earlier into the oven to reheat. Once she'd set the table for two and checked on Dawdi again, she wandered to the sitting area in the kitchen alcove and noticed her Mammi's devotional book open and lying upside down. Looking at it, Joanna began to read the selection for the day from Psalm 29:11, surprised by its pertinence. *"The Lord will give strength unto his people; the Lord will bless his people with peace."*

Still holding the book, she sat down in Mammi's chair. "I long for your peace, O Lord . . . I truly do." She stifled her urge to cry as she looked with fondness around this little corner where Mammi loved to sit and read. "With God's help, I'll get through this unbearable time," she whispered, wishing Eben Troyer safe travels home. She did not harbor any bitterness toward him, not one speck: Eben was a good man, she knew. But she was hurt terribly and longed to receive the peace spoken of in the psalm. She leaned her head back, hoping her grandmother would be all right. *Let her know you're with her, O Lord.*

After a time, Joanna went to stir the casserole, making sure it was hot enough to serve. And she burst into tears, realizing she would never cook such a supper for Eben.

The man in front of Eben on the bus smelled of cigarettes. Now that he thought of it, Eben realized that Leroy had smelled a bit like smoke, too. Surely his brother hadn't gravitated toward that kind of habit. But then, Leroy had dabbled in plenty of things since he'd attended high school and college.

Eben looked out the window, the sky already dimming as the sun dropped low, flicking light between thousands of tree trunks as they headed west.

Back to where I came from . . .

He'd learned more about the Hickory Hollow church district in a few short moments with Jake than he had in all the months of courting Joanna by letter. But then, Eben hadn't probed about her community, so it wasn't fair to measure in that way. Joanna was a responder—she had never been pushy or forward like some girls. No, Joanna was kind and patient, and she certainly hadn't deserved being put through the wringer today. What a rotten outcome for someone so wonderful.

Squinting into the fading sunlight, Eben thought it served him right if Jake Lantz *was* interested in Joanna. Considering how forthright and congenial the young man was, Eben almost hoped he'd pursue her. At least then he'd know Joanna would have a fine husband.

He closed his eyes, again seeing Joanna's sweet face when first she'd seen him sitting there on the back porch. Repeatedly, he made himself remember only her demure and cheerful expression . . . the way she looked before he'd opened his mouth and ruined everything. He resented the pain in his heart, for it was his own doing.

Rest eluded him. Eben opened his eyes and stared out the window at the landscape along the highway, a greenish-brown blur as the bus sped along faster and faster toward home. *Away from my dearest love*, he thought as the wind rushed past the windows.

··· ➣➢ ···

After supper, Joanna sat in her grandmother's chair and listened as Dawdi Kurtz read the old German Bible. She wondered when someone might return to give some word of Mammi.

Not surprisingly, Dawdi eventually called it an early night and headed off to bed in the downstairs sleeping room. Her grandfather was a quiet man who lived his life inside his head and disliked engaging in much conversation—like Joanna's own father. Sleep was Dawdi's way of coping with his great concern for Mammi, now far away in the hospital. *Amongst Englischers . . .*

Feeling restless, Joanna wandered upstairs to look at the rooms that had been set up by Fannie and her husband to look nearly identical to those in the main farmhouse, where decades before, Joanna's grandparents had nurtured and raised their children. The more spacious bedroom was presently arranged as a comfortable guest room, and the smallest was a sewing room. Just as in the bigger house next door, the larger bedroom was situated directly over the kitchen for the best warmth during the cold months. The room still looked the same as when Mammi and Dawdi had moved here to the slightly smaller Dawdi Haus, right after Cora Jane was born. Joanna's mother had needed some extra care from her own mother, so Joanna was brought here at the age of seven to spend a week. At that time, Mammi Kurtz had shown her a secret opening in the wall, a concealed bookshelf where she'd kept her diaries and a New Testament in English. There was also a file of old letters—*"relics,"* Mammi had called them—and an assortment of books, including one titled *Voice of the Heart*, by John Newton.

Knowing Mammi wouldn't mind if she poked around a bit, Joanna made her way to the crevice in the wall. There, just as she remembered, was the small hideaway, now filled with still more books. Joanna looked more closely and noticed that some were novels—*"made-up stories,"* as Preacher Yoder had described them. Then, opening one of the devotional books, Joanna saw two letters tucked inside, both on parchment. The words *Aunt Joanna* were beautifully written on the strip of paper wrapped around them.

"Is this my namesake?" Joanna whispered, noting the June 1932 date on the letter. Surely this confirmed it was written by the aunt who'd made the double wedding ring quilt. Joanna sighed. *I'll ask Mammi if I can read these sometime.*

She slipped the letters back into the book and closed the small door. The discovery of letters from the other Joanna was so interesting, especially right on the heels of having received the quilt. Why *had* Mamma chosen to name her after this woman whose letters were so special that Mammi Kurtz had saved them all these years?

Sitting on her grandparents' old bed, Joanna contemplated her heritage—so many devout folk, like her two sets of grandparents. Wise folk . . . like Ella Mae Zook.

She leaned back on the bed and looked up at the ceiling. She thought again of the Wise Woman's surprising advice. "She was right," Joanna whispered, letting her tears flow freely now that she was alone.

Chapter 28

In many ways, Joanna was thankful she hadn't told Cora Jane or Mamma about Eben Troyer's recent visit. She was an emotional mess, and while she did her best to conceal her heartache, she was also aware of her parents' concern. So she tried to hide how she felt during the day, grateful for the time she had to herself while Mamma went to the hospital to visit Mammi Kurtz, who had indeed shattered her hip and was facing a lengthy recovery.

Adding to Joanna's pain was the rift between her and her sister. Never before had Joanna known such discord in their home. She and Cora Jane actively avoided each other. Mamm had stepped in to keep the flame from blazing out of control, ordering housework so that the two sisters were never thrown together—at least, not alone. The girls' work outdoors was even more conducive to the standoff, as they rarely crossed paths. If one was weeding and hoeing the vegetable garden, the other carried feed or water to the barn animals. Joanna wondered if things could ever be made right between them.

After two solid months of melancholy, Joanna was exhausted from crying each night, weary of her grief. She decided to make the effort to go on a van trip with other youth in the church district in mid-June—a tour of the Ephrata Cloister National Historic Landmark. The tour would help her get her mind off herself. Besides, it was time to dismiss Eben Troyer and get on with living.

On the way back from Ephrata, Freckles Jake asked to sit beside her, and amidst inquisitive looks from the other girls, Joanna agreed. *They think he's trouble*. But Joanna wasn't the sort of young woman who would put up with anything inappropriate from a fellow, so she ignored the initial stares. As for her opinion, thus far the only real drawback was his age. Jake was turning twenty-four in the fall, a full year younger than Joanna.

Pretty soon, Jake was telling her one story after another, weaving together people and places until everything else around them seemed to fade. She was thoroughly entertained and amused, though she hadn't the least idea if the stories were true or not. Really, it didn't matter—she'd so desperately needed to laugh again!

Jake appeared delighted by her response and asked if she'd go riding with him. Joanna agreed but didn't commit to when that might be—still, she found herself actually looking forward to some more time with this fellow storyteller.

As for her own stories, Joanna had managed by sheer willpower to refrain from writing since Preacher Yoder's visit, but her resolve was waning—she was that eager to express herself once more. And late that night, after returning from the trip to Ephrata, she could hold off no longer. Jake's remarkable tales had stirred up her creativity all over again.

She pressed a doorstop beneath her closed door and pulled out the writing notebook from the binder in the hope chest. What if she could replace the first pages of her most recent story by rewriting the opening? And as she recast it, she realized her turns of phrase were actually better than those in the former attempt. *How strange is that?* Joanna mused, happily writing for more than an hour, the words pouring onto the page. As before, she was transported to another place, losing all sense of time . . . and loving every minute.

Never once did she consider the need to be repentant for this breach, nor did she feel guilty. If she could just finish this one last love story, she would cease her writing for good.

The very next night, and the next, Joanna engaged in the same activity, writing frantically in the secret haven of her room until she was helplessly drawn back into her old pattern of daily creating a make-believe world on paper. But she'd wised up considerably, vigilant now to hide her notebook, not wanting anyone to read the sad pages of her fictitious love story and guess that her own romance had also come to a painful end.

On a sultry Saturday near the close of June, Joanna longed for a breeze as she dressed for her first real date with Jake. Oh, to have a nice big overhead fan, like the one Ephraim Yoder had recently installed at the General Store! Not electric, of course, but run by an air compressor.

She eyed two recent notes on her dresser, both from Jake. He'd sent them in the last week, mostly humorous anecdotes intended, she was sure, to make her smile. She guessed he'd picked up on her appreciation for his "tellin's"—the snippets of stories he so obviously delighted in sharing.

Before checking her hair one last time, she lightly dabbed a rose scent behind each ear, then walked primly downstairs. Cora Jane had already left to meet her beau, or so Joanna assumed, and Mamma sat on the back porch with Dat, both eating tapioca pudding as Joanna made her way outside. She waved shyly as she left, catching Mamma's eye. "I won't be late," she said softly, and Dat nodded, fidgeting.

They must suspect I'm going out with a new fellow, she thought. *If so, they must be relieved.* She'd moped around the house long enough. *That's all behind me now.* She wished she hadn't put all her eggs in one basket with Eben. But there had never been anyone else for her . . . till now.

Presently, she walked barefoot down the lane, the evening still warm enough that no wrap was needed for later. An owl hooted somewhere high in the dusky cottonwood, and Joanna felt his keen gaze on her.

Will Jake entertain me with his stories again? she wondered as flecks of the past crossed her mind. *Will he help me forget Eben?*

Eben felt like he was swimming underwater as he trotted his driving horse on the way to pick up Ada Kemp. It was his first social outing since he'd returned from Lancaster County. At the thought, he heaved a sigh. "Wonder what Joanna's doing tonight," he said aloud, realizing he'd have to quit thinking about his former sweetheart. Wouldn't be fair to any other girl he started seeing.

The evening sky was a hazy blue, and the sound of crickets already filled the air. He forced himself to think about nineteen-year-old Ada Kemp, his date tonight. *Ain't the smartest thing I've ever done*, he decided, knowing the pickle he'd gotten himself in by smiling at Ada last week at Sunday Singing. Ada's older brother had taken notice and twisted Eben's arm into asking her out. *Well, not actually twisted*, Eben thought.

He urged the horse onward as he grew closer to Ada's green-shuttered farmhouse. If she even remembered to show up at the preappointed spot, he hardly knew what to say to her.

Maybe she'll forget. . . .

He was out of practice; it had been some time since he'd gone through the motions of a typical courtship. Eben frowned, still disgusted with himself for unintentionally leading Joanna on for so long. For that he was the most sorry of all.

"If I could just go back and do everything differently," he muttered, yet he realized the end result would be the same. The exact same wretched outcome. He shook his head at the depressing thought, and just then spotted Ada walking this way, wearing a bright lavender dress—a salve for sore eyes.

She smiled demurely but didn't wave . . . and he couldn't help himself: He missed Joanna all the more.

Joanna hadn't realized how strong Jake Lantz was until he offered his hand to help her into his open buggy. She felt featherlight as he pulled her up, and she was soon at ease as he remarked on the especially warm temperatures and the fact that there were no storms brewing tonight in any direction. "It'll make for a nice buggy ride." The way he said it, so casual like, made her feel even more relaxed.

She was equally surprised to see the black leather bucket seats and plush carpet he'd installed. Trying not to smile too broadly, she thought, *You just never know what a day will bring!*

"Did ya have a nice big supper?" Jake asked, looking mighty fit in his black broadfall trousers, white shirt, and black vest. He hadn't worn his straw hat this time, his clean hair blowing gently in the slight breeze.

Was he asking if she wanted a snack? Joanna wanted to be polite, not sound like a pig. "I had plenty to eat, jah."

"That so?" He gave her a mischievous grin. "I've noticed you always make room for ice cream."

"Really, now?"

"Well, you've eaten your fair share at the youth gatherings."

She chuckled but felt a little embarrassed, realizing he had been watching her for quite some time.

They talked about other things. Then Jake brought up

her grandmother's fall and the day he'd met Eben. "Do you mind if I ask if you're still in touch with him?"

He certainly had every right to know if she was free to date. And for some reason she felt comfortable enough to say that Eben was gone from her life. "We wrote back and forth for a long time, though," Joanna added.

Jake looked at her again, concern in his eyes. "You sound upset."

"I sure am!"

He smiled quickly. "That's all right—I don't mind bein' your punching bag . . . if that's what ya need."

She shook her head, looking away. "Sorry. It ain't like that. Shouldn't've said anything."

"'Tis all right. You're feelin' better already, jah?"

Goodness, he'd seen right through her. "Guess I do."

The horse pulled them faster, nearly at a gallop, and Joanna glimpsed flashes of black soil between the rows of soybeans on either side of the road. No question, Jake was showing off. And just how had he known she loved a good joyride? *What else does he know about me, for pity's sake?*

Chapter 29

Joanna thoroughly enjoyed a double-scoop peach ice cream cone at Lapp Valley Farm, where she and Jake used the convenient drive-through. Jake was determined to treat her, which was quite nice, even though she suspected he was hungry for some dessert himself.

Over the course of the next few hours, they managed to talk about everything from English tourists they'd met to what it would be like to live in a house with air-conditioning on such a humid night. She was especially relieved that Jake hadn't spoiled things by reaching for her hand or slipping his arm around her. Had the Wise Woman counseled him on the proper way to date, just maybe?

And Jake did not bring up Eben again during the zippy ride past Amish farmland. For that, Joanna was grateful. She was even more surprised later, when Jake pulled over on the side of the road, near Weaver's Creek—the very spot she'd wanted to bring her former beau.

"What're we doin' here?" she asked.

"You'll see." He offered to help her down. "Follow me."

They walked single file through the high grass, toward the wide, wooded creek bed. He scrambled to the top of the largest boulder and sat there like a tall bird. He smiled, watching her from his perch. "Oh, here, do ya need some help?"

"I'm fine," she said, laughing. And she was. She could easily climb up there to join him.

When she'd sat down in the small spot left for her, she soon saw why he'd brought her here.

"Shh, just watch," he whispered.

As the light dimmed, the sun melted the sky into pinks and gold, the rosy hue filling the shadows and the stream itself. Colors she'd never seen before were reflected in the water. Adding to that near-magical glow were the sparkles of hundreds of lightning bugs. *Fireflies*, Eben had called them in a letter. But Joanna had never seen them like this with Eben. No, her evening with Jake was far different than a date with a letter . . . or a phone booth! And Joanna rather liked it.

Eben initially thought Ada might be rather shy, but as the evening progressed, he discovered he'd been quite wrong. She seemed to feel the need to fill even the smallest gaps of silence. She also had a strange habit of wringing her hands, just like his tetchy *Grossmammi* on his mother's side. Both habits made him wish he'd stayed home.

Ada was saying something now about her best friend

planting an extra big crop of celery seedlings, starting tomorrow. "Ya know what that means, ain't?" Her voice rose to a crescendo.

He knew, all right.

She jabbered on about this unnamed friend of hers, even though Eben knew perfectly well it was Dottie Miller, having seen Ada come into Singings and other get-togethers with her sisters and this good friend. *So Dottie's getting hitched,* he thought, guessing one young woman after another would marry during this November. And if Eben didn't get on the stick and get serious about finding a bride, he'd end up having to look at the new crop of sixteen-year-olds next thing.

He must've chuckled at the thought, because Ada looked over at him. Then, oh, the laugh she gave! It was the most harsh-sounding, peculiar laugh he'd ever heard before, sharp as shattered glass. Why hadn't he noticed this prior to asking her out? Eben held tightly to the reins and reminded himself that he'd been the one who'd asked her to go riding tonight.

By the time they arrived at his brother-in-law's place to meet another couple for a tournament of Ping-Pong, Eben was annoyed, though he knew he must be a gentleman and make the evening pleasant for her. He was not one to throw in the towel quickly.

So they played doubles in the cool basement—girls against the guys, and later couples against each other. The beautiful girl opposite Ada reminded him of Joanna in looks and demeanor, and he had to be careful not to stare, lest her boyfriend think he was coveting.

As the Ping-Pong wound down, Eben's sister-in-law made popcorn and surprised them with some homemade strawberry ice cream for the occasion. The time of refreshment and visiting was dominated by Ada, yet in spite of the chatty girl by his side, Eben felt downright lonely. Was this how he'd always feel without Joanna in his life?

There was talk of another tournament—some other evening—and Ada leaped up a little in what Eben assumed was excitement at the idea. The other couple readily agreed, but Eben was reluctant. He saw the disappointment in Ada's dark brown eyes but had to be true to himself. He was not going anywhere again with Ada Kemp. It was wrong to let her think he was interested in anything more than friendship.

Minutes after Eben had seen her home, he removed his black vest and rolled up his white shirt sleeves, nearly as tired as if he'd filled silo all day. The leisurely ride home was just what he needed . . . and the blessed silence. "What a mistake," he whispered, vowing not to get himself into such a pickle again.

Cora Jane surprised Joanna by waiting up for her that night, perched on the edge of Joanna's own bed. "Heard you might've gone out with Freckles Jake," Cora Jane said, eyes wide. "Did ya?"

"I'm awful tired, if ya don't mind."

"You sure don't look it."

Joanna went to the window, her back to her sister. "Well,

I *am.*" Did her sister suddenly think that all was well between them because Eben was no longer a part of Joanna's life?

"Did he kiss ya?"

Joanna whirled around. "You know better than that!" She caught her breath. "Takes two for that."

Cora Jane began to laugh, then clapped her hand over her mouth, stifling her own giggles. "You should see your face, sister. I mean, honestly!"

"This isn't funny."

"Ach, your face is."

"I'd like to get ready for bed now, Cora Jane." Joanna didn't even think to ask if she'd had a good time with Gid. It was the last thing on her mind with her sister acting so foolish.

But Cora Jane continued to sit there, calming down some and looking more serious.

Joanna pointed toward the door. "I mean it," she said. "I'd like some privacy."

"What . . . so you can dream 'bout Jake Lantz?"

Joanna shook her head in disgust. "When will you ever grow up?"

"Are you just too *old* to have fun . . . is that it?" Cora Jane rose and stood at the door, leaning her head against the doorjamb. "How could you possibly go out with the likes of that boy?"

"He's a gentleman, that's how."

"Well, ain't what our cousins are sayin'. . . . Goodness, all the girls are avoiding him."

"People can change."

"But not Jake," said Cora Jane.

"How would you know?"

"I'm smart enough to listen to *gut* advice," Cora Jane shot back.

Joanna stood her ground. "I'm tellin' you he's nothin' at all like the rumors."

The two of them glared at each other, but the resentment Joanna felt wasn't because of Jake. "I think you owe me an apology, sister." She'd endured Cora Jane's silence and near gloomy outlook for far too long . . . holding in her hurt the best she could. "You know precisely what I'm talking about."

"Why, because I called the preacher's attention to your disobedience?"

"Wasn't necessary and you know it."

"No?" Cora Jane shrugged. "Since when are you the rule maker?"

It was all Joanna could do not to retaliate and say, *Since when are you?* But she bit her lip and kept silent. She turned away. The encounter with Cora Jane was beginning to cloud her special time away. Not wanting to ask her sister to leave the room again, Joanna went to sit in the chair near the window, and when she turned around, wondering how she was going to keep her peace, Cora Jane was gone.

Joanna wished for a lock on her door as she wrote long into the night, remembering the beauty surrounding her at Weaver's Creek. Yet the evening's charms mingled with sadness at her loss of Eben, and she wrote with all the more fervor—only *this* story must have a happy ending.

She felt carried away to her lovely fictional world, like a character snatched away from another completely different place, where things of the heart were shared and treasured for always. Where there was no speck of pain or sadness over lost love. Just as always before, Joanna reveled in her precious creation.

Sometime later, after she'd put away her notebook, she dressed for bed, slipping into the lightweight blue gown she'd sewn a few weeks ago. Then she pulled out a box of greeting cards and found one to send to Mammi Kurtz, who was still in a rehab hospital in Lancaster. Each week, Joanna enjoyed sending a card with her own special made-up poem, hoping it might bring her grandmother some cheer. Joanna's mother had commented on the cards, which she'd seen when she'd gone to visit, saying how pleased Mammi was to receive them.

While writing this poem, Joanna wondered if anyone else amongst the People might see her poetry. If so, would they report her to the ministerial brethren the way Cora Jane had? She hoped it wasn't against the church ordinance to write little rhyming encouragements, too!

When she was finished, she pulled out the wooden letter box in the hope chest and contemplated what to do with Eben's many letters and cards. But the more she considered it, the more she knew she couldn't part with any of it just yet. Maybe someday.

Something else weighed on her. Pleasant as he was, she didn't know if she ought to go out with Jake again, except that all the other fellows who were unspoken for were even younger than he was. She'd so wanted to be married this wedding season. *But not to just anyone . . .*

Joanna turned out the gas lantern and slipped into bed, sighing. As her eyes slowly grew accustomed to the dark, it struck her that she might simply enjoy occasional dates with Jake Lantz, if he was willing. What could it hurt? But she should let him know next time they saw each other that she was only interested in a casual friendship until she was completely over Eben Troyer.

How will Jake feel about that? she wondered. *Is that fair to him?*

Chapter 30

The following Wednesday morning, Joanna worked with Cora Jane and Mamma—and Ella Mae's daughter-in-law, Mattie Beiler—to transplant celery seedlings from the nearby Amish greenhouse. Afterward, Joanna stopped at the end of the lane to mail a get-well card to Mammi Kurtz. Then, setting off on foot so she wouldn't tie up the family carriage, she went to visit Cousin Malinda.

A quarter mile along, here came Jake Lantz in his pony cart, waving to beat the band. He slowed and stopped in the middle of the road. "Hullo," she said. It was clear by his smile he was happy to see her.

"We meet again," he said.

Recalling what she'd wanted to tell him, she suddenly felt bashful. "Nice day, jah?"

"Ideal for helping the deacon. He's still under the weather, ya know."

She knew all too well. He'd been ill since April.

"Thought I'd take up some of the slack over there with barn chores and whatnot."

Nodding, she smiled. "*Gut* of you."

He glanced up the road like he had something on his mind. "I sure had a great time last Saturday. I'd like to take you out again, if that's all right."

Here was her moment to speak up, but by the happiness in his eyes, he surely wouldn't want to hear anything but a positive response. "When were ya thinkin'?" She amazed herself.

"How 'bout we go riding after the Singing this coming Sunday night?"

She'd guessed that's what he might suggest. "Preaching's at Andy and Malinda's, ya know."

"Jah, heard Andy's sweepin' out the upper level of his barn come Saturday, so I'll go over there and lend a hand."

"I was just headin' there now . . . to help Malinda wash down the walls and whatnot," she added.

"Nearly forgot you're kin to them," Jake said as he reined in the anxious pony. "So will ya go with me, then . . . Sunday night?"

Another carriage was coming this way, so she had to make up her mind. Joanna smiled right quick. "Jah, I'll go."

His face burst into a grin and off he went. And, if Joanna wasn't mistaken, she heard him say, "Glory be."

"What *am* I doin'?" she whispered, moving back to the side of the road to let the coming horse and carriage pass.

Joanna enjoyed the walk to Cousin Malinda's less for having bumped into Jake, and she stewed now about not having the courage to say what she should. *This Sunday I will, for certain*, she promised herself as she took in the stands of hardwood trees near the white horse fences of Andy King's land and the open pasture beyond. Indeed, it was a splendid day.

Malinda was outside weeding her marigolds and asters, a patch of yellows and purples, when Joanna came up the driveway. "I've come to give you a hand," Joanna called.

Malinda was red cheeked in the blazing sun. She wiped her damp brow with the back of her palm, her plain blue scarf having slipped back. "Ach, so *gut* to see ya. Sure, you can help."

They worked together to finish up the bed so that it was free of even a single weed for the coming Lord's Day. Of course, knowing Malinda, by Saturday she would go back and do the same thing where needed.

Once inside, they cleaned the house from the top of each room down, dusting, sweeping, washing, and making everything tidy and spotless. Joanna felt a hushed reverence about their work, knowing that this farmhouse would become a temporary place of worship this Sunday.

After the noon meal, Malinda's twin sisters, Anna and Becky, joined them in beating rugs and sweeping every inch of the front and back porches before hosing them down. They finished off by cleaning the windows and screens, as well.

Later, once Joanna and Malinda were alone again, they enjoyed a tall glass of meadow tea, which hit the spot, as Mamma liked to say. Malinda dropped into the rocking chair on the shady back porch with a sigh. "Thanks to you and my sisters, I'm a little ahead of things," she said, fanning herself.

"Glad we could pitch in."

Malinda asked about her family and Cora Jane, and Joanna told her about planting the celery.

"Oh, Joanna . . . I hope Cora Jane's getting married this fall isn't hard on you," said Malinda.

"Bein' she's younger than me by a mile?"

There was a sweetness in Malinda's concerned expression. "Maybe I shouldn't have said anything."

"No . . . no, that's all right." *We're more than cousins . . . we're friends.*

They sipped their iced tea, watching the breeze move through the tops of trees and the birds flitting about.

Then Malinda said softly, "I'm afraid I've got a rather prickly topic to bring up. I heard something the other week that's hard to believe."

Joanna froze and stared at her glass, wondering what on earth.

"Did Preacher Yoder come and talk to you?"

"Jah, he dropped by a couple months ago . . . about my stories."

Malinda studied her. "Is everything all right?"

"For now, jah."

"I've been concerned awhile but wasn't sure if it was true."

"Oh, true enough." Joanna told on herself. Somehow it was different talking about difficult things with Malinda. *A far cry from talking to Cora Jane.*

"You must have a real gift for writing."

Stunned, she looked at Malinda. "What?"

"Evidently the deacon's wife read part of your story and was quite taken by your talent."

"She did—she *is?*"

Malinda nodded and took a sip from her glass.

"How'd ya hear this?"

"My mother mentioned it last weekend, when she was over to help me put up beans."

"Good grief, I wonder who else knows?" Joanna felt it strange to hear someone talk about her private writing like this.

"Word spreads, ya know?" Malinda encouraged her.

Jah, ain't that the truth.

Joanna watched Malinda closely, wishing she hadn't said anything just now. So, was everyone talking about this? Had it gotten to the grapevine? She cringed at the thought.

Malinda continued along the same lines. "Seems kind of peculiar that on one hand, the preacher wants you to put a stop to your creativity, and on the other, the deacon's wife is praising your work."

"Odd, indeed." And that, Joanna thought, was all she ought to say.

Chapter 31

Joanna could hardly wait to see her grandmother that Friday when she learned Mammi Kurtz had at last been released from rehab. Fannie and the rest of the family had requested permission for the rehabilitation hospital to dismiss her to their aid. With the help of a home care nurse several times a week, they planned to look after Mammi together.

Hurrying through her morning chores, Joanna got a ride to Mammi Kurtz's with her father, who was on his way to see the smithy. "Mammi must be delighted to be back home again," she said, making small talk.

He nodded so slightly she almost missed it.

"Do ya happen to know anything 'bout my namesake?" she asked, wondering if she might be able to get him talking. "The aunt I was named after?"

"You might ask your grandmother Kurtz. She'd know best. I don't remember her so well."

"I hope to but don't want to tire Mammi out, ya know."

He neither nodded nor commented.

After that, she remained quiet till they pulled over onto the side of the road, at the turnoff to the driveway. "Denki, Dat . . . I'll walk home later."

His eyes registered her words, and he gave another nod. "See ya then."

From the street, the white clapboard house looked tall and narrow. Large oak trees flanked the east side of the lawn. A small shed and big barn out back, as well as the curing house over near a grove of trees, rounded out the property. The lawn had been recently cut; whoever had used the push mower last needed to sharpen the blade before the next mowing.

Three small children came running out the front door to meet Joanna—her married sister Salina's three—Stephen, Sylvia, and Susan—all adorable towheads. "*Aendi* Joanna!" they called, flinging their arms around her long skirt.

"Come see the sweets Mamma made. Hurry!" said almost six-year-old Stephen in *Deitsch*.

"Could it be sugar cookies, maybe?" Joanna played along.

"Nee . . . come see," said Sylvia, her eyes dancing.

"What can it be?" Joanna scampered after them, hurrying around the side of the house to go in the back way. "Sticky buns, maybe?"

"Whoopie pies—chocolate ones!" tiny Susan exclaimed as all of them burst into the kitchen.

Salina gently shushed them as they entered, then greeted Joanna.

"Hullo, sister," Joanna said, the little girls still hanging on her.

"A warm welcome, jah?" Salina fanned herself with a white hankie.

"How's Mammi Kurtz?" Joanna asked once the children were settled at the table, swinging their bare legs beneath the blue-and-white-checkered oilcloth.

Salina set a large whoopie pie on a napkin in front of each of them. Then she motioned for Joanna to follow her to the bedroom just around the corner. There sat her grandmother in a straight-backed cane chair, head bowed and sound asleep. "She's all tuckered out, which is understandable," whispered Salina, leaning near.

"Can she walk without help?"

"She uses a walker okay, but she shouldn't be alone . . . that's why I'm here today." Salina smiled and touched Joanna's arm. "Would ya mind checkin' on Dawdi for me?"

"Front room?"

"Jah, there by the screen door, to get the best breeze. He's not too keen on sittin' on the back porch when the children are here."

"No doubt the commotion wears on him." Joanna could understand that—Salina's busy three were definitely a handful. She went to the largest room and found her grandfather sitting there, wide-awake. "You all right, Dawdi?" she asked, going over to him.

He said nothing but blinked his eyes at her, and a small smile inched past his lips.

"Okay, then."

Going back to the bedroom, she stood in the doorway. "Dawdi looks to be just fine."

"*Gut*," Salina replied. "Never hurts to check, ya know . . . at their age." She looked lovingly down at Mammi. "Pains me to see them suffer like this." She sighed.

Joanna agreed. "So the family's takin' turns with Mammi?"

Salina nodded and moved toward the door to join Joanna. "We have it all arranged. I'll show you the chart."

Joanna hoped she might be called upon to help, too.

"Here 'tis." Salina found the paper on the kitchen counter, next to the whoopie pies. "Help yourself," she said as Joanna eyed the goodies.

"Denki, think I will." Joanna took a bite and, oh, it was heavenly . . . melted in her mouth.

"Before I forget, Mammi mentioned how much your cards—especially your poems—meant to her in the hospital. In case she forgets to tell ya, I thought you should know."

"That's why I wrote them," Joanna replied. "To bring some cheer."

"Well, they surely did that," Salina said. "She even read two of them to me. Saved each and every one."

Joanna was pleased but didn't want to let on. All this talk about her writing here lately had her unnerved.

The children were giggling and becoming rambunctious now.

"Too much sugar," Salina was quick to say.

As much as their silliness seemed to annoy Salina, it had the opposite effect on Joanna. Watching them act up, poking one another and bursting into laughter, made her yearn even more for children of her own one day. "How 'bout I get them washed up and take them out to see the new calves? Leave ya be with Mammi for a while?"

Salina looked relieved. "You're a lifesaver, Joanna."

"Not to worry." She set to work wiping off each little set of hands before permitting them to leave the table.

Salina picked up a basket of mending, then headed back to Mammi Kurtz.

They had been observing the new calves for a good twenty minutes or so when Stephen said, "I'm awful hungry, Aendi Joanna."

"Didn't ya just have a snack?" She smiled down at him, ruffling his flaxen hair.

"Can't remember," he said, straight-faced.

"He's *always* hungry," Sylvia piped up from where she was crouched near the smallest calf.

Spoken like a little sister! Joanna got a kick out of the interaction between those two. "Is he, now?" she asked.

"Oh, jah." Sylvia dramatically nodded her head up and down.

"I'm hungry, too," little Susan said, blinking her blue eyes at Joanna.

"I know!" Stephen announced. "Let's get some milk from the cooler."

Joanna agreed, thinking that would stall the children from returning to the house just yet. Salina had looked tired, like she might enjoy a bit more time alone with their grandparents. Joanna, too, was eager for a visit with her grandmother, but that could wait if necessary.

While they were in the milk house, Stephen gulped down a full glass of the fresh raw milk. Then, looking at her with a white moustache, he asked, "Will you tell us a story, Aendi?"

She began to protest. "I'm not a storyteller like Rebecca Lapp or . . ." She stopped before saying Jake Lantz's name.

"*I* heard ya were." Stephen was frowning.

"Well, now, who's sayin' that?"

"The deacon's wife," Stephen said, standing on tiptoes now as he held his empty glass up for more milk. "Heard her tell Grandmammi Mast so."

Joanna found this ever so curious. *So much for that!*

"So will ya tell us a story?" he pleaded.

She guessed it would be all right, especially if she told a Bible story. What could that hurt?

Eben had already spent too much time at the harness shop, overhearing his neighbor Micah Hershberger talk enthusiastically about a group of older folk from their community who were thinking of buying up a row of condos in Virginia Beach.

Where I met Joanna, thought Eben.

"When's this?" he asked, though he needed to get back to the farm. Still, Eben was mighty curious.

"Oh, in the next month or so," Levi, the harness shopkeeper, replied.

"'Least before wedding season, anyways," another neighbor, Elias Schrock, remarked.

At this, Micah shook his head. "Seems there must be quite a few condos available right now . . . same thing's goin' on in Florida."

"The housing market's in a heap of hurt," Eben offered.

"Might be the ideal time to snatch up some property, then," Micah said with a tug on his peppery beard.

Levi nodded. "Wouldn't wait too long to seal the deal, either. Not if you're serious."

"Well, these folks certainly are," Micah said.

Eben wondered just who he was talking about. He hadn't heard anyone mention this. "Well, my Daed's goin' to think I'm playin' hooky," he said, then moseyed toward the door.

"Say, I heard Leroy got married," said Levi, following him.

"That he did."

"So the world got him, then?"

Eben nodded. "Sorry to say."

"Well, now, I'll bet you are." Levi gave him a sympathetic smile. "Word has it you had someone mighty special over in Lancaster County."

Eben wouldn't deny it.

"So is she comin' out here sooner or later . . . or is that all over now?" Levi was known to pry, and he was doing a mighty fine job of it.

It wouldn't do any good to explain the problem. Besides, it wasn't Levi's place to ask. Eben shrugged off the question. "Best be headin' on home."

"Tell your Daed hullo for me, ya hear?" Levi called, turning to greet the man who'd just entered the shop.

"I'll do that." Eben closed the door behind him and made his way to the horse and carriage parked behind the shop. He looked to the east, wondering what Joanna was up to this hot summer day. Were they having a Preaching Sunday this weekend? Was she going to Singings yet again?

Eben untied his horse, then hopped into the enclosed black buggy and backed out of the spot. All the way home, he smelled the fragrance of honeysuckle and wondered if he'd been right about Jake Lantz's seeming admiration for Joanna. And if so, had Jake made a move to court her? The questions in his head continued until he saw Ada Kemp and her mother in another buggy, coming this way. Ada leaned forward suddenly when she caught his eye, smiling and waving at him. He was polite and gave a slow wave of his own. After their first and only date, he'd taken two other girls out, and knowing how fast the grapevine was, Ada most likely had heard about it.

Eben wasn't interested in leaving a long line of spurned women. But the truth was, none of them compared with Joanna . . . not a one. Maybe he just needed to continue his search. For sure and for certain, he needed someone to fill up Joanna's place in his heart.

I have no other choice.

Chapter 32

Joanna was very sure Salina's threesome had grown taller just in the space of two days. Mamma often said children grew faster in the summer months—"*like weeds*"—and looking at her nieces and nephew, Joanna couldn't help but agree.

Strolling about the backyard between the time Preaching service ended and the shared meal began, Joanna enjoyed the shade from several tall trees. She spied Salina and a couple other young mothers with their youngsters and went over to talk to them. Joanna's nephew Stephen was on the verge of being grouped with other boys his age—first graders come this fall. For now, though, he still played with his little sisters and young cousins, chasing them around the tree trunks and teasing the girls, some of whom were playing with their little white handkerchief dollies.

Joanna noticed Cora Jane on the other side of the yard with a few teenage girls, including Mattie Beiler's granddaughters

Martha, Julia, and Susie. Martha and Julia looked at Jake Lantz and his younger brother, Jesse, with disdain when the guys walked by with a handful of other courting-age young men. Joanna wondered if Susie and Julia had perhaps been two of the girls who'd complained about Jake's forwardness. Would he behave differently now, were he to go riding with either of them?

Over on the long back porch, Mary Beiler crept alongside her elderly grandfather Abram Stoltzfus, searching for a chair for him. *Bless their hearts*. Joanna watched them tenderly, missing her own grandparents today. Dawdi Joseph hadn't felt well enough to attend, so Mammi Sadie had stayed home with him. And of course her Kurtz grandparents hadn't come, either, and probably wouldn't until Mammi was more sure of herself with her walker. Dawdi Kurtz refused to leave her, even though someone was there caring for her—he'd missed her terribly while she was in the hospital. Joanna wondered what Bishop John thought of that. Did he ever send the preachers out to talk to elderly and infirm members about missing church?

"You're deep in thought, ain't?" Salina leaned to whisper to Joanna.

"Guess I am . . . sorry."

"Couldn't help but notice you and Cora Jane sitting far apart during church today," Salina said, moving closer to Joanna beneath the shade tree to talk more privately. "You girls still at odds?"

"It'll pass."

"Well, I should hope so, after all this time . . . ain't the best example for the other young folk, ya know."

"No, s'pose not."

Salina frowned and made eye contact. "There *is* something bothering you, Joanna. I hear it in your voice."

She didn't want to criticize her younger sister on the Lord's Day, especially. "Best just pray 'bout it, jah?"

"Watch and pray, Scripture says." Salina was smiling too broadly.

"Ach, don't be so *labbich*, sister."

"Ya think I'm silly, do ya?" Salina said, rolling her eyes. "Hard not to see what's goin' on round us, jah?"

Joanna had never thought of her older sister as a *Schnuffel-box*—busybody—but today she certainly did seem to know what was going on with nearly everyone.

The two of them laughed softly, and then Salina really cut loose, which made Joanna laugh even harder. Laughter felt good; she couldn't deny it. And she knew it was wrong to harbor bitterness toward Cora Jane . . . or anyone.

Eben willingly helped his older brothers construct the temporary tables for the common Sunday meal at their father's house, using three wooden church benches for each table. First, they placed the benches side by side, then raised them using a hidden trestle. The very moment each table was put together, the womenfolk began setting down plates and drinking glasses.

When the tables were in place, Eben spotted Daed come inside and remove his straw hat out of reverence. His eyebrows rose when he caught Eben's eye. He came right over and patted him on the back, saying nary a word. It was Daed's way of expressing gratitude. And it was still interesting to Eben that nearly the minute Leroy and his wife left for their own home, Daed's demeanor had returned to normal. Although it *was* clear his parents were pained through to the heart over Leroy's decision to leave the Amish life for good. Daed wore the regret on his face every waking hour.

To think Leroy's offspring will never experience the Plain life . . . never be taught the Old Ways. Eben couldn't begin to imagine that.

"Have ya heard 'bout the birthday doin's for the bishop's wife next month?" Salina asked Joanna.

"Didn't know. Does Mamma?"

"I think so. Everyone's talking 'bout it."

Everyone? Once again, Salina was in the know. "Where and when will it be held?"

"At Bishop John's—on August eighteenth. A Saturday."

"Must not be a surprise party, then."

"Oh, believe me, it was supposed to be." Salina smiled. "But the cat managed to get out of the bag."

Joanna understood. "Must be a special birthday, ain't?" She'd lost track, since birthdays weren't celebrated all too often, particularly not too fancy-like.

"Mary's turnin' twenty-five."

My age, thought Joanna with a shock, watching young

Stephen pull on Sylvia's apron strings. How could she have forgotten?

A light breeze swept over the lawn, rustling leaves above her head, letting dappled light through. A squirrel scampered to the highest branch and daringly pattered out to nearly the end of the limb. Joanna enjoyed watching the little animals and thought suddenly of Eben, who'd once written about caring for a wounded squirrel when he was a boy.

Oh, Eben . . .

Would he forever be just on the edge of her thoughts? He had been such a huge part of her life for too long to expect that she was over him. No, she couldn't fool herself into thinking she was fine, because she was far from it.

"Before I forget, can ya help Mammi Kurtz this Tuesday for a few hours—get the noon meal started and whatnot?" asked Salina, bringing Joanna out of her reverie. "She's already doin' so much better since returning home."

"Sure . . . I'd like that."

"All right, then, I'll let Fannie know. She has to run an errand for the deacon's wife."

Joanna perked up her ears. Fannie Kurtz rarely interacted with Sallie, the deacon's shy wife. "What's Dawdi doin' to keep himself busy?"

"Hovering, mostly, like a worried old hen."

"Aw, so sweet, jah?"

Salina nodded. "Still lovebirds after all these years."

Lovebirds . . . The word whirled in her head. *Will I ever know that kind of love?*

··· ➣ ➣ ···

The noontime siren sounded in the distance, reminding Eben that along with the sun's progress across the sky each day—and the occasional pocket watch—there was more than one way to tell the time on Peaceful Acres Lane this Lord's Day. He'd heard, though, that the siren wasn't always prompt—sometimes it was early, depending on the fellow who was in charge of pulling the lanyard. Eben grinned at the very notion as he stood over near the woodshed with other young men his age, waiting till the first seating of ministerial brethren and older couples had an opportunity to eat the light meal inside.

It was such a beastly hot day, Eben wondered why they hadn't set up the tables on the lawn, like two weeks ago when church was held at his uncle Isaac's place, just a mile up the road.

Eben stood with hands clasped behind him, like several of the more pious young men did, determined not to let hunger pangs get the best of them on the Lord's Day. He listened as Cousin Chester talked about having just landed a job on the west side of Elkhart, doing some welding work. But it wasn't hard to notice the faltering way Chester was describing this sudden change of work. It was almost like he was leaving the area.

Then Eben began to piece things together. Anyone would have to be blind not to have seen Emma Miller's swollen eyes earlier as she waited in line for the service with her mother and younger sisters. Had Chester broken up with his longtime girlfriend? Eben observed his cousin gesturing with his big hands, apparently overcompensating as he told about the "wunnerbaar-*gut* job" he'd landed.

Eben felt downright sorry for him, and for poor Emma, too, knowing something of what they were going through. *If* he was correct about their circumstances.

Emma Miller was an attractive girl and awfully nice, but Chester had gotten to her first, years ago, preventing Eben from pursuing her himself. But now . . .

His head was spinning with what to do. How long should he wait for Emma to get over Chester? Eben had his own reasons for not rushing into something serious. It hadn't been long since he'd hoped to make Joanna his bride.

Even so, he hoped Emma might be at the Singing tonight, although he seriously doubted it. *Girls tend to wait awhile*, he thought and wondered how long before Emma might go out again . . . or was she so upset with Chester that it didn't matter?

Chapter 33

After the Singing in Andy King's big barn, Joanna discreetly slipped out with Jake to his courting carriage. He set her at ease at once by sharing a funny anecdote about what a sound sleeper his brother Jesse was, even during an afternoon nap. He insisted that Jesse could sleep through thunder and lightning, and even a tornado. Jake described the scene, just today, prior to coming to Singing—how he'd shaken Jesse and hollered at him, finally resorting to pulling him across the floor by one leg. At last, Jesse woke up. "What're ya doin' to me, Bruder?" he'd yelled. "Couldn't ya see I was sleepin'?"

Laughing as she pictured the scene, Joanna momentarily forgot her plan to come clean about wanting no more than a friendship with Jake.

They talked in a relaxed manner as they rode behind several other carriages, the sounds of chatter and laughter filling up the night. He asked her what sorts of things she liked to read, and whether she liked to cook or bake better. So many questions . . . he sure seemed eager to get to know her.

But Jake wasn't Eben, and Joanna knew it wasn't right to keep accepting dates with him. So, breathing a silent prayer for wisdom, she pressed forward. "I've enjoyed spendin' time with you, Jake," she said so softly she scarcely heard herself.

He looked at her with a smile. "Same here."

"And I like you—"

"I like you, too, Joanna," he broke in.

She felt so bad for him . . . hated saying what must be said. "But I'd prefer to just be friends, if ya don't mind."

"Well, we're already that, jah?"

She nodded. "But how would ya feel if we were to stay only friends for a while? Till I have enough time to—"

"To forget about Eben?" He turned away and looked at the road now; the horse's head bobbed up and down.

"I'm sorry, Jake . . . I really am."

"No need," he said, sounding more upbeat. "Why don't we see where this leads?"

She pondered that. "Maybe in time, jah. I don't want to be thinking 'bout him when I'm with you."

"Well, then?" He chuckled, breaking the tension.

She paused. "I hope you understand, Jake."

"I certainly do," he replied. "But I'd like to keep seein' you, Joanna . . . as a friend, of course." He smiled over at her. "All right?"

As long as he understands, what can it hurt?

Much later, when they were heading back toward Hickory

Lane, Jake mentioned how much he appreciated her honesty. "I truly do," he said.

Then, turning into her lane, Jake said, "I can see why Eben was so taken with you, Joanna."

She blushed and was glad he couldn't really see her face in the darkness.

He leaped out of the carriage and raced around to help her down on the left side. "Sweet dreams," he said as he walked her around toward the back door. Then, turning, he told her good-night and made his way back to the waiting horse and open buggy.

Joanna realized she felt relieved to have a good friend in Jake, and that he understood. *I did the right thing by telling him*. She went to sit on one of the rockers on the back porch and watched ten thousand stars light up the summer sky. It made her think again of Eben and wonder if he, too, was stargazing this warm, muggy night.

Mammi Kurtz's face shone with joy as Joanna walked into the kitchen the following Tuesday morning. "I'm Fannie's substitute today," Joanna said, going over to greet her grandmother with a smile. "Did Salina tell ya?"

"No, but Fannie did, before she left." Mammi sat in a comfortable chair near the wide-open window, drinking root beer. She held up her glass. "Would ya care for some?"

Joanna thanked her and went to get a glass from the cupboard. She reached for the pitcher from the counter and poured a half glass, then returned to pull out Dawdi's chair from the table and turned it to face Mammi. "How're ya feelin' today?"

"So much better. Fannie insists I walk back and forth the whole length of the driveway now." Mammi told of the home-care nurse's visits, as well. "I do believe I'm getting back to normal. Slow but sure."

"And Dawdi—how is he?"

A beautiful smile appeared. "Since I've been home, he's doin' all right." Mammi mentioned he was in their room resting, having his morning nap. "A bit clingy, though, I have to say."

Joanna was pleased they were alone—the perfect chance to mention the quilt from Cousin Malinda. And after they'd talked about Mammi's hospital experience and all the kindly Englischers she'd met there, Joanna asked about the tale behind the quilt made by her great-great-aunt. "I'm really curious, Mammi. Why'd you want *me* to have it?"

Mammi nodded and looked more serious now. "Well, because your namesake—I'll call her Aunt Joanna to make things simpler—made that double wedding ring quilt in the midst of great disappointment . . . out of sheer faith."

"What do ya mean?" Joanna was determined to persuade Mammi to at last tell her everything she knew.

"She was nearing her fortieth birthday and had never married," Mammi explained. "And although it was her heart's desire, your aunt had been labeled a Maidel by then."

Joanna listened intently, her heart breaking for a relative she'd never known.

"Aunt Joanna wrote all about 'the ache' in her heart, as she described her disillusionment at being passed over during her courting-age years."

Joanna was intrigued—it sounded like the seeds for a good story. "Where'd she write this?"

"In two letters to her younger sister."

"Did she also keep a diary?"

"Oh, I'm sure. Most folk did in that day."

Joanna admitted that she'd looked in the special cubby in the wall upstairs, in their former bedroom. "I saw a devotional book with two letters in it. Were they hers?"

"Snoopin', were ya?" Mammi teased.

"Well, I didn't read them."

"That's all right. I've nothin' to hide, dear girl. Least of all from you." Mammi readjusted herself in her chair. "I'm surprised I never thought to have ya read them."

"Oh, could I?"

"Sure, go on up and get them. But before ya do, I'd like you to know why you were named after this particular relative."

Ever so delighted, Joanna said, "I understand the name Joanna was rather unusual in her time. Cousin Malinda said as much."

"Oh my, was it ever. But it certainly fit her—she was a pretty unique soul," Mammi said. "And such faith was involved in makin' a wedding quilt for herself. Unheard of in those days."

"Because everyone had given up on her marrying?"

Mammi's eyes glistened. "That's right."

Joanna felt even more drawn to this woman who'd left such a precious spiritual inheritance. *For me*. "So it must've been hearing about Aunt Joanna's courage that caught Mamma's attention, and the reason she decided to name me after her."

"Jah—ain't it the dearest thing?"

"And kind of peculiar, too, if ya think 'bout it," Joanna said softly.

"Why's that, honey-girl?"

Joanna took a deep breath. "Well, because my own beau and I parted ways."

"Ach, I'm so sorry. Shouldn't have said anything."

"No, no, it's all right. Hadn't you heard this, Mammi?"

"Jah, I believe I did." Mammi sighed. "But it was some time ago now."

"Well, to be honest, it seems like just yesterday to me. I'm still struggling with it."

Mammi frowned amiably. "This young man . . . you must've loved him very much."

Joanna nodded thoughtfully as she remembered all the letters, the good times she and Eben had spent together, however short. "I know he loved me, too." Joanna opened up even more and explained that Eben had been hoping to come here to live and work, to become established in the community while courting her. "But all of that fell through when his youngest brother married an Englischer and refused the partnership with his father."

"No wonder you're sad. Sounds to me like the two of you had your future all planned out."

"We did." Joanna was relieved to share with her grandmother, who seemed to understand. *At last someone cares.* Mammi Kurtz was quite sympathetic about Eben, unlike Ella Mae Zook had been.

"Have you ever considered goin' out there to be with *him?*" Mammi asked, surprising her.

"I really don't see how." *Not with Preacher Yoder's warning to me.*

"If he still loves you, I mean," Mammi added.

"He tried to ask if I would, but at the time, well . . ." Joanna's voice trailed off as she remembered again the dreadful moment. Eben *had* asked her about moving, hadn't he? Yet he'd seemed so hesitant, almost apologetic. And she . . . she knew it would never be allowed, though she hadn't explained why. "We haven't even written each other since April," she murmured. "I'd thought of it—but I don't want to be forward."

Mammi shrugged. "Well, you should read the letters your namesake wrote to her sister if you think that."

Hearing this, Joanna got up from her chair that quick. "I'll be right back!" She hurried upstairs, opened the hidden spot in the wall, and found the letters. Then, returning to the kitchen, she placed them in front of her on the table, suddenly feeling nervous.

"Go on, it's all right," Mammi coaxed. "Read them in the right order."

Joanna looked at the dates in each postmark and opened the earliest one. She began to read with great interest this account from the past, from one sister's heart to another.

My dear sister Miriam,

Since our visit, I've been a-pondering many things. For one, I realize it is important for each of us to become humble, like a little child, so much so that we cry out to our Father in heaven, looking to Him for guidance first and foremost. We must reach for His hand each and every day. Just as you said, it's the only way to live a happy life in the midst of disappointment. And I say, it's the only way to live life, period.

Joanna finished the letter, which continued in a similar vein. But apart from what Mammi Kurtz had just told her about this woman of great faith, Joanna didn't know why her great-great-aunt had written in such devout terms. Had her sister counseled her about being single?

"Are ya ready for the next one?" Mammi asked, her voice gentle.

Joanna removed the letter from its envelope and unfolded it, suddenly trembling as she began to read.

Dearest Miriam,

Since your last letter, I've taken your advice and decided to put out a fleece of sorts, like Gideon of old. I realize some folk will think I'm all but ferhoodled. But to demonstrate my belief that God will hear and answer my heart's cry, even now as I've just marked forty years of life, I've started to piece together a double wedding ring quilt. Some might poke fun behind my back, but that's all right. And I'm not superstitious enough to think that once it's finished, I shouldn't spread it on my own bed, even though at my age I have no prospects for a beau. Fact is, I'm going to do just that!

So, coupled with my earnest prayers, I'm putting my confidence to work, so to speak. "Faith with feet," I read somewhere. True, this is not the typical Amish way. Even so, I believe that when the Lord God puts a desire in a person's heart—remember Psalm 37:4?—it's there for a reason and ought to be acted upon.

I'll keep you informed as time goes along. And I'm telling you right now, I won't be shy when the Good Lord brings a beau to my door!

I wait and pray with expectancy for the husband He has chosen for me.

With love,
Your sister, Joanna

Blinking back tears, Joanna looked over at her grandmother. "What an amazing woman, jah?"

Mammi nodded her head, face solemn. "She certainly was . . . and God not only heard her heart's prayer, but gave her two children—twins, a boy and a girl—a double blessing, to be sure."

Joanna couldn't help asking—she had to know. "How long after the quilt was completed did she wed?"

"One year," Mammi said. "She married a lovely man, a widower who was only three years older . . . and a respected preacher, as well."

"With that kind of faith, she must've been a wonderful-*gut* preacher's wife."

Now Mammi was brushing away tears. "We have an inspiring heritage, ain't so?"

The Good Lord had known, all the way back to the day her great-great-aunt Joanna was threading her little quilting needle, that on this day, these many years later, another much younger Joanna would be deeply touched by the unseen yet very real bond between them.

Joanna remembered the line toward the end of the last letter. *I won't be shy. . . .* "With as much pluck as she seemed to have . . . did Aunt Joanna pop the question to the widowed preacher, just maybe?"

"As the story goes," Mammi said, the most encouraging smile on her pink face.

"Denki for sharing this with me."

"Happy to, dear girl."

"Aunt Joanna's quilt is a mighty special one, I'll say."

"Special indeed," said Mammi, a twinkle in her eye.

Chapter 34

Eben had lined up two dates with two different girls for the next couple of weekends, well into the middle of July. Maybe filling up his free time might help him recover more quickly from his loss of Joanna, though so far that plan hadn't been working. And since Emma Miller, Cousin Chester's former fiancée, was by no means interested in mingling with any new fellows, Eben was stuck with asking out much younger, and rather immature, girls.

Each Friday since returning home, he'd thought of Joanna when the usual time rolled around to call her. By now, though, he had lost track of which Friday it was, and for that he was sorry. He'd thought he would always remember the every-other-week pattern.

Life had plodded along for him. He scarcely had any leisure, what with threshing in full swing and his father depending more and more on Eben's decision making.

Since Leroy's visit, his letters had become increasingly frequent, which Eben found curious. Now that Leroy was married and had completely severed himself from Amish life, did he miss it?

But it was a mistake to entertain such thoughts. Besides, Eben had gotten a good look at Leroy's Mustang convertible and his English wife. Mrs. Debbie Troyer was by no means inclined to think of becoming Plain, even if her husband might begin to regret his decision in years to come. No, it was hard to comprehend why Leroy now wrote to Eben each week. Was he merely making up for lost time?

One night in mid-July, a couple weeks after Joanna's enlightening visit with Mammi Kurtz, she gently removed the large double wedding ring quilt from her hope chest and placed it on her bed. Of course, with the summer heat almost unbearable upstairs, there was no way she'd use it to cover herself, but placing it there felt like a celebratory act.

When she'd taken care to lay it out just so, she knelt beside her bed and prayed as earnestly as Great-Great-Aunt Joanna had prayed so many years ago. Silently, she poured out her heart to God, sorry for not having prayed for His will in her life before now, especially in regard to a husband. She asked for a broken and contrite spirit, acknowledging her part in the wall that had come between her and her sister. *Please, Lord, forgive me for my own unkind attitude. . . .*

In the quiet, Joanna also confessed her repeated defiance

toward the ministerial brethren when it came to her writing—whatever she might think of it. *Lead me in every aspect of my life . . . just as you led my namesake.*

After a while, Joanna rose and sat on the only chair in the room. Her heart felt lighter somehow as she began to knit soft white baby booties for Cousin Malinda's coming child. She had also been crocheting a pale-yellow-and-mint-green cradle afghan, which she picked up now and then, taking her time and praying all the while for this new little one.

The minutes passed, and she glanced up to see Cora Jane lingering in the hallway, her long hair down and clad in her lightweight house robe. Her sister looked like she wanted to come in. "It's all right," Joanna said, motioning to her.

Cora Jane blinked her eyes as she gawked at the quilt. "I must've missed something," she said, face puzzled. "Did ya secretly get married?"

Joanna laughed softly. "No."

"Well, what's this doin' here?"

"I've decided, why not just enjoy it while I wait?"

Cora Jane's eyes fluttered. "Wait for what?"

"Well, for a husband."

"And you think this quilt will make that happen?"

"Nee—not at all." She smiled at her sister. "But it will happen in God's time." Quickly, she shared the story behind the old quilt, glad for the opportunity to finally tell her.

Nodding slowly, Cora Jane gathered up her hair and pushed it over one shoulder. "You wonder me, sister."

I understand that feeling. But Joanna kept the thought to herself.

…⊱⊰…

In the following days, Joanna wished there was a way to broach the topic of her namesake with Mamma. On one of the last Tuesdays in July, she helped finish up the ironing while baking several loaves of bread. Her mother put up a batch of green beans with Cora Jane and talked about the peaches and plums that were coming on soon. Mamma hoped they'd make lots of extra jam, along with canning the fruit.

The heat was so sweltering, Joanna suggested they take their noon meal under the shade tree in the backyard. "How about a nice picnic instead of a hot meal today?"

Cora Jane nixed the idea, arguing that Dat and their older brothers helping cultivate the cornfield needed a big, tasty meal to keep up their strength. "A sandwich just isn't enough."

Mamma gave Joanna an agreeable look. "What a nice idea, though," she said while Cora Jane glowered. "Another day, maybe?"

"Well, Dat's not goin' to want to sit on a blanket on the ground anytime soon, is he?" Cora Jane piped up again. "His back's out of whack again, what with all the field work."

"That's true," Mamma said. "But still, it was a lovely thought your sister had. And your father and I can always sit on lawn chairs out there, ya know." She wasn't going to let Cora Jane have the final say on this—that was clear.

Joanna braced for another spirited remark from her sister, but when none came, she offered her best smile to Cora Jane, who held her gaze, then suddenly looked sad.

"So what should we make for dinner, then?" asked Mamma.

Joanna observed her sister more closely. Something wasn't right. Cora Jane's lower lip quivered as she moved to the window and stood there looking out, her shoulders heaving.

Then, of all things, she left the kitchen and went running across the side lawn to the celery patch.

"What on earth?" Mamma said.

"I'll see to her," Joanna said, leaving the ironing board set up. She rushed out the back door.

It was so stifling out there under the noontime sun, Joanna hardly wanted to move, let alone run after her surly sister. But run she did, determined to talk to Cora Jane . . . and find out why she'd gone to stand in the middle of the celery patch, holding herself around the middle and weeping like she'd lost her best friend.

"Cora Jane . . . honey, what's a-matter?" Joanna said softly, standing back a ways.

"Leave me be!"

"I just want to help."

"Ain't nothin' you or anyone can do," Cora Jane sobbed.

Joanna saw Mamma step out on the back porch down yonder. "You're terribly upset," Joanna said more softly. "I know you are."

Cora Jane leaned over, still holding her stomach like she might be sick. Then she did a strange thing. She fell to her knees and began to yank up young celery stalks, as many as she could grab with both hands, weeping. "I never should've planted these! Never!"

"Aw, sister . . ." Joanna felt like crying now, too. "I'm ever so sorry."

Cora Jane turned to look at her, letting the plants fall on the rich, dark soil. "I was a fool." She wiped her tear-streaked face with her grimy hands. "That's all I am. A fool, I tell ya."

"Come with me." Joanna held out her arms, moving closer. "Won't ya, please?"

Her poor sister sat back on her heels in the dirt, surrounded by uprooted plants. "We'll never need this much celery come fall."

"Maybe things'll turn around."

"That's impossible." Cora Jane pulled her tan-colored bandana off and sat there with her soiled hands on her head. "Just leave me be."

"You're in no shape to sit out here. Besides, you'll get cooked by the sun," Joanna persisted, stepping near. "I want you to come inside with me. How about I draw you a nice cool bath?"

"I don't deserve that. I'm *gut* for nothin'!"

"That's not true," Joanna said gently. "You heard me, Cora Jane. Get up and come inside."

"I'm done for, that's what."

Joanna reached down and assisted her sister into a standing position. "Your heart's all broken apart, but you won't let whatever's happened get the best of ya. I know you, sister."

Cora Jane turned, her lower lip trembling, and looked at Joanna. Then she flung her arms around her, just as Joanna had done with Cousin Malinda, crying like she might never stop. Joanna held on to her as she sobbed, her whole body quaking with every gasp. The day had come crashing down around them.

"Go ahead and cry," Joanna managed to say. "That's all right. . . ."

Once she could gently pry Cora Jane loose enough to walk her back toward the house, Joanna knew it was a good thing the noon meal wouldn't be outside with their father and brothers relaxing on the back lawn in the shade of ancient trees. No, a picnic was not a good idea on this wretched day.

Chapter 35

Cora Jane went to lie down in her room that afternoon, needing some time alone. Joanna truly hoped she'd find a way to rest.

Returning to her own room, Joanna looked up at the creak of floorboards and saw Mamma standing in the doorway, a frown on her face as she stared down at the bed.

"I've noticed you put the quilt on your bed," Mamma observed. "Can't help but wonder if that has something to do with Cora Jane's tears today."

"I decided to bring out the quilt from my hope chest is all," Joanna explained, standing at the foot of her bed. "A while after Mammi Kurtz told me the story behind it." She tried to keep her voice calm, her sister's cries still in her ears. "And I hope you understand, Mamma, my quilt isn't what set Cora Jane off." She looked toward the ceiling and heaved a sigh. "I feel sure this was coming on for a while now."

"What was?" Mamma's eyes narrowed as she stood near the dresser, her arms folded.

Joanna sighed, feeling a bit hesitant. "Apparently my sister's without a beau."

Mamma's jaw dropped. She glanced toward the hallway, to Cora Jane's bedroom. "So there'll be no wedding?"

"Jah . . . she didn't tell me a lot, but she made that much clear."

Mamma looked fatigued, dark circles beneath her eyes. "I didn't mean to make it sound like I was accusing you, dear." Her mother lowered herself onto the bed and sat there gingerly, as if she didn't want to mash the heirloom quilt. "Since we're alone, I'd like to talk to you 'bout something else altogether."

Joanna went around the bed and sat on the other side, wondering.

"I want to tell you a little something about your namesake, Great-Aunt Joanna Kurtz."

"I'd like that." Joanna didn't need to say that Mammi Kurtz had already told her a few things when she'd shared about the quilt itself.

For a moment, Mamma was very still, looking out the window, then back at the quilt, smoothing it gently with her right hand. "Your father mentioned you'd brought it up to him once."

Joanna remembered. "Jah, I've been curious for a long time."

"From what I knew of your father's great-aunt, well, I'd have to say I was impressed. She was a unique woman, and in some ways, a woman who put me to shame . . . her unusually strong faith and all." Mamma sighed. "She knew what she wanted and clung to prayer."

"You've given me a special gift, Mamma . . . with my name." Joanna felt the lump in her throat.

"The name suits ya," Mamma said, looking at her from across the bed. "As does this quilt."

Joanna ran her fingers over one of the double wedding ring patterns. Then, pausing, she covered Mamma's hand with her own. "This time together, talkin' like this, I mean . . . it's just awful nice. Denki."

Mamma rose and came around the bed, placing both hands lightly on Joanna's shoulders. "I see your faith at work in displaying this quilt, even without a serious beau," she said quietly. "You surely do resemble your namesake, Joanna. I'm ever so thankful for that."

Joanna raised her eyes to Mamma's and held her gaze. "I believe the Lord God has a plan for me," she whispered. "Just as He did for my namesake."

Mamma nodded sweetly. "I believe that, too, Joanna, dear."

Truly, she had never felt so close to her mother.

Cora Jane stayed home from all youth-related activities for the next few weekends, as did Joanna. Not knowing how to draw her sister out, Joanna wrote short poems of encouragement and slipped them under her bedroom door at night. Rhyming poems with such titles as "My Sister, My Friend," and "From My Heart to Yours."

Cora Jane actually brought up the "nice poetry" one night in mid-August after their parents had gone to bed. Joanna had drifted over to her room, hoping to strike up a conversation, and with a small smile, Cora Jane had invited her in. Ever so slowly, Cora Jane began to open up, sharing what she believed had gone wrong between her and Gideon. "But I can't blame my beau for everything. It takes two to make things work well," Cora Jane said, grimacing.

"Now that I'm this far away from our breakup, I can see better that we weren't right together." Cora Jane tilted her head and looked hard at Joanna. She opened her mouth, then shook her head.

"What is it, sister?"

Cora Jane pursed her lips for a moment. "Well, since we're talking so openly . . . but I really hesitate to bring this up."

"Say what's on your mind."

"Just wondered if ya think Eben was well suited to you."

Joanna pressed her fingers to her temples, then ran her hands through her long hair. "I know we'd be engaged by now, or possibly even married . . . if it weren't for his father's need for a farming partner."

Cora Jane nodded sympathetically. "Seems like something should've worked out for you two." She sighed. "*Something.*"

Joanna couldn't let herself think that way. "The past is behind us."

"Did he ever ask you to move there, even though it would take some doin'?"

"He mentioned it, but I knew it was out of the question." She stopped for a moment, realizing that what she was about to say surely implicated Cora Jane. "After Preacher Yoder talked so straight to me, I knew I couldn't leave Hickory Hollow."

"The preacher said you couldn't?" Cora Jane's eyes grew wide as quarters.

"He suggested it, jah. Said I shouldn't get any ideas to transfer my membership out to Indiana . . . not with my story writing."

Her sister's gaze dropped, her face losing its color. "And to think I caused much of that."

"Not entirely. I should've taken heed, thought twice about it, for sure. It's not easy, believe me, turning my back on something I've enjoyed so much. The writer's muse is a powerful thing. But I have stopped writing stories—I don't want to continue doing something others dear to me consider wrong. Lately I've been writing poetry instead, hoping maybe I can honor the Lord in that."

Cora Jane turned and held out her hand. "Do you still resent me for tellin' on you?"

Joanna's breath caught in her throat. She reached for her sister's hand and pressed it gently, letting the gesture speak the loving truth. "I forgave ya some weeks ago. And . . . are you still angry with me for pushing you away after Eben came along?"

Cora Jane shook her head slowly. "Who could ever stay angry at a sister like you?"

"I should've told ya from the first, but my relationship

with Eben seemed so fragile and new. 'Specially with the distance between us, I was afraid things wouldn't work out if we were watched too closely."

"Truth be known, I was jealous of you for bein' so self-assured, as if you thought you could just keep accepting invitations from brides like that, always bein' a bridesmaid . . . and not heeding tradition."

It felt good to set things right. Cora Jane had made it clear she was sorry, and in time, the sting from her sister's betrayal would surely lessen.

But it was Cora Jane's remark that something should've worked out with Eben that gave Joanna a fleeting feeling of warmth. At the same time, it was also a miserable reminder of what had been lost. Even if she had a glint of hope, she could see no way to fan it into flame.

Chapter 36

August peaches were coming on almost faster than Mamma could keep up. For that reason, neighbors Mattie, Ella Mae, and Rachel came over for a canning bee right after breakfast Tuesday. Mamma, Joanna, and Cora Jane helped set up an assembly line for peeling and pitting. They gave Ella Mae the most comfortable chair in the house, situating her away from the sunny windows.

They jabbered in Pennsylvania Dutch, midwife Mattie telling stories about the babies she'd delivered—and three she'd nearly lost—over the many years. Rachel and Mamma listened but blushed and rolled their eyes at times, no doubt because Joanna and Cora Jane were present.

Once Rachel could get a word in, she shared the plans for her daughter Mary's upcoming birthday. "The children are all makin' little cards to hang up on a string, over the kitchen doorway . . . like at Christmastime."

"Aw, that's nice," Mamma said, placing the sliced peaches in slightly salty water to preserve their natural color.

"The bishop's son Levi is quite the artist," Rachel added. "Hard to know how that'll turn out, with his father overseein' things."

"Just maybe he'll see the benefit of this wondrous gift from the Good Lord," Ella Mae said. "That's what."

The room went silent, and Rachel and Mamma exchanged concerned glances. But Joanna knew, as did all the others, that the Wise Woman exercised no restraint in speaking her mind.

Eventually, the talk turned to putting up pears and plums in the coming days and weeks, and making jam, too. Mattie complained a little about needing to patch her husband's work pants by hand. "An unpleasant task, ya know," she said, sighing.

"Ach, just be thankful your husband still lives," widow Ella Mae muttered to her daughter, though they'd all heard.

Later, Rachel mentioned *der Debbich*—the bedspread—she was looking forward to making come fall. "I'm doing it in blues and yellows, with a perty black border that'll make the colors stand right out."

Ella Mae said she'd laid eyes on a hand-woven coverlet made from wool at an antique shop in Bird-in-Hand recently. "Carded and spun by hand, too," she said, dimples showing.

"That'd be a real chore, spinning," Cora Jane said pleasantly. Though still somewhat downcast at times, her overall mood seemed much better since her heart-to-heart with Joanna a couple nights ago.

When it came time to stop and make the noon meal, Mamma took charge of the kitchen, requesting some help from Cora Jane, Rachel, and Mattie. She'd asked Joanna in advance to keep Ella Mae company, so Joanna led the older woman into the small sitting area around the corner from the kitchen.

"How you doin', dearie?" Ella Mae asked once she was settled in Mamma's chair.

"All right some days . . . others, not so *gut*. It's the way of life, I'm learning."

"Heard your young man came twice to see ya, ain't?"

Jake must've told her. . . .

"Well, once to visit and once to part ways."

"That so?" Ella Mae scratched her head. "Now, wait a minute . . . didn't I hear that, too?"

Everyone's heard by now, thought Joanna.

"Thing is, I can't seem to forget him, even though I've tried." She shared that she'd gone out with a fellow from around here. "Someone lots of fun, and a really convincing storyteller, too." She wondered if Ella Mae might guess whom she meant, although that wasn't why she'd mentioned Jake in so many words.

"Ah, I daresay I know just who you're talking 'bout. A right nice boy, he is."

Joanna wouldn't say Jake's name, thinking it could tempt Ella Mae to divulge a confidence. But she gave a little nod. "Honestly, though, it'll be mighty hard to forget Eben Troyer."

By the look in Ella Mae's eyes, the wheels inside her head were turning. "Are ya wantin' to know what I'll say to that?"

Joanna was taken off guard. "I didn't bring it up for counsel, no."

"Why don't you tell me more 'bout this young man who's captured your heart."

This time Joanna did not hesitate from beginning to end, every last detail she felt comfortable sharing. "But now I don't know how to be round anyone but him."

Ella Mae observed her intently, then asked if she'd ever thought of going out to Indiana. "To meet his family, I mean. Surprise him like he did you, maybe?"

"I'm stuck here, I'm afraid."

"Well, that just ain't true, dear girl. No one's stuck anywhere unless they choose to be. The Lord God guides those who are moving forward." Such startling words . . . words that resonated in the depths of Joanna's heart.

In that moment, she remembered how impressed Eben had been with Cora Jane's frankness—he'd even indicated that he liked a woman with gumption.

"Ever ponder Ruth's pledge to her mother-in-law, Naomi, in the book of Ruth?" Ella Mae asked, seemingly out of the blue.

"Not really, why?"

"Well, just listen to this." Ella Mae wore a smile on her wrinkled face. "'For whither thou goest, I will go; and where thou lodgest, I will lodge: thy people shall be my people, and thy God my God,'" Ella Mae recited.

Joanna recalled hearing that plenty of times in Preacher Yoder's wedding sermons.

"So now, if it was *gut* enough for a young widow to declare to her mother-in-law, why not a girl to the man she loves?" Ella Mae locked eyes with hers. "Chust think 'bout it, Joanna. That, and pray 'bout it, too."

All the rest of the day, and throughout that week, Joanna thought and prayed and thought some more, until that Friday evening. She'd purposely gone walking on the field lanes where she and Eben had strolled together, hand in hand. Again, Ella Mae's words came back to her, like an echo. Then suddenly, they stopped.

The phone was ringing in the little shanty in Dat's field.

Joanna froze right there. *Is Eben calling? Can it be?*

Heart hammering, she ran through the cornfield, rushing past the countless rows, thrusting the stalks away from her face as she ran faster and faster.

The phone continued its ringing, like a clanging cowbell in the distance, as she groped her way toward its beautiful sound.

Think, think, Joanna! Which Friday is it? Which?

Then, stopping for a second, she knew. "Oh, Eben . . ."

The ringing continued as she peered on tiptoe over the tops of the tasseled corn, the tall telephone shack before her like a lighthouse in a vast green sea.

She moved forward, dashing to the shack. There, she pushed open the wooden door as the phone continued to ring. Reaching for it, she felt faint at the prospect of Eben's voice on the line. But wasn't he long gone from her?

Still, she had to know. Lifting the receiver off its cradle, she managed a hello.

Just then, like a feather flying away in the breeze, Joanna heard the line click as the phone went dead. And her heart sank.

Was it you, Eben?

She couldn't help wondering how long the phone had been ringing, perhaps even before she'd come within earshot. Feeling weak, Joanna leaned against the familiar wall, staring straight out the only window at the sky with its billowing clouds. And she cried, unashamed.

"O dear Lord in heaven," she wept. "I don't know what to do . . . or where to turn. Eben's in my constant thoughts. Please remove my love for him, if it's your will." She reached to touch the black receiver, recalling Eben's voice in her ear, oh, so many times. "If you have a different plan, will you make that path clear and ever so straight . . . and lead me back to Eben? Amen."

When she'd managed to dry her eyes and gather her wits, Joanna headed through the maze of cornstalks, over the field lanes, and past the corncrib toward home.

Chapter 37

The afternoon birthday celebration for the bishop's wife the next day turned out to be a hen's party with a mystery meal, complete with cryptic descriptions of the menu items and various group games, including Dutch Blitz for all twenty or so women present. The atmosphere was as festive as any Joanna had ever been a part of, and jovial, too. For a while she actually forgot herself and entered into the gaiety, relishing the fun.

Dear Mary, wearing her best royal blue dress and matching cape apron, looked a bit sheepish about receiving so many pretty cards, as well as a few handmade gifts from close relatives and friends. As gracious as Joanna had always known her to be, Mary dutifully thanked each of them before the party disbanded.

On the way out the back door, Joanna was surprised when Preacher Yoder's round-faced wife, Lovina, stopped her and quietly said her husband wanted to meet with her again. "But he's goin' on a trip, so it won't be for a week or so."

Why's she telling me this now—so I can worry myself sick?

"He wants you to know he'll contact your father when the time is right," the older woman added, a serious look on her face.

Joanna felt self-conscious about being singled out like this, especially at such a happy gathering. "Is this concerning—"

"He'll speak directly to *you*," Lovina Yoder said, touching her arm. "All in *gut* time."

Nodding, Joanna said she'd wait to hear further from her father about this. But now her stomach was churning. How long would she have to wait for the next scolding? At least she could honestly tell the preacher about her prayer of contrition . . . and about having turned her back on writing make-believe stories, hard as it was. Something she'd decided to do to demonstrate her willing heart before God, and her love for the People.

"Denki," Joanna said softly, though really there was nothing to thank her for.

"Have a nice day," the preacher's wife said, smiling now.

Nice day? How on earth?

Joanna was relieved Cora Jane hadn't attended this get-together. Cora Jane was feeling crushed enough for having started all this by going to the deacon in the first place. But Salina was there, although she hadn't observed Joanna's encounter with Lovina. Here she came just now, out the back door, having stayed inside a bit longer to visit with the birthday girl.

"Can I get a ride home?" Salina asked Joanna, hurrying her pace. "I should prob'ly walk, but I need to start supper soon."

"Sure."

On the ride there, Joanna relived the unpleasant encounter with Lovina Yoder, whom she rarely spoke to, considering the woman's age and stature in the community.

"You're awful quiet," Salina said. "Hope ya don't mind goin' out of your way."

"Not at all."

Up ahead, Joanna noticed Jake and his brother Jesse driving their market wagon home. Jake spotted her and waved.

She watched as Jake headed down the way, toward the Lantz home. *Are we merely friends?* she mused, wondering if this was a swift answer to yesterday's prayer in the phone shack. *Should I let him court me after all?*

Salina sighed and it brought Joanna's attention back inside the buggy. "I'm feelin' tired today."

"The heat's getting to all of us, jah?"

Salina agreed. "Ain't that the truth, though we can't complain compared to the high temperatures they've been having in Ohio and Indiana this week."

Indiana . . . Had Salina mentioned that state for any particular reason?

But her sister went on to talk about a number of circle letters she was writing to distant cousins out there in the Midwest. "Didja know we have a third cousin named Maria Riegsecker who lives in Shipshewana?"

Joanna sucked in a breath at the mention of Eben's hometown. "Never heard of her," she managed to say.

"Jah, she was a Witmer like Mamma but married into an Indiana family. She's been askin' for Noah and me to come visit and bring the children, too. She runs a candle store and wants me to come and pick out whatever I'd like."

"How nice," Joanna replied absently. *Maria?* Had Eben ever mentioned her before? She didn't recall. "How long have you been writing circle letters with her?"

"Four years now. Maria's awful nice—kindhearted and generous. Says she has lots of empty bedrooms just waiting to be filled up when we visit."

"Sounds like you'd have a *gut* time."

"I think so, too, but getting Noah to take off during the summer is out of the question."

"How old a woman is Maria?"

"Mamma's age, I'd guess, although I really don't know."

"She makes candles, ya say?"

"All kinds of colors and scents. Hundreds of 'em, and they sell right off the shelves in her little shop above their stable."

"Sounds pretty," Joanna said. "I hope you can go sometime, Salina."

"Maria lives right off the main street, she says, within walking distance of the Blue Gate Bakery, where she likes to go to purchase apple dumplings and pecan rolls."

"Now you're makin' my mouth water!" Joanna smiled. "If you go, I'll send along some money for you to pick out a candle or two for me, all right?"

"Well, by the sound of it, Maria would be happy to treat anyone in the family," Salina said. "You could come, too . . . help look after the children, maybe?"

Just thinking of being anywhere in the vicinity of Eben's

neighborhood and not seeing him tore at Joanna's heart. "I don't know how I could get away, even in the fall," she said.

They were coming up on Salina's house—Joanna could see the front yard jutting into view, just around the next bend. All this talk of Shipshewana was making her head spin. It was a good thing she was close to dropping Salina off.

"Nice to see you havin' a *gut* time today at Mary's."

Joanna nodded. "I did." *Except for the preacher's wife.*

"Say, if you'd ever like to join in on Maria's circle letter, just let me know." Salina paused, then opened her pocketbook and fished for a notepad and pen. "Here, I'll jot down her address for ya, if you'd like."

It was funny seeing Salina so insistent, but Joanna did like the idea of writing to someone who was creative with something other than flowers or quilts. "Sure, I'll be glad to write her," she said, not sure when she'd have time.

"Denki for the ride, sister!" With that, Salina got out of the carriage and walked toward the house, waving without turning around.

Looking at the slip of paper in her hand, Joanna saw that the street name was Peaceful Acres Lane. *Same as Eben's address!*

"First the phone rings nearly off the hook . . . then I spot Jake. And now this," she said to herself as she hurried the horse toward home. She thought of the beautiful quilt and smiled as she recalled her prayer last night, asking God to make the path clear. Goodness, but the path, if it could be called that, was all *ranklich*—tangled up!

Chapter 38

The following Saturday, Joanna went riding again with Jake. When she asked, he confessed that the tales he told were true ones, some of which he'd heard from his grandfather. "He liked to embellish nearly everything," Jake told her.

"So they're family stories, then?"

"Oh jah, who'd ever think of makin' such things up? Real life is much stranger than fiction, ain't?"

Fiction. There it was again.

"Have you ever read a made-up book?" she asked.

"Oh, maybe a handful of mystery novels." He glanced at her, looking mighty dapper in his white dress shirt and black vest. "Have you?"

"Well, since we're becoming such *gut* friends, I'll tell ya a little secret."

He leaned his head over. "I'm all ears."

"I've read quite a few novels, actually."

"Love stories, maybe?" He chuckled. "Make-believe—all lies, ya know."

"But a reflection of our relationship with the great Lover of our souls, I like to think," she stated.

He looked surprised, then nodded, evidently in agreement.

They were getting along so well, Joanna was thankful she'd agreed to continue seeing him. Maybe Jake *was* the answer to her prayer. Maybe in time he could help her forget Eben, once and for all.

That night, she and Cora Jane whispered and giggled, and Joanna told her all about Jake's convincing tellings. But she kept back their discussion about fiction, still sensitive about her former story writing. Would she be up to facing Preacher Yoder when he returned? Joanna couldn't help but worry about what he had up his sleeve.

After the ironing was done on Tuesday, Joanna and Cora Jane went over to Mammi Sadie's and helped her put up sweet corn all afternoon. It was the hottest day in August thus far, but none of them complained, not with the thought of delicious canned corn to enjoy come autumn and winter.

While the corn was simmering, Joanna slipped her grandmother a little poem of encouragement she'd written earlier that morning upon arising, knowing how stressful Dawdi's situation was for dear Mammi. His mind was slipping more often these days.

"Well, aren't *you* nice!" Mammi Sadie said, opening the

poem. She read it silently, tears springing to her eyes, then opened her ample arms to Joanna, who couldn't help feeling ever so joyful at this heartfelt response.

"Heard you've written a lot of these poems for various folks," she said.

Joanna was reticent to own up. "Oh, it's just something I do to spread cheer." *And keeps me honest before the Lord God, too,* she thought, wishing her passion for story writing would fade for good.

Dawdi Joseph began to babble about his brothers and other relatives who'd passed away. But when he talked of his school days, his eyes sparkled, especially as he recalled the happy memory of helping raise cocker spaniel puppies to sell.

"Did ya ever get attached to any of the pups?" Cora Jane asked, drawing him out as he sat near the back door, just rocking.

"Oh jah . . . there was one black one with the saddest eyes you ever did see, and the way he'd just sit and look at ya, cock his little head, and nearly talk to ya . . . well, it warms my heart." Dawdi's shoulders rose and fell as he took a deep breath, revisiting the past. "In the end, that one went to our neighbors down the way. Mighty nice, too."

"You must've visited him sometimes, then, jah?" Joanna asked, hoping to keep their grandfather with them in the present a while longer.

"Why, sure I did."

"What did you name him—or did you?" Cora Jane asked, smiling at Joanna and giving her a knowing glance.

Dawdi nodded. "Called him Jigger. My, my, what an active pup he was. It seemed right."

"'Cause he nearly danced a jig when you saw him?" asked Joanna. She enjoyed seeing Dawdi so caught up in the recollection.

"Oh, goodness, did he ever." Dawdi went quiet and stopped rocking. Then, stretching his arms, he yawned and started murmuring, like he was talking to himself again—the way he often did these days.

"When was the last time you saw Jigger, Dawdi?" asked Cora Jane.

"Well, now, I 'spect he's round here somewheres." He scooted back his chair, straining his head to look. "Here, Jigger, ol' boy . . . c'mon to your friend Joseph. Here, Jigger . . . Jigger."

Heart breaking, Joanna had to turn away. She wondered if Mary Beiler's own Dawdi Abram ever lost track like this. As she recalled, Mary hadn't mentioned him at her birthday party. Perhaps because it was meant to be a very happy day.

Only eight women showed up at Mary's for the weekly quilting frolic. Joanna and Cora Jane helped stretch out the quilt, and then all of them worked to put it into the big frame. Because Mary was left-handed, she sat at one of the corners of her choosing and the rest of them filled in, finding their spots across from or near sisters or cousins. Cora Jane whispered that she wanted to sit right next to Joanna, which pleased Joanna no end. In time it would be like they'd never had a falling out at all.

Neither Ella Mae nor Mattie was in attendance. When Joanna asked about both women, Mary said Ella Mae was suffering with a miserable summer cold, and Mattie had stayed home to look after her. "A woman that age has to be careful, ya know?" Mary said as she picked up her thimble and needle.

Joanna agreed and smiled over at her. *Dear Mary, always thinking of others.*

And then, as though Mary had been privy to Joanna and Ella Mae's talk the day they'd put up peaches with Mamma, she said she'd been reading in the Old Testament. "The book of Ruth, actually . . . and it just struck me again how much love Ruth had for Naomi."

"*For whither thou goest, I will go. . . .*" Joanna hadn't forgotten that verse, either. It felt to her like yet another nudge back to Eben, and she wondered if she ought to make a list of everything pointing in his direction. *Then maybe I should make another list for Jake.*

"What're you thinking 'bout?" Cora Jane leaned over to ask.

"Why, was I smiling at nothin' again?"

Cora Jane giggled a little. "It's like I can read your expressions anymore."

"Well, that's what sisters do, jah?"

Cora Jane nodded and glanced at her again, all smiles.

That night after family worship, Joanna read the entire book of Ruth, lingering on the verse Ella Mae had quoted.

"*Is* this a sign from God?" she whispered, staring at the tall gas lamp with its shiny glass chimney from her spot on the bed.

Then, admiring the old wedding quilt again, she thanked

the Lord God for this legacy of faith passed down to her. And for divine guidance in her life.

She rose and placed her Bible back on the dresser, and as she turned, her eyes fell on the hope chest. *I ought to put my writing notebooks somewhere else*, she thought. They were such a temptation. So many feelings raced through her, she scarcely knew what to think.

She started when a knock came at the door. "Come in, Cora Jane," she said.

"Well, it's Mamma."

Stepping to the door, Joanna opened it. "Jah?"

"Your father's receiving a visit from Preacher Yoder on behalf of our elderly deacon." Mamma's face looked pale in the lamp's amber light. "Preacher wants you there, too."

Lovina Yoder's words flew back to her, and Joanna dreaded what was to come. "When's he comin' by?"

"One of these mornings, your father says."

"I'll be ready."

Mamma frowned hard, her lower lip trembling. "Sorry to be the one to tell ya. Your father, well . . ."

"I know—he's a busy man," Joanna said, excusing his wariness.

Nodding, Mamma patted Joanna's arm. "I'm here, if ya want to talk 'bout it."

These were the gentle words she needed to hear. "I'm not afraid, Mamma. All right? Please don't worry."

"I'll pray." Mamma turned to leave.

"Denki," Joanna said, wishing her story writing hadn't caused such a stir and put an ache in her mother's heart. *And poor Dat's, as well.*

Chapter 39

The light coming from within the barn Thursday evening was a stark contrast to that of the gas lamp in the kitchen. Eben's father had summoned him to the makeshift office in one corner of the old barn for an unexpected "*meeting, of sorts*"—or so Daed had called it. The lantern light glowed eerily on such a dark night, and the animals were restless. Eben could sense something amiss, and not only in the atmosphere. His father's face was unusually grim.

For the past few weeks, Eben had noticed something quite different about his father and even considered perhaps Daed might be ill. Yet it was the oddest thing—some days he seemed entirely optimistic, then the next day downright dreary. Eben had never known Daed to be unsettled like this, and he wondered what might be on his mind. Maybe he was going to bring up some newfangled gadget that would make work easier for them both. If so, was it something the bishop approved?

Daed awaited him, sitting slumped at his beat-up wooden desk. He looked tired . . . defeated.

What's troubling him?

Immediately, Eben thought of Leroy. Had his father received news from him? But then again, what could be worse than Leroy's leaving the People, his heart no longer kneeling in contrition before almighty God?

So why'd Mamm urge me here on his behalf? Eben wondered as he entered the murky glow of light. "You wanted to see me, Daed?"

"Pull up a chair, son." His father sat straighter, filling his lungs slowly. "Need to bend your ear awhile."

Eben took a seat, ready to listen.

"I've come to a hard decision. One I've been mulling over for long enough now."

Eben's shoulders tensed into knots as he braced for the news that, nearly overnight, had the power to grow gray hair in his father's beard, and plant more crinkles around Daed's eyes and mouth. The weight of it had seemingly cloaked him with a gray pallor.

"Some days ya get the bear, other days the bear gets you," Daed began.

Never before had Eben heard this saying from Daed's lips—so uncharacteristic of him. What could it possibly mean?

Even though Joanna had pleaded with her mother not to worry, she had tossed about for half the night, doing plenty of that herself. And upon rising the next morning, her legs felt as wobbly as newborn calves. She made her way downstairs to shower and dress, then helped Mamma make breakfast. All the while, she kept her eye out for an early arrival by Preacher Yoder, in case he chose to appear today. It was well-known in the hollow that Preacher Yoder liked to arrive early, often surprising folk as he checked up a bit.

But Preacher didn't come that day or the next, and Joanna couldn't have been more apprehensive if she were expecting the bishop himself.

After the Sunday Singing, the first one in September, Joanna noticed Cora Jane talking with Mary Rose Witmer and two other cousins across the barn. Joanna managed to catch her sister's eye and motioned to her. "Come join us," she mouthed, thinking it might be fun to include Cora Jane in small talk with her and Jake.

Once Cora Jane came over and made a little circle of three, Jake told a story about a bunch of fellows who'd gotten their feet tied up while they were sleeping at a campout one night. They'd ended up tripping all over themselves when they got up in the morning—falling flat on their faces.

"Why on earth?" Cora Jane asked, inching in closer.

Jake grinned. "Well, it's like this: They were all getting hitched that comin' week. The single fellas tend to pick on the ones who are published to be married, ya know."

"There are so many pranks for the groom, ain't so?" Cora Jane said. "Oh, tell us another prank you've heard."

With that, Jake was off, this time with a tale about another cousin. Cora Jane's eyes were big as he wrapped up, and then one topic of conversation shifted effortlessly into another, until they were talking easily about shared interests. Cora Jane seemed to be genuinely enjoying herself, and Joanna could see how exceptionally taken Jake was with Cora Jane's spunk.

Joanna felt amused at being left far behind in this exchange. And later, when Jake asked if Joanna minded if they gave Cora Jane a ride home, too, Cora Jane protested demurely. But it was quite obvious there was a real spark between her and Jake, and Joanna realized she didn't mind in the least.

Jake seemed to enjoy the attention of both girls as they rode along in his handsome open carriage. Joanna couldn't keep from smiling as she looked back and forth between Jake and Cora Jane, like a witness to a Ping-Pong match. She was smashed like cheese in a sandwich between the two of them, and as they talked animatedly, she noticed that this was the third time they'd passed the house and not stopped to let Cora Jane out.

Eventually, as the hour grew late, Cora Jane graciously suggested she should be getting home. Joanna didn't object because she wanted to talk with Jake for a bit once her sister left for the house. She would be ever so cautious, though, in how she phrased things.

When asked, Jake didn't deny the attraction. Joanna gave him the green light to pursue courting Cora Jane. "If you'd like to."

"Are you sure 'bout this?" he asked, leaning closer. "I'd never want to hurt you, Joanna."

"We have a deal, remember? Just friends."

He nodded much too emphatically, and she couldn't help but laugh. "I'm perfectly fine if you want to take my sister out."

Jake studied her. "Only if you're absolutely certain."

"I am. And just think, if you two end up together, we'll be brother and sister, which is even better than friends, jah?"

He chuckled. "Not always. Sometimes siblings can be a pain in the neck, if you know what I mean."

While that was certainly true enough, Joanna didn't admit to it—not now, given the way Cora Jane and she were getting along so well.

A crescent moon appeared over the cornfield to the east, and Jake kindly mentioned that it was probably time to call it a night. He came around the open carriage, helped Joanna down, and walked her partway up the lane, just as he had always done before. But tonight, Joanna guessed, was to be the very last time.

Cora Jane's lantern was still lit and burning when Joanna slipped over to her room. Her sister's hair was a sheet of flowing flaxen over one side of her pale pink nightgown. She sat in bed and smiled immediately. "Did Jake tell more stories after I left? I must've missed some *gut* ones, jah?"

"Are you honestly sayin' that's what you want to know?"

Cora Jane's eyes glimmered. "What else is there to ask?"

"Oh, well . . . I wouldn't want to spoil the fun."

"For me or for you?" Laughing softly, Cora Jane reached for her hand. "You do know something, don't you?"

"Maybe."

"Goodness' sake!" Cora Jane blushed.

They were both laughing now, and it felt like old times. Cora Jane patted her side of the bed, inviting Joanna to stay awhile longer.

"Jake is *gut* for you, ain't so?" Cora Jane said as she turned on her side to look Joanna square in the face.

"I never thought I could be friends with a fella, ya know? It's kind of peculiar."

Cora Jane was suddenly quiet.

"He's learned some important courting lessons," Joanna said. "Knows how to behave on a date, for sure."

"I wondered 'bout that. But it's pretty obvious he got some *gut* advice from somewhere."

Joanna didn't mention Ella Mae Zook or that she knew Jake had gone to talk to her last April.

"He's grown up a lot—maybe because of bein' friends with you, Joanna."

She shrugged. "Who's to say?"

"And the two of you have something big in common, jah?" said Cora Jane. "A real love of stories."

"That we do." Sliding her hand beneath the pillow, Joanna began to relax. "He tells them so freely."

"Do you miss your story writing terribly?" Cora Jane's voice was soft, even regretful.

"Not as much as at first. If I didn't have my poetry to fall back on, I'd miss it even more. The Lord's given me another way to express my creativity, I guess."

"Well, no matter what you write, it's a gift."

This surprised Joanna. "What a nice thing to say."

"Nice . . . and mighty confusing, too, ain't?" Cora Jane glanced at the small clock on her bed shelf.

Nodding, Joanna refused to think about the confusing part, feeling quite sure she knew what was coming with Preacher Yoder's impending visit.

"You'd better head for bed," Cora Jane said, "or you'll end up falling asleep in your clothes right here."

Joanna opened her sleepy eyes and looked over at her sister. "I'm glad we can talk like this again."

"Me too."

With that, Joanna got up, said good-night, and walked to her own room. Once there, although feeling tired, she lit her lantern and settled into bed to read from the book of Proverbs. After a time, she bowed her head and folded her hands in a prayer of thanksgiving for God's goodness and grace in all of their lives. Then she outened the gas lamp.

But sleep did not come quickly. For one thing, she had a hard time dismissing the conversation with Ella Mae the day they'd canned peaches. For another, she couldn't forget the letters her namesake had written to her own sister Miriam.

Lying there in the darkened room, Joanna stared at the open window, welcoming the cool night air. She had carefully folded back the heirloom quilt, along with the sheet, and relished the slight breeze on her cotton gown.

And then, as if a nudge had come from heaven, an unexpected idea dropped into her heart. *Oh jah.* Joanna knew exactly what she wanted to tell Preacher Yoder, Lord willing, once he revealed what was on his mind. It was ever so plain to her just now.

But dare she speak up yet again?

Chapter 40

A single blunt knock came at the back door the next day, just as Joanna and her mother were sitting down to catch a breath after having hung out an extra large washing. They'd also baked two more loaves of bread than usual, and on such a warm day, too.

Mamma looked sideways at Joanna and got up to move toward the screen door, where Preacher Yoder stood in his usual black attire, his straw hat in hand, jaw set.

I must surely be in trouble again. Joanna slunk down in her chair at the table, where she'd fluted the edges of two pie shells she planned to fill with early apples. When she glanced up, she could see the old well pump behind the preacher, in the backyard. She cringed, remembering the minister's last visit.

Meanwhile, Mamma was telling him Dat had gone. "Went over to Noah's place not fifteen minutes ago."

Joanna held her breath and hoped Preacher Yoder might simply offer to return at a more suitable time.

"Joanna, dear," Mamma called, turning to reveal a flushed face.

She left the piecrusts there on the table. *I'll hear what he has to say and be done with it,* Joanna told herself.

But before she could get out to the utility room door, Preacher Yoder strode into the kitchen with Mamma following behind like a chubby little bird.

"Joanna," he said, not cracking a smile. "I have something to tell you."

She refused the urge to flinch and instead met him at the table when Mamma gave a slight shift of her hand, indicating they should sit. Joanna sat where Cora Jane usually did, on the long bench facing the windows, and Mamma sat across from her in her own chair, with Preacher Yoder presumptuously at the head of the table, in Dat's place.

Preacher folded his callused hands on the table and stared at them for a moment. "You are quite fond of writing, as I understand it."

Joanna slowly raised her eyes to his. This was ground they'd already covered.

"And you continue to write even now, according to the deacon's wife, Sallie, and others."

"Only poetry." She took the risk and defended herself in what she dearly hoped was a respectful tone. "Little poems to cheer folk up."

He nodded, his expression less severe than at the last visit. "So I hear."

"I've given up my story writing—gave it up before the Lord God and heavenly Father." She longed to jump ahead and tell him what had helped to prompt her decision, but she refrained, thinking it unwise. She curled her toes under the table.

"Sallie is so impressed by those little poems, she's suggested I encourage you to submit some of them to the *Ladies Journal.*" He pulled out a piece of paper and handed it to her. It gave an editor's name and the address for submissions.

Joanna could hardly speak. "My writings . . . published?"

"Your *poetry*."

She was stunned at this turn of events. Mamma beamed at her across the table, and her short, quick nod of the head meant that Joanna should say something. But news of this sort had been the farthest thing from her mind on such a day. "Are *you* . . . is she ever so sure?"

"Sallie?" Preacher grinned. "I'm told several women were in agreement with her."

Joanna thought then of the way Fannie's visit to the deacon's wife had been somewhat downplayed by Mammi Kurtz. Now that Joanna thought of it, she wondered if Cora Jane might also have been involved.

Beyond pleased, Joanna shook her head as she tried to absorb all of this. And, lo and behold, the very question she'd so wanted to ask just flew from her mind. Gone in the wake of this wonderful-*gut* surprise.

"I'll leave it up to you to pursue this, if you wish," Preacher added. "With my blessing . . . and Bishop John's, too."

The bishop's?

She nodded, still overwhelmed at this turn of events. It wasn't difficult to think of which poem to present to the magazine editors. A pleasant tremor went through her. What if it ended up in print for the whole world to see? *Her* world . . . the Plain community at large.

Then, before Joanna could say more, Mamma offered to bring each of them a slice of warm bread with strawberry jam, and soon Joanna and the preacher found themselves sitting alone at the table, just looking at each other.

Something about the way he ran his fingers up and down his suspenders made her think of Eben. And in that moment, Joanna knew she could indeed confide in Preacher Yoder.

Eben enjoyed nibbling the fresh cinnamon sticky bun his mother had made earlier that morning, though he allowed himself only one. He hadn't second-guessed the things Daed had put to him the other night in the barn. None of his older brothers had blinked an eye at Daed's decision, which still surprised Eben. Yet he reeled with the news and felt it was only right to contact Leroy about it, as well.

"You and your father have to fill silo yet," his mother said, offering more to eat.

"That and the vet's comin' to check the cows' blood for TB and brucellosis in a couple of days," Eben mentioned. Knowing how sluggish eating between meals made him, he politely refused any more mouthwatering treats and hurried back out to help his father.

Eyeing the phone shack, a brown dot in the distance, he determined it was time to give Leroy a call.

Later tonight.

***

The time had come for Joanna to share with Preacher Yoder what she'd felt led to do. "No matter how things turn out, I want to do this for the Lord God . . . and out of respect for the brethren," she began.

A confused frown crossed the minister's brow. "Speak plainly," he urged.

She glanced at Mamma, now over at the sink, then back at the minister. "After prayer, I am willing to sacrifice my story writing for the rest of my life, for a transfer of membership to another state," she said with all the courage she could gather.

"To which church?"

She told him quietly.

"Well, I can't promise, but I'll bring it up with Bishop John." His composed countenance spoke volumes, and she felt heartened.

Mamma returned to the table carrying a plate with two thick slices of bread and set it down, along with a jar of jam.

Joanna continued, being more direct than she'd ever been with anyone in spiritual authority. In turn, the preacher made it equally clear that she was permitted to continue writing her poetry as long as it was done to offer encouragement.

"Daughter?" Mamma said after a time, looking baffled as she sat there. "Why a request to transfer to another church?"

Holding off on revealing her entire plan, Joanna explained that she didn't know yet if transferring would even be necessary. "But I'll know soon enough."

It was only then that Joanna saw the bewilderment lift, and tenderness and understanding shone in Mamma's dear eyes.

Chapter 41

Joanna hadn't really foreseen how anxious she would be to locate the Troyer farm in thriving, green Shipshewana. By the time she arrived Friday—in a van full of other Amish heading for various towns in Indiana—and had acquired a taxicab, she was beginning to feel the effects of the exceedingly long day, tired yet buoyed by the excitement of her surprise visit. The worry came from not knowing what her former beau might do or say when she arrived without warning.

What if he has a steady girlfriend by now? Joanna asked herself, then attempted to squash the dreadful notion. Oh, surely not! Yet the voice of reason crept back in, and she realized that Eben could very well have moved on with a new sweetheart. What would keep him from doing so?

Either way, she had to know for certain. And if not, was he still thinking of her, missing her . . . wishing there was a miraculous way for them to be together? Well, here she was, and all of their distance keeping was behind them. Although Joanna no longer wrote down her romantic imaginings about happily-ever-afters, she still liked to contemplate different scenarios. No one could keep her from writing stories in her head, so to speak. And she did just that as she enjoyed the ride along the rural roads, all of which were numbered county roads rather than streets with names, like those in Hickory Hollow.

Weary as she was, she longed to lean her head back in the cab, but she would not have time to undo her hair bun and tidy it up before seeing Eben and meeting his family. *If that even happens*. The thought of being introduced to his parents hadn't been something she'd mentally prepared herself for at all. And thinking just now how awkward that might turn out to be for all of them, Joanna wondered why she hadn't considered it before now. *Was I in too much of a hurry?* she wondered, thinking back to last Monday and the preacher's visit.

Mamma had quizzed her at length after their minister left with strawberry jam on his shirt. She'd been unable to suppress her smile or her animation. In fact, Joanna had never imagined her mother so aflutter about Joanna's hope of reuniting with Eben. Mamma, of course, had mixed feelings of both joy and sadness—and, oh, how she fretted about the risk Joanna was taking!

"I *have* to do this," Joanna had explained, citing her namesake as the inspiration for her daring plan to go to Indiana. "Did ya know my ancestor proposed marriage to the man she eventually married?"

Mamma grimaced and said she wasn't certain that information was factual, but Joanna insisted Mammi Kurtz knew all about it.

Once Joanna had finished sharing her intention, she asked Mamma not to tell Dat. "Only you and Cora Jane will know," Joanna said. "Promise?"

Mamma looked askance, as if to say, *"You're asking this?"*

"I'll tell Cora Jane myself," she assured Mamma.

"Well, and that's far better, I daresay. Sister to sister." Mamma fell silent for a time. "Your father would never agree to let you go, if he knew."

"Another reason why it's probably best for him not to. After all, aren't I old enough to decide?"

"He'd say it isn't becoming of you to chase after a beau."

Doubtless Mamma was right. Except that Eben Troyer hadn't been just any beau. Joanna wholly trusted that God had planted this desire in her heart . . . and now she must fulfill it.

The cabbie pulled into a long, tree-lined lane. "Here we are, miss."

She paid the bill and double-checked the address she'd come to know so well. "Denki," she said and got out.

The cab pulled away quickly, and she was left appraising the grand lawns and the Troyer house itself. There was a strange hush surrounding the place as Joanna walked timidly up the lane, carrying her small overnight case. Was it just her imagination, or was her heartbeat audible?

Flecks of sunlight dappled the flower gardens beneath

enormous, leafy oak trees along the left side of the house and the wraparound porch. And, now that she was nearer, Joanna noticed several Amishmen strolling along the opposite side yard, talking in Deitsch. If she wasn't mistaken, one of them mentioned something about a "big doin's" coming up soon on these premises. What could that mean? Perhaps a landmark birthday for either of Eben's parents, like the celebration thrown for Mary Beiler? Or someone's wedding anniversary?

She focused again on the three-story house, noting the arch of a tree limb reaching like a protective wing over a white gazebo with gingerbread latticework along the bottom. The air was fragrant with climbing pink roses on two white arbors, and there were several martin birdhouses positioned on the lawn. She searched for any sign of Eben, hoping she might spot him near the barn set off to the west.

There was a white sports car parked in the very back, and surprised, she wondered whose it was. A black-and-white tabby meowed loudly at her, then ran and hid under the back porch, as if daring her to play hide-and-seek.

With a knock on the screen door, Joanna peered into the wide summer porch and beyond, into the long kitchen. She saw no one. Then, just as she was wondering if anyone was at home, she heard someone calling and turned to see a red-haired English woman wearing white walking shorts and a bright red sleeveless blouse. A cross pendant hung around her slender neck.

"May I help you?" the young woman asked, pushing her lovely hair behind one ear.

Joanna noticed the sparkling diamond ring on her left hand and wondered if this might be Leroy's bride. "I'm a friend of Eben's," she said. "Thought I'd surprise him with a visit."

The petite woman glanced curiously at Joanna's overnight bag and shook her head. "I'm sorry, but Eben's out of town for a few days. Left this morning."

"Oh," Joanna said, heart sinking. "I've missed him, I guess."

Looking her over, the younger woman frowned for a moment, her eyes searching Joanna's face. Then she turned as if she was going to call to someone, but just as suddenly turning back. She touched Joanna's hand. "Excuse me, but you wouldn't be . . ." She paused. "Are you Joanna?"

"Jah." She shook her head enthusiastically, pleased the woman knew her name. *A gut sign, for sure!* "And might you be Eben's new sister-in-law?"

"I am." The pretty woman nodded, smiling now. "Debbie's my name." She shook Joanna's hand. "I'm just along for the ride, I guess you could say . . . here to help my husband and his family organize and sort through a lifetime of accumulation."

Sort through?

"What do you mean?" Joanna asked, astonished.

"Leroy's parents are auctioning off the farm this coming week—moving to Virginia Beach. So we're dividing up the items they don't want to sell. Sentimental things, you know . . . things that should remain in the family."

Joanna wondered when this had come about, and how it would impact Eben. Her head was whirling. She wanted to ask if Debbie truly knew what she was talking about, because it sounded unbelievable. Such strange things she was telling her . . . so very hard to comprehend. Eben's father was selling his farm?

Just then a young man in blue jeans and a gray T-shirt appeared from the barn, heading this way. He looked enough like Eben to be his brother, and his gait reminded Joanna of the first time she'd seen Eben walking along the beach, snapping pictures. In that surreal moment, she wondered what had ever become of those pictures. Had Eben saved them? She so yearned to see them . . . to see him.

Debbie introduced Leroy to her, and he was quick to offer a handshake in greeting. Then he slapped his forehead, laughing hard. When he'd managed to stop long enough to speak, he said, "You'll never guess where Eben is right now." He paused a moment. "He hopped on an early-morning van to Lancaster."

Joanna thought her heart might stop right then and there.

Leroy was still chuckling, and Debbie looked as shocked as Joanna felt, obviously just hearing about this amazing coincidence for the first time. "Well, like we say here, don't this beat all?" Leroy said amidst more laughter.

"What's he plannin' to do there?" Joanna's voice sounded far away to her.

Leroy ran his hands through his hair and looked at the sky, then back at her, a glint in his eye.

Suddenly, she knew. Debbie had mentioned an auction here. So Eben had gone looking for her—to tell her the news that he was unshackled at last!

But Joanna didn't wish to hear any more of the details

from either Leroy or his wife. No, she wanted to wait to hear all of this from Eben himself. *Dear, dear Eben!*

She noticed the cell phone clipped to Leroy's pocket. "Might I use your phone right quick?" she asked, wanting to contact Cousin Maria before it got dark.

Leroy gladly handed it to her and showed her how to use it. She made the call to see if she could spend the night with the candlemaker before catching an early van home tomorrow, explaining that she was Salina's sister, which opened the door to Maria's heart extra wide. Or so it seemed by the sound of delight in her voice.

Still flabbergasted by the day's unfolding events, Joanna thanked Leroy for the use of his phone. When he offered to drive her to Maria's, with Debbie accompanying them, she wasn't sure what to say. This was the man whose foolishness, his discarding of his Amish heritage, had kept her and Eben apart. But forgiveness was a way of life, the very core of their beliefs. She had to overlook what he'd done, knowing people made their own choices, whether for God or the world. "All right," she said, agreeing. "I appreciate it."

"Won't Eben be surprised when he finds out you're *here*?" Debbie said over her shoulder as they climbed into the sporty car.

The realization shook Joanna anew.

Chapter 42

Eben quickened his pace up the driveway, anticipating seeing Joanna after all their months apart. He dismissed any notions of her being engaged to Jake Lantz or any other young man, for that matter, although if he were honest with himself, he knew he should be worried. Right now his entire focus was on winning back her heart, if that's what it took, now that he was finally able to relocate here to Joanna's splendid little corner of the world.

A low stone wall along one side of the lane leading to the house was coated with thick moss, and behind it a long double row of marigolds flourished. The windmill beyond the barnyard creaked in a cadence that reminded him of Daed's own, and Eben breathed in the familiar aroma of soil mixed with the fertilizer of more than two hundred years as the sun leaned toward the horizon.

Rhoda Kurtz was sitting out on the back porch when he

arrived at the door. She let out a gasp when she spotted him, getting up from her chair right quick to come over and babble something about Joanna's not being home. "She's out of town," Rhoda said, seemingly too shy to meet his eyes.

"I should've written to say I was comin'. . . ." Eben felt his shoulders slump as the breath left him for a moment. "When will she return?"

Again, Rhoda acted altogether bashful. Was she the type of woman who needed the cushion of others? Eben knew plenty of womenfolk like that, but this apparent change in Rhoda took him aback.

"Not exactly sure when she'll be home," Rhoda said hesitantly.

"Well, I'll be glad to wait and see her, if you don't think she'd mind."

She nodded, again behaving in a completely different manner than the first time he'd visited here.

Eben asked if she knew where he might spend the night. Immediately, Rhoda mentioned Rachel Stoltzfus, saying she'd be more than happy to go over there with him. "They'll be pleased to put you up again," she insisted.

"Don't want to put anyone out."

"Oh, no worries 'bout that," she was quick to say. "Let me get you something cold to drink—you look all in."

He lowered his duffel bag onto the porch and turned to gaze out toward the barn, perspiring as he stood in the dying sunlight. It had been equally as hot back home. He wondered how Leroy and Debbie and all the other family members were getting along while dividing up the spoils. He was actually relieved not to be present for all of that, although he wouldn't have minded having some of the garden tools—shovels, trowels, and such. Things his father's hands had touched all the many years. As for personal effects and furnishings, he desired nothing like that from Daed, who'd given him steady employment since his late teens while asking very little by way of room and board, allowing Eben to stash away much of his earnings.

Eben sighed and realized how tired he was. He watched Nate Kurtz bringing in the field mules, a dark profile against the meadow, where lightning bugs twinkled as far as the eye could see. Eben guessed he'd gone back out to labor after supper, just as Eben's own father often did. *No more*, he thought, wondering how long it would take for his parents to adjust to retirement once the farm sold next week at auction to another Plain family. Daed had been winding down awhile, he'd told Eben that night in the glow of the barn's lantern. And he'd waited for several years, just to be sure this was what he and Mamm wanted. And now, he said, it was.

Eben knew all too well the daily strain, year after year, required in farming the old way—using mule or horsepower to plow, cultivate, and harvest, instead of tractors like the English. Lots of Amish farmers lasted only twenty or twenty-five years anymore before selling their land to their youngest son, or other kin, to keep the fertile soil in the family.

"Here's something to wet your whistle," Rhoda said as she handed him a tall glass of ice-cold root beer. "Made it just last week."

"Denki." He felt terribly nervous around Joanna's mother,

just as she seemed to be around him. Joanna was the important ingredient in the social equation, and she was absent. But gone where?

Rhoda asked if he'd like to sit a spell till Nate came in and washed up. "He'll be surprised to see ya, too."

Eben didn't have to guess what that meant. And he hardly knew where to look, because when Rhoda spoke, she avoided his eyes, which signaled something. *What?*

Then a terrible fear gripped him. Was Joanna spoken for? Could that be the reason for her mother's peculiar manner?

Rhoda seemed restless as she got up yet again. "Would ya like some pie, maybe?"

"Oh, that's not necessary," Eben said, trying to be polite, although he was hungry, having devoured his sandwich, apple, and nearly a whole stalk of celery in the van hours ago.

But Rhoda didn't seem to pay any mind and headed back inside again, fanning herself now with her black apron.

Cora Jane was wandering through the meadow when he looked that way, barefoot and swinging her arms. Strands of her blond hair hung out from beneath her royal blue bandana. She had been picking golden daisies and was waving them in the breeze as she came closer. Then, just that quick, she caught sight of him and began to run toward the house.

"What on earth are ya doin' here?" Her expression was one of total disbelief.

He laughed. "That's an interesting way to say hullo." This was the plucky sister, he recalled.

"No, I'm *serious* . . . why are ya here, Eben Troyer?"

"Came to see Joanna."

"I see that." She blinked her eyes and frowned toward the back door. Then, coming closer, she whispered behind her free hand, "I was told not to tell a soul this . . . but I think you should know that my sister has gone lookin' for *you*."

"She what?"

"She's out in your neck of the woods." Cora Jane nodded her head. "She made us all promise not to say anything. Not even Dat knows where she went."

Eben couldn't believe it. "I'm here and she's there?"

"Jah, but remember, you never heard it from me."

"Glad for the tip."

She stood there looking at him, a smile on her face now. "Something else," she whispered again, then paused, weighing her words, he thought. "Joanna's in love with you, Eben—she never stopped."

With that, she hurried to open the screen door and headed inside.

He couldn't have imagined this in his best dreams. Yet what had precipitated this sudden move by Joanna toward him? And what on earth had possessed her to go to Shipshewana without letting him know first?

Rhoda reappeared with a tray of goodies—pie and cookies. Must Eben now pretend he didn't know Joanna's whereabouts while he made small talk? He accepted a generous slice of peach pie and thanked her, picking up a fork from the tray, as well.

No wonder Joanna's mother acted so strange!

He could hardly sit there and eat his pie, even though it tasted truly terrific. Rhoda said hardly a word, and he wondered how much longer before Nate came and joined them, as Rhoda had suggested he might.

Out of habit, Eben pulled out his pocket watch, the light in the sky diminishing with every tick of a second. It was just a few minutes till seven o'clock—he'd been traveling nearly all day.

Has Joanna really gone to Indiana . . . could it be?

"Such a quiet evening, ain't?" Rhoda said for lack of anything else much to say. "Ever so peaceful here."

"Fridays are like this back home, too," he said, thinking of his family. Would they come here to meet Joanna and her kin someday?

Friday!

The awareness was an alarm bell in his memory. Eben nearly leaped out of his chair, spilling a bit of his pie, which he leaned down to pick up before returning his dessert plate to the tray on a small table nearby. Then, despite the fact that most likely he'd raise Rhoda's eyebrows by his impulsive actions, Eben hastily excused himself, not looking back to see the startled expression that surely played across her face.

He took off running across the yard, toward the dusty field road. Though the little phone shanty was now nearly hidden by cornstalks taller than his head, he knew the way.

Chapter 43

Joanna sighed, shaking away the doubts. No, she was not as outspoken as Cora Jane . . . nor was she as self-assured as her forebear Aunt Joanna. Still, she couldn't reject the curious pull she felt toward the phone booth down Peaceful Acres Lane from Maria Riegsecker's house. Joanna had to see where Eben went to call her, thinking it might make her feel a little closer to him tonight.

"You might have to wait to use it, though," Maria had said with a smile. "Sometimes that happens, 'specially on a Friday evening." She meant the more traditional young men used it as a matter of course to connect with their girls. Others less adhering to the church ordinance used cell phones.

Joanna had not commented on that one iota. Now that she was here in Eben's neighborhood—now that she knew Eben was free to court her and move to Hickory Hollow if he chose to—she felt compelled to see the shanty where he had always phoned her on Fridays at seven o'clock.

It was close to that time even now.

As she walked along the roadside, she saw that the door to the small lean-to was standing open. Once inside, she pushed the door shut. Then, without thinking or second-guessing herself, she raised her hand to the black receiver. Slowly, she lifted it out of its cradle and dialed the operator, ready to use the code Maria had given her for the eventual billing.

There was little hope that anyone would be in the area of the cornstalk-concealed phone shed to even hear the phone ring, let alone answer and go to track Eben down at her parents' house. But Joanna wasn't thinking like herself just now; she was doing what Cora Jane might do. "Or my namesake," she said aloud.

Eben literally jumped when he heard the phone jangle the first time. He shoved the wooden door open at the second ring and picked the receiver right up. "Hullo?"

Silence.

"Anybody there?" he asked.

Then softly, he heard her voice. "Is that you, Eben?"

"Jah . . . Joanna?"

She said it was. "I came to see you in Shipshewana."

"And I'm here in Hickory Hollow, as you now know."

They laughed at the wonderful unlikeliness of it all.

She told him of having met Leroy and Debbie and sounded like she was starting to cry, and trying not to. "I'm standing in your phone booth, not far from your father's house."

"Ach, Joanna . . . this is *erschtaunlich*—astonishing!"

"I came to Indiana to let you know I might be able to transfer my membership to your church." Her voice cracked.

He contemplated what all this meant and wished he were next to her now, able to show her how pleased he was. "Well, whoever thought we'd go to see each other . . . and on the same day?" he managed to say, wanting to sound strong so that she could be.

"Stranger than what ya might read in a storybook, ain't?"

"I want you in my life, Joanna. I'd rather talk to you this way or write to you by letter than be with any other girl. But all that's goin' to change, if you'll have me."

"Have you? Oh, Eben, don't ya know . . . I love you?" she said, warming his heart.

"I wanted to wait to say those words to you in person." He wished she were here in his arms this minute.

"Well, I want to hear them *now*," she declared.

Cora Jane's spirit had rubbed off on her. "All right," he said, grinning into the phone. "I love you, Joanna Kurtz, with all of my heart. And I want to make you my bride."

There was a sudden, poignant silence. He held his breath.

"Will ya ask me again when I see you tomorrow?" she said, surprising him once more.

"I certainly will," he said. "And you know what I think? We need to preserve these phone shacks somehow. Maybe I could take a few pictures."

Her laughter was so sweet. "For posterity, jah."

They laughed together, blending their mirth as the Friday

evening sun set. And it was all Eben could do to say goodbye when the time came.

...

Joanna spied Eben sitting on the front porch waiting for her as she arrived home the next day. She made herself walk, not run, across the front lawn, and when he saw her, he fairly flew off the porch swing and hurried down the steps to meet her.

"Willkumm home," he said, looking well rested and as handsome as she'd remembered.

"You too." She smiled as she moved into his open arms, letting him hold her. "I thought I'd never get here."

"I know *that* feeling." He chuckled. "My sweet Joanna."

She loved being so close to him, after having been apart all this time. But this was not the place to be so intimate.

Soon they were walking back to the porch, where he told her all that he'd been doing today. "I've lined up a place to start workin'—for Smithy Riehl. I'll start next week, just as soon as I get my things moved here."

She was thrilled, hanging on to his every word. "Will you stay with him and his wife, maybe?"

"That's part of the deal, too." Eben seemed mighty pleased.

She kept waiting to hear the longed-for words but was happy to take in the exciting plans he'd set in place in such a short time.

Eben also talked further about his father's decision to sell the farm. "It's such backbreaking work for my poor Daed," he concluded.

She fully understood yet was stunned at how this had all come together . . . and for their benefit, of all things!

"And, just so ya know, he did offer me the farm to purchase. But I turned it down, hoping you were still single."

"You gave it up for me?"

This took her breath away. And now her heart yearned to tell what she'd sacrificed for God—and for him, as well—but Joanna thought better of it. *Maybe I'll wait till my poems are published in the magazine . . . Lord willing!*

"You and I—this whole thing—is an answer to prayer," he told her.

She nodded in agreement, wanting to pinch herself.

He reached for her hand. "So now that we're together here . . . will you marry me, Joanna?"

The words startled her briefly. But then she smiled into his dear face. "What took ya so long?" she replied.

He winked at her, clearly enjoying her spunk. He leaned over and kissed her lightly, and then again. "Is the coming wedding season too soon?" His eyes still lingered on hers. "All right with you?"

"Can we possibly be ready by then?" There were so many plans to be made—where they would live, most important. Suddenly, Joanna remembered the ample celery patch and wondered if Cora Jane would mind if she used it.

"I'll work to make that happen, my love." He slipped his arm around her and pulled her ever so near, kissing her again for even longer, not seeming to care what the neighbors thought.

And snuggling next to him . . . neither did she.

Epilogue

Within weeks of Eben's move to Hickory Hollow, my younger sister confided that Jake Lantz was quickly becoming a serious beau. Cora Jane also said it was more than all right to use her celery crop for the traditional creamed-celery casserole at my wedding feast. I couldn't help myself—I slipped in my all-important question then and there. "Will ya consider bein' my bridesmaid, sister? It would mean ever so much."

A mischievous smile appeared on her pretty face. "Why, sure, I'd love to." She reached to hug me, and we laughed till tears clouded our eyes.

Both Eben and Jake have had numerous opportunities to get acquainted at church and at youth gatherings. We've even talked of going on double dates here before too long. Such *gut* times we'll have together!

Meanwhile, Mammi Kurtz has shown a great deal of

interest in Eben, asking me about his attendance at Preaching services and the like. She, too, suspects we'll be published after church one of these November weeks. And I know Mamma and Dat do, too.

As for the double wedding ring quilt that has graced my bed, I've decided to wash it up real nice and set it aside for Eben's and my wedding night. I'll tell my darling the story of the determined woman in my family tree who wholeheartedly believed that we're all here by design . . . that none of us is an accident in God's eyes. Our heavenly Father's hand is at work in all of our comings and goings—and in the choice of a life mate.

Prior to their move to Virginia, I went with Eben to Shipshewana to meet his congenial parents. They were so encouraging about our eventual union, they even invited us to come visit them once they're settled there. That way, we'll come full circle and go walking along the beach where we met. Eben says we might want to go for our first wedding anniversary, as well.

Thinking of anniversaries, Cousin Malinda had her first baby, a boy, the week before her anniversary. Andy said it was right fine with him whenever the Good Lord wanted to bless them with such a healthy baby. And Malinda says Baby Aaron's day of birth definitely ties for first place in happiness with the day she and Andy married.

As for me, I've continued to attend the weekly quilting frolics, where Mamma says a wedding quilt is in the making. I haven't had the heart to tell them I already have one that I cherish, instead letting Mamma guide the decision as to the pattern and color scheme. It's something I will look forward to as a thoughtful gesture, to be sure. Besides, a bride can always use more than one quilt in the house!

Once Eben and I are wed, we will stay with my parents till springtime, as is our custom. Eben has been hard at work with Smitty Riehl, so he's already making money here, adding to his savings, along with some funds his kindly parents gave us from the sale of their farm. Even though there is no land available to purchase in the hollow, we've got our eye on a smaller house not far from the bishop's.

Yesterday, the deacon's wife, Sallie, and Fannie surprised me when they showed up at the house, bringing several copies of the *Ladies Journal*. They could hardly quit chattering and quickly turned to the page featuring two of my poems.

Zwee—two! Who would ever have thought this possible?

When I showed Eben later, he asked me to sit near him and read them aloud, which I happily did, although toward the last stanza I could scarcely see the words through my joyful tears. It was a good thing I'd memorized the rest. He kissed my cheek and I cried all the harder, such happy tears.

Then he showed me the numerous digital pictures on his camera, including the ones he took that first night on the beach—a striking series of the ocean, sky, and the dark ship on the horizon. And one more: a distant shot of a forlorn-looking Amish girl sitting with her feet pushed deep into the sand.

"So you *did* take my picture," I teased.

"But I never got it printed—in keeping with the Ordnung, ya know." He smiled as he showed me the zoom button on his fancy camera. "I couldn't say how many times I looked at this picture of you up close. First thing every morning and the last thing at night," he admitted.

His picture taking reminded me of my story writing, a lovely yet swiftly fading memory. After all, I was too busy living my happy ending to have any regrets.

Now, if I *were* still writing fiction, I'd start by penning something like this for the opening lines to my own personal love story: *"Three times a bridesmaid, never a bride." That's just what my younger sister said about me—in front of our engaged cousins, no less. . . .*

Author's Note

Since my early teens, I've heard the saying "Always a bridesmaid, never a bride," but I didn't know all those years ago how that well-known saying might entice me as a novelist to discover Joanna's unique story path. I delighted in developing the characters of Joanna Kurtz (oh, the writing side of her!) and her feisty younger sister, Cora Jane. Not to mention their devoted mother, Rhoda . . . and the *wunnerbaar* Eben Troyer. I also especially enjoyed revisiting the character of Ella Mae Zook, Hickory Hollow's Wise Woman.

I offer enduring gratitude to my dear husband, Dave, my brainstorming partner and first editor, who in every way helps make my deadlines achievable.

My sincerest appreciation also extends to the stellar staff at Bethany House Publishers, whose collective expertise guides and encourages me, and who ultimately share the pleasure of publishing stories for legions of devoted reader-friends.

Thanks primarily to Jim and Ann Parrish, David Horton, Steve Oates, Rochelle Glöege, Debra Larsen, and Helen Motter—you are all truly gifted!

Many thanks to Mary Jane Hoober, gracious innkeeper of the Peaceful Acres Bed-and-Breakfast in Shipshewana, Indiana, who offered invaluable insights into the Indiana Amish for this particular book. During an autumn respite, my family and I thoroughly enjoyed staying at this lovely inn, the source of Eben Troyer's fictitious street address: Peaceful Acres Lane.

The brief reference to John Newton's book *Voice of the Heart* was inspired by the cherished copy given to me by Aunt Ada Reba Bachman before her Homegoing nearly three years ago.

Special thanks to my cousin Dave Buchwalter for the gift of an heirloom friendship quilt made in 1927 for my maternal grandparents . . . the seed that planted the family quilt subplot in this story. I am so grateful!

Denki to my faithful assistants and consultants—Amish and Mennonite alike. I am forever thankful for your prayers and encouragement, as well as to Barbara Birch for meticulous proofreading, and to Dale Birch and Dave and Janet Buchwalter for research help and faithful prayers.

To our magnificent and all-wise heavenly Father be all blessing and honor . . . *Soli deo Gloria.*

Beverly Lewis, born in the heart of Pennsylvania Dutch country, is the *New York Times* bestselling author of more than ninety books. Her stories have been published in eleven languages worldwide. A keen interest in her mother's Plain heritage has inspired Beverly to write many Amish-related novels, beginning with *The Shunning*, which has sold more than a million copies. *The Brethren* was honored with a 2007 Christy Award.

Beverly lives with her husband, David, in Colorado.

The Guardian

The third book in the Home to Hickory Hollow *series*

AVAILABLE APRIL 2, 2013

More From *NY Times* Bestselling Author Beverly Lewis

To find out more about Beverly and her books, visit beverlylewis.com or find her on Facebook!

When Amelia Devries, thoroughly modern and equally disillusioned, takes a wrong turn during a rainstorm, she unexpectedly meets an Amishman—and a community—that might just change her life forever.

The Fiddler
HOME TO HICKORY HOLLOW

As two Amish sisters find themselves on the fringes of their Lancaster community, will they be forced to choose between their beloved People and true love?

THE ROSE TRILOGY: *The Thorn, The Judgment, The Mercy*

When her mother's secret threatens to destroy their peaceful Amish family, will Grace's search for the truth lead to more heartache or the love she longs for?

SEASONS OF GRACE: *The Secret, The Missing, The Telling*

BETHANYHOUSE

Stay up-to-date on your favorite books and authors with our *free* e-newsletters. Sign up today at bethanyhouse.com.

Find us on Facebook.

Free, exclusive resources for your book group! bethanyhouse.com/AnOpenBook